A SPIRIT MADE OF MEMORIES.

The Book:

This book is about a spirit made from PTSD and many other mental illnesses combined. It haunts a soldier fresh from war. The only one that can see this monster is the soldier, but the spirit can touch everyone. How will he deal with this monster? Will he find a way to kill it? Will he find a way to co-exist with it? Will it kill him?

The Author:

I am an author who grew up in a small town in North Carolina. Mental illness is no stranger to me from seeing it with others and with personal experience. Writing has been a way to cope with it myself. This book was written in hopes to help people see what PTSD can be like. I am not a therapist, so I can't give a perfect description of the illness itself. This is just a way to share how it seems to me in my own personal way. I hope you enjoy the story and thank you for reading it.

A Spirit Made Of Memories

A psychological paranormal horror

by

Caleb D. Walker

Distributed by: IngramSpark   La Vergne, TN

A Spirit Made Of Memories

1st Edition 2021

Caleb Walker– North Carolina

Table of Contents

Chapter 1: On The Front

My name is Travis Marvic. I am a soldier in the United States Army. I have been in Iraq for six months for my second tour of war. I feel that I have nothing left in the states, so I keep coming back here even if it sucks. It is better than being back home and haunted by what I have done over here. I don't think any soldier truly escapes the wars they fight in. It seems that it goes home with you, and you live in that moment for the rest of your life till age or medicine takes your mind. I just want to get away from it all, as many soldiers tend to feel. This is my way to make sure that my story is not forgotten. This is my story.

Travis makes his way across the tarmac to the mess hall. He is supposed to report to duty in an hour, but he wanted to get something to eat before his patrol. This day felt different, but he could say for sure what it was. He could see the air about the tarmac rippling from the heat that surrounded the base.

"Good evening Travis, are you ready for the night patrol you have today?" The voice came from behind Travis as he turned around, he saw it was SGT. Spooner clad in his uniform freshly pressed, and his polished boots.

"Oh yeah, I forgot." Travis let out a small chuckle of embarrassment. Spooner put an arm around him, and they both laughed while they continued into the mess hall.

"I took on an extra patrol today it seems." Travis said, while grabbing a steaming potato off the tray in front of him.

"It appears you did my friend, or did you forget that you had the night shift or something?" Spooner asked while filling his plate with junk foods.

Spooner donned a grim and serious look on his face and stopped Travis by putting a hand on his shoulder. You could tell by the look on his face that he could feel something in the air. He moved to be face to face with Travis. When he finally spoke, Travis was a bit shaken by his words.

"We both know why you are over here. You are trying to run away from the fact that we do bad things over here and you don't want to do the coping part of being at home." Spooner locked eyes with Travis trying to read his response before it came.

"Yes, I am Spooner, but I also have nothing over there anymore. My closest family died in the last attack on our hometown." Travis said, turning to head to a table. As he took his seat, he let out a sigh.

"I miss them every day, but I think if I stop fighting, I will let them down." Travis lowered his head while he waited on a response from Spooner.

"You know that you don't have to beat yourself up over them dying. You had been on deployment at the time." Spooner gave Travis a supportive look. He started to take a bite of his food when the alarm went off.

"Looks like something is happening." Spooner said, sitting down on his fork.

An explosion went off shaking the building violently. Glass shattered as a fireball smacked the side of the building. Men began to scream outside some of them covered in fire. Someone had just blown open the wall of the base. Travis went to exit the mess hall but found that rubble had blocked the door, and no one can exit the building now.

"We can't open this goddamn door fuck!" Travis yelled out of frustration just as he kicked the door.

"Well, we have to have a possible way out of here." Spooner said hoping someone would have an answer for him.

No one spoke up so Spooner and Travis began going around checking every door of the building just as another explosion went off outside. You could fell it shake the entire building as flames broke through the windows. Everyone fell to the ground coughing as smoke and dust filled the room. You could see cracks in the wall shortly before it collapsed on top of the only door that lead out of the building. "Well, I guess that is our way out." Spooner said in a condescending attitude. Travis gave him a nod before they started to head toward the collapsed wall.

"We need to be cautious because we don't know if the enemy is still out there." Travis said as he stopped them both short of the wall.

Travis took a deep breath and just as his foot went past the wall another explosion knocked him back into the mess hall. His vision went blurry, and his ears rang as the bright flash started to fade away from view. The only thing he could feel through the adrenaline was a pain in his chest where the blast knocked the air out of him.

"Son of a fucking bitch that hurt!" Travis yelled holding the back of his head.

Travis struggled to his feet just as gunfire ignited outside. He could hear bullets bouncing off the outside of the mess hall and people could be heard yelling orders to each other at the gates. It was a sight of both beauty and horror as blood met fire. Men running at each other being cut down by shrapnel and bullets. Some bodies laid burned from the fire's bombs had caused across the base. Others screamed looking at their missing limbs laying out of their reach. He let out a pained breath he didn't know he had been holding before turning to look at Spooner.

"Looks like we are missing all of the fun Spooner." Travis said with a laugh.

Spooner and Travis both looked around to see many people that needed medical attention. The ones that had the least injuries started to see if they could help the others. It looked to Travis like a scene out of a horror movie. The room had been filled with the smell of blood and smoke. It was thick enough in the air to choke everyone that took a deep breath.

"Travis, I think we need to help some of these guys out." Spooner said walking over to one of the guys and knelt down checking their wounds.

Spooner took a rag to clean the wound while Travis brought over a first-aid kit. The best they could do was disinfectant and a band aid. Their lack of medical skill was becoming more apparent to them. They started to feel their hope slipping away from them.

"Spooner use your belt to cut off this man's bleeding!" Travis yelled from across the room as another explosion shook the building.

Men started screaming as the sound of one thousand feet charged at the base. The sight of the army struck fear into our soldiers. They started being taken prisoner under a hail of led rain. As the bullets flew slowly you could hear the voices slowly begin to vanish from the surrounding area. Travis risked looking out the window of the mess hall. What he saw was everyone else in the base had been killed and the Afghan army had come in and started stacking bodies.

"Fuck! Spooner, we need to get out of here now!" Travis yelled as the soldiers started towards the mess hall.

He ran to the backroom and started breaking out the windows. As he struggled to break the windows, looking down to see his knuckles had begun to bleed. He searched for anything he can use to break the window when he saw a shine from under a nearby shelf. Throwing it to the side he found a metal bar. He grabbed and began using finally breaking the window after a few swings throwing his blood across the walls.

"Hurry Spooner get these fucking men out of here right this goddamn minute!" Travis yelled as he picked people up and ran them to the backroom.

As they lifted people through the back window sounds of the rubble being cleared away echoed through the building. The process was one that felt like it was taking forever as the sounds of men talking could be heard. This made everyone panic. They began to rush out of the broken window causing some people to get cut.

"Who is in here!" A voice in a thick Arabic accent yelled as the rubble was cleared away from the front door.

They started digging through what was left of the mess hall only to not find a single thing remaining in the building.

Travis and Spooner managed to get everyone out just in time. The only thought that ran through their minds was the thought of surviving and getting to the closest base that they could find.

They piled everyone they could into the back of one of the few surviving trucks and stomped the gas pedal. With the roar of the engine sand kicked up a trail behind them as they sped off into the distance. They drove as fast as they could not knowing if the gas would run out first or if the radiator would blow first. From around them rose four dust clouds as the enemy started to close in around them.

"I will not die in this fucking desert Spooner! Shoot those fucking bastards!" Travis yelled as the enemy trucks closed in.

Spooner grabbed his rifle and started firing at the trucks without hitting any useful shots on them. He held steady to the truck trying to support his rifle for a better shot. Even in the excitement of the situation he tried to focus his breathing. His focus was broken when Travis hit his leg to get his attention. In response Spooner threw up one hand.

"Where the fuck did you learn to shoot Spooner?!" Travis yelled.

"The goddamned United States Military goddamn it!" Spooner yelled back as he fired a second spray at the trucks.

The only difference is this time he hit the driver in one tuck. It went flying into a sand dune sending up a large cloud of sand and smoke as it exploded. They didn't stop to make sure no one had lived through the crash as they kept speeding through the desert. Spooner got back into a position he felt was safe.

"That's how it is fucking done you son of a bitch!" Spooner yelled smiling at Travis.

Another truck came into view, but before Spooner or Travis could start firing again. The enemy truck unloaded with a machine gun into the cargo area of their truck. This caused both of the men to jerk in a panic. They traded looks between each other and the truck that just opened fire on them.

"What the fuck!?" Travis yelled as he rammed into the Afghan truck trying to shove them into a sand dune.

"These fuckers will not stop coming at us!" Travis yelled as they slammed into the enemy truck again.

As the trucks hit sparks came from the metal each time. As the enemy truck started to come back at them Travis put his pistol out the window and fired shots into their tires. As the tires gave out it caused the Afghan truck to slam into Travis and the others putting both trucks out of commission. The trucks flipped into the sand dunes causing the trucks to lose some of their parts. The injured men fell out of the back of their truck. As Travis came back to consciousness his vision was blurry and he had a headache. He assumed he had suffered a concussion of some form. He still had a job to finish so he staggered to his feet.

As his head cleared the wreckage, he saw one Afghan soldier was starting to stand as well. With a hand on his pistol, he got the soldier's attention. "Hey you stupid fuck!" As the last word left Travis's mouth he shot. With a bang the bullet went through the head of his enemy killing him instantly. After that act Travis collapsed onto the wrecked truck.

"Well Spooner this may just be our blazing end." Travis let out a chuckle as he passed out again.

The sound of helicopter rotors cut the air above them as a man yelled over a megaphone.

"Is anyone alive down there?" The voice of an unknown man called out causing Travis to stir.

"We got a live one!" The man yelled as ropes and a gurney dropped onto the ground beside Travis spooking him.

He tried to run, but his body wouldn't move.

"Don't worry man we are getting you home and another helicopter will be here soon for your friends." Though it was blurry Travis could tell the man was smiling after he finished his sentence.

As Travis lost his consciousness again the air went across his face giving a soothing cold feel to him. The helicopter had no issue getting Travis back to a nearby base. As they landed, he was rushed into the medical bay. When they got him into the bay he was swarmed by doctors and nurses. He didn't realize the extent of his injuries. He had a large cut across his chest causing an extreme loss of blood along with a spike in his back. These injuries had caused him to have to be medically discharged from the military.

"Welcome everyone to our medal assigning ceremony. We are here to give SGT. Marvic the medal of honor. He was giving this honor to him for his bravery in the attempted rescue of his fellow soldiers after the attack on his station." The general ended his speech with pinning the star to Travis's uniform.

With his head held high Travis limped out of the building. Travis went as fast as he could to his car and collapsed into the driver seat finally allowing the tears to escape his eyes. In the back of his mind, he didn't deserve the award he was given. To him the star was weighed down by the souls of the dead.

"Travis, are you okay?" Said a voice from just over his car door.

Travis looked up to see his sister Vinessa Marvic walking over to him. Travis just shook his head before the tears returned. Vinessa placed a hand on his shoulder before speaking again. The warmth of her hand brought him to a place of happiness with the memories it dug up.

"Travis if something happened over there it isn't your fault, and you need to understand that. War is a bloody and disgusting mess." She tried to say it in a comforting voice, but it wasn't received that way.

Travis couldn't bring himself to change from blaming himself for the deaths of his comrades. It was so fresh in his mind, that it was the only thing he could think about. He could still see their bloodied faces each time he closed his eyes. The sounds of their names brought screams of pain to his ears. He felt like he had failed every single one of those families.

"I killed them when I engaged those goddamned trucks." Travis said trying to hold back the sobs in his throat.

Ever since he got put in the hospital and given the news that SGT.Spooner died he learned how to hold back those feelings. He was proud of the fact that Spooner was promoted after his death. At the same time, he felt that it didn't fix anything because of everything he did while Spooner was still alive. As they once again looked at each other a voice called for Vinessa from the building's exit door.

"I will call you later big bro." Vinessa called back as she walked away.

Before she got too far Travis groaned and then let out a small chuckle. Travis pulled a cigarette out of the pack he kept in his center console. With a sigh he lit it and took a long draw. As he blew out the smoke he focused on the smoke and could swear he saw Spooner smiling at him from the smoke. As it dissipated, he just called himself crazy.

"He won't leave my memory, but I can't go seeing him everywhere now." He laughed at himself as he took another draw.

Travis sat back trying to be more comfortable. He had no plan on moving anytime soon. After about fifteen minutes he finally felt comfortable enough to think. What he started to think about was what he could have done to save everyone. No matter what solution he tried in his memories he knew it wouldn't bring them back in real life.

"I am sorry I got you killed Spooner but save me a seat at that bar up there." He said quietly before the sound of singing crickets came in.

"Don't worry man I will keep your spot warm." A voice spoke in his ear out of nowhere.

Travis jumped out of his car screaming as he pulled out his pistol. He checked the back seat and all around his car, but he couldn't see anyone.

"No one is here but us Travis." The voice was in his ear again, and he spun around still finding no one.

"Leave me the fuck alone, whoever you fucking are!" Travis yelled his voice echoing around the parking lot.

No one came out of the building for him but that was no surprise because music was blasting from the open windows. From what Travis could see everyone was slow dancing. Instead of being in there dancing with everyone Travis collapsed in the parking lot with a lit cigarette crying.

"Why are you doing this to me?" Travis asked with his eyes to the sky.

Tears rolled from his eyes while the rain began to move in. He let all his anger and sadness out as the rain fell. To him it felt safer to cry while it rained. Something cut him off. In the distance he could see a figure. It was tall and dark. He couldn't see any features due to it wearing a dark cloak. All it did was point at him before it vanished.

Chapter 2: Therapy Visit One

As Travis entered the therapist's office, he marked off the third day since his ceremony. He had already put the medal in a drawer in his room. "Hello Dr. Marron, how are you today?" Travis asked as he took a seat on that stereotypical couch. The therapist just adjusted himself in his chair and smiled at Travis with a warm look on his face.

"I am good Travis, how are you doing?" He gestured to Travis and his posture. Travis just didn't know how to respond to that because no one has ever really asked him and meant it. All the doctor got in response was a shrug. The therapist wrote down a quick note in his file and put his gaze back on Travis. Which in turn made him fix himself differently on the couch.

"Three days ago, doc I was in the parking lot after getting my medal and I could have sworn I could hear SGT. Spooner in my car." Travis said not meeting the gaze of the therapist. Travis took a deep breath and continued. "After the first sentence I got out of my car and heard him again. I then broke down crying then when I looked up a figure was standing beside the building watching me but, it had no eyes. It did wear a cloak shadowing over any features it had or could have had."

"I see what you are saying. Is it possible that you are forming something in your mind? Say for instance that you are hearing what you think he might have said if he was there with you? Maybe you are holding onto his memory and your mind is mixing several things that he has said in the past so that they fit the current situation." The therapist said as he wrote another small note in his pad.

"You might have a point and I guess at this point I should say that I blame myself for him and the others dying in that fucking desert. I have also had a lack of sleep since I got back. I did try to go back, but they won't let me go back because of the injuries that I had gotten from the crash." Travis laughed a small amount before focusing on the therapist. "I guess you think I am crazy now that you are hearing this." Travis cracked a small smile before it faded soon after.

"I think that you are having some instances of post-traumatic stress disorder or PTSD. Which means you are being sent back to the war zone not physically but mentally." He grabbed a blue pad from his desk and made some scribbles on it then handed it to Travis.

"This a medication you can take to help keep the episodes away so to speak." He gave Travis a small smile before leaning back into his chair and writing another little note in his folder.

"I don't understand. You have only seen me for not even a whole session yet. How can you already know what is wrong with me? For all you know I am fucking insane, and you could be giving me a medication that could make me worse than I already was when I came in." Travis was starting to get angry at the Doctor who sat across from him. To Travis he was a fake and only giving out meds so he could make a paycheck. In his mind Travis felt that if he took the medication, he could end up in a mental hospital drooling life away.

"It is my job to know what is wrong with you. I have seen and still see a lot of soldiers. This most recent conflict has given me a lot of patients with similar symptoms." The therapist sat back in his chair with a smug look on his face. This only drove Travis closer to the edge and almost over it. Somehow Travis held it together long enough to sit until the end of the session.

Travis took the card that told him about his next visit, and he left the Valhon Veterans Hospital. As he left, he couldn't help but think about how everyone told him not to go to the V.A. hospital. "The government funded stuff is a fucking joke!" He yelled as he put the card into his pocket. As he looked towards his car a woman stood behind it with a bag over her head and a flowing black gown on. "Who are you and why are you near my car?!" Travis yelled at the woman.

As he approached her the woman reached up and ripped the bag from around her mouth. As the bag ripped away her bottom jaw fell open, and she let out an ear-splitting scream that shattered the windows on his car. Slowly Travis stumbled to his car and put his hand on his window only to find the windows in one piece and the woman gone. "What the fuck just happened?" Travis asked as his vision started to clear, and he got into his car.

As he pulled out of the parking lot, he got out his phone to call his sister. "Vinessa can I come over? I have something I need to talk to you about." Travis sat silent as a whisper came over the line. It sounded like many voices at one time. Out of nowhere Spooner's voice screamed causing Travis to swerve into the curb and lose his phone to the floor. He slammed on the brakes taking deep breaths.

As Travis picked up his phone, he could hear his sister on the other line. "Hello? Travis, are you there? Are you okay?" Vinesssa got louder slower as she continued to ask. As he got the phone to his ear, he took a big gulp of air so loud his sister could hear it. "Get your ass over here right fucking now Travis!" Vinessa yelled over the phone.

The drive over to his sister's house had no big developments. "I am so happy to see you little sister." Travis said as he put his arms around her almost in tears over what just happened. Vinessa escorted him to her couch and sat him down with a cup of tea. As she took the seat across from him, she cleared her throat and flattened out the wrinkles in her skirt.

"What happened Travis?" Vinessa asked.

"You wouldn't believe me if I told you sis." Travis said with a small laugh.

"Try me big brother. I have heard a lot of crazy things." Vinessa responded with a smile on his face.

"Well, the doctor prescribed me medicine for PTSD. I came out of the office and saw a woman standing beside my car. As I approached her, she ripped the bag from around her head which I have no idea why she was wearing. When she ripped it away her bottom jaw fell limp, and she screamed. When she did it shattered my car windows and made my vision bad. When I got to my car she was gone, and my car had no damage to it." Travis said with it sounding crazy to himself also.

"You are right, that does sound crazy." Vinessa laughed but kept a serious look on her face. She didn't think he was crazy, because she didn't think it was anything outside of his PTSD. She got up and all she could think was to hug her brother. She hugged him and fell into tears before she could even tell she was crying. Travis hugged her back and tried to calm her down by singing the lullaby that their mom used to sing to them when they had been children.

"Sis you don't need to cry. I am going to be okay. I promise that I will because it comes with the job I had." Travis gave her a kiss on the cheek and got up to leave. "I love you sis and I will see you later." Travis gave her a smile, and he walked out to his car. As he exited his sister's home in the woods, he saw the bag headed woman again, but she was wearing a cloak over her bag. When a car went by the bag headed woman was gone and there stood SGT.Spooner wearing the black cloak, but he had a broken smile.

"Spooner what are you doing here! You're supposed to be dead!" Travis yelled with tears in his eyes. His sister busted out of the door behind him; she had a confused look on her face. When he turned around, she slowly backed up into her house and locked her door.

"Please leave Travis. Go home and then go get help at a hospital. Not that useless fucking V.A. please!" Vinessa yelled through the doors screen. She grabbed her phone and came back to the door showing it to him. "If you don't drive yourself, I will be forced to call you a ride myself." She held her gaze to her brothers. Travis could always tell when she was bluffing and at this time she was not. He pulled the keys out of his pocket and walked slowly to his car.

He didn't know where to go. He sold his house before his last deployment. He sold it because he had no plans on ever coming back home. He had told this to the people that bought his house when he had them make the check out to a charity that houses homeless people. "Where the fuck am, I going to stay tonight?" Travis cursed at the steering wheel before pulling into a motel that was nearby. He couldn't bring himself to drive much further than needed. The lady at the check-in desk was probably in her mid 40's. The 80's style hair was a giveaway besides the loud makeup and nail polish. He placed his bets that if she stood up, she would have tights and leg warmers.

That thought made him laugh. He laughed so loud that he was glad he was in an empty car. As he got out, he tried to make himself look better than he felt. With a deep breath he opened the door and stepped into the room. As he walked in, he was hit with a blast of cold air that carried the smell of nail polish and acetone. "Hello ma'am I would like to rent a room please." He said with the warmest smile he could muster up.

The lady looked up at him loudly chewing on a piece of gum. "We don't give rooms to the homeless." She said in an infuriating nasally voice, and she paired it with an eye roll. She went back to loudly chewing on her gum and pretending to write papers. The comment made Travis look at himself. He saw that his clothes had been dirty, so he reached into his bag for the one thing he thought would help. Travis took a deep breath and pulled out his medal. He cleared his throat and started tapping it on the counter in front of the desk.

The lady glared at him and in a mocking tone she began to speak again. "Oh, I am so sorry oh mighty hero. I didn't mean to be oh so disrespectful. We still don't serve the homeless no matter how many fake medals you have on you." She picked up the phone and called the police on him.

"Yes, I have a man here pretending to be a soldier and need him removed from the premises." She hung up the phone and laughed at him. "Got you a room sir but please wait outside." She said as she walked Travis outside and locked the door behind him.

As the police showed up and got out of their car one of the police recognized Travis. He had seen him in the letters his son sent from Afghanistan. Each letter described him saving everyone over and over again. These memories caused the policeman to walk over to him with a smile on his face.

"Hey man what are you doing out here? You are a hero and you have you seen a homeless man around here?" As the policeman finished his sentence Travis pointed at himself and told them he was the homeless man she called about.

The police brought Travis back into the building and rang the bell on the counter. He felt frustrated with having to pull Travis off of the sidewalk outside. He put look professional look on his face trying to not show his frustration. His hand already in his pocket that held his wallet.

"Ma'am you do realize this man is a hero, right?" the policeman asked the bitch at the counter as Travis thinks of her now.

"He just flashed a medal and didn't say anything else." She tripped over her words as she spoke.

"He is the only reason I got to see my son again." The policeman sat down his debit card and paid for Travis to have a room as long as he needed one.

With a large amount of disdain in her eyes she handed Travis a room key and told him to get out of her face. He turned to the police officer to argue over buying him the room, but the policeman stopped him. "You have done more for me than I could repay you for. I don't have to worry about what could have happened to my son over there, and he is home now." With a smile they parted ways.

Travis went to his room and the first thing he did was take a shower. In the shower he collapsed to the floor of the bathtub and began to cry. He cried harder than he had ever cried in his life. "I am so sorry Spooner I could have done so much more to save you and the others." He choked on the tears that had been coming out without challenge.

As his tears began to stop the whispers started up again. This time he didn't have the phone on at all. He turned it off shortly after leaving his sister's house. He looked around to see if a vent was nearby or not. When he couldn't find anyone, he curled up in the far corner of the tub trying to comfort himself. A large menacing shadow appeared against the curtain, but the strange thing is where the eyes are supposed to be, you could see the light from the room. "Go away goddamn it. you are just a figment of my trauma." He repeated to himself over and over. The shadow stood there for about an hour of cornering him in the tub doing nothing it just vanished.

He began to hyperventilate as the light poured back into the tub. "Fuck my life. Maybe I do need to go get those meds." He said to himself as he got out and wrapped a towel around his waist. He quickly got a set of sleeping clothes and went to lay in his bed. As he found himself unable to sleep, he picked up a book he brought with him. He would have gotten his phone, but he doesn't feel like having people talking to him. He opened the novel to the last page he read when a figure crept up the wall and settled in a corner. It sat in silence staring at him as tendrils of shadows snaked off of it in different directions. He tried to not acknowledge it, but the chattering of teeth began to get to him.

Chapter 3: Volatile Shadows

"I can't sleep with this fucking shadow looking at me all night." Travis said rolling over in his bed. He threw the cover over his head trying to ignore the shadow watching over him. The whispers continued to Echo through the room throughout the night. Travis slowly managed to drift off to sleep despite the sound of his friends talking to him from the grave. As he slipped deeper and deeper into sleep he began to dream.

As he opened his eyes he was in a hut in Afghanistan. The smell of black powder filled his nose. The sounds of gunfire surrounded him. Everyone around him was screaming and yelling orders at each other. "Where are we?" Travis asked the soldier closest to him.

"We are in the middle of a gun fight to hold our lines." The soldier said without turning to him

"That seems about right." Travis said to himself.

A shot rang out above his head and a soldier fell in front of him. It shook Travis to his core because the soldier had no face. It was just a pit of darkness. Travis covered his mouth to stifle a scream from coming out. The gunfire got more intense, and more men fell. More men without faces. Travis raised his weapon and peaked out from behind the wall. A long line of those cloaked figures stood there pointing. He didn't see any weapons in their hands.

As bullets began to fly at him his alarm clock rang out. He shot up in his bed with sweat pooled up around him and pouring down his forehead. He got up and ran to the bathroom before collapsing over the toilet and puking his guts up. Travis took a deep breath before getting water from the nearby sink.

"What is happening to me?" He asked as he took a good look in the mirror at himself.

He splashed water on his face before getting into the shower. As he was there all he wanted to do was sit there and let the water wash over him. The wish that the water could wash away all the stuff that has been happening Filled his mind. Quickly he washed his body and hair then quickly got out. As Travis got dressed the whispers continued, but they stopped as he left the hotel. Travis headed straight for a nearby bar, and quickly found a seat at the bar.

"One whiskey please." Travis asked, sitting down a ten-dollar bill.

The bartender sat down a glass in front of him without speaking to him. Travis stole a look into the mirror across from him. What he saw was a cloaked shadow sitting behind him. It locked eyes with him and didn't wave; this caused him to become rigid with fear. He asked for drink after drink after drink. He wanted to make the shadow disappear but even with the drinks it wouldn't vanish. It began to get closer as his vision became blurry from the effects of the alcohol.

"Can I get another one please?" Travis asked, slurring his words.

"I am sorry friend. I cannot give you any more drinks, but I can call you a cab." The bartender said for the first time since Travis sat down at the bar.

Travis struggled to get up but still managed to make it out of the bar doors. He pulled out his phone and dialed his sister. The phone rang out the dial tone four times before the voicemail came up. He let out a sigh as the beep came to record his message.

"Hey sis, I know I messed up when I was over at your place. I have scheduled a new appointment and decided to continue to see the therapist. I have started looking for a place to go to that is outside of the V.A. I am just under so much stress and I still can't believe that all those men died. I do blame myself for what had happened to them. I was driving the truck when all of that happened and my actions are responsible for the truck going into the sand dune when it did." Travis stopped as the phone cut him off.

Travis called his sister back hoping to get the voicemail again. To his surprise his sister actually answered the phone. Travis could hear the tears in her eyes but not in her eyes, it was in her voice. It brought tears to his eyes hearing her the way she is.

"Travis, I heard the voicemail you left me, and I was about to call you when you called me." Vinessa said before Travis continued.

"I have more to add to it. Don't say anything but I have more to tell you. I take the responsibility of their deaths upon myself. When I shot the tire out or well went to shoot the tire, I fully understood what direction the truck was going to go. I did feel that the result would have been the same even if I would have shot the driver. I didn't mean for anyone to die. I didn't want them to die but I understood the risk of it all. I had hope that we would have all made it home living and breathing." Travis began to choke on the tears in his voice as he continued to think about everything he just said.

"Listen to me and listen to me good Travis. It was war and every one of those men knew what they had signed up for. It doesn't matter how you slice it. Those boys knew that they had more of a chance coming home in a box. They knew what happened that day when the explosions started. You did the best you could, but I am not in your head. Only you can help yourself Travis." Vinessa tried to hold back the emotions in her voice.

Travis began to cry without being able to stop it. He cautiously makes his way to a nearby bench as he begins to buckle under his own weight. As he cried, he kept the phone close to his ear because he didn't want to feel alone. To Vinessa's credit she stayed on the phone with him while he cried.

Vinessa hung up her phone and quickly got into her car to retrieve her brother from the bar. Soon she was in front of the bar, her brother crying out in the open. Vinessa got out of the car and placed a hand on Travis's shoulder. Travis looked up and slowly met his sister's eyes. With a smile Travis got up and dried his eyes as they got in the car to leave.

"Are your hungry big bro?" Vinessa asked Travis with a smile.

"I am always hungry." Travis laughed at this question.

They had stopped in the parking lot of their local pizza parlor when the whispers started. Travis tried to ignore the whispers, but they caused him to lean against the window with how loud they are. He found his sister's hand on his shoulder trying to comfort him. He went to look her in the eyes but when he did her face was gone. It was replaced with a bag that had a whole ripped around the mouth showing a hanging jaw. While his eyes had been locked on the gaping mouth, he could see hordes of flies in her airway.

Soon the drone of the whispers had been replaced with an assault of buzzing from the wings of flies. Both of the hands of what used to be his sister had both of its hands on his shoulders. He could have sworn that through the buzzing of the flies he could hear his name being called. He began to focus on that sound of what he hoped was his name reality began to come back into focus.

"Travis!" Vinessa yelled, shaking him back into the current world.

"Sorry I don't know what happened to me there." Travis said as he took a deep breath to make sure he was level-headed.

"Are you sure you are okay to go in?" Vinessa asked, taking her hands off her shoulders and sat back in her seat.

"Yes, I am sure that I am." Travis said with a smile on his face.

They exited the car and slowly made their way into the restaurant. Out of the corner of his eye Travis saw the female figure with the bag over her head making rapid twitching motions. The figure made no noises while it twitched. With a deep gulp of air, he looked forward at his menu trying to ignore it.

Travis and Vinessa ordered their food within a few minutes of the figure appearing. Surprising himself Travis managed to ignore the figure for the entire meal. As they got up to leave the figure had gone but every customer in the restaurant had dawned the bag of the bag headed woman. Seeing the sight of all the bags caused Travis's heart to race and sweat to pour from his forehead. He began to hyperventilate the closer he got to the exit.

He tried to take deep calming breaths but each breath he took the more his vision began to leave him. It was like he was beginning to become drunk again. His legs as well began to buckle again. Before he knew it his sister caught him under the arm. He was not present in the current world. He was being carried off of the battlefield.

When he looked over, he was being carried by himself. He saw the pain that was written on his face when he was carrying away those men. As Vinessa helped Travis into her car he was seeing something different. Travis saw himself being tossed into the back of that truck he had driven into the desert. While his sister drove him home Travis saw the entire scene of leaving in the truck and hearing the guns being fired at the enemy.

Before he knew it, he was witnessing the truck flip into the sand dune. He could hear the gunfire and see himself fall onto the truck through a cut on the covering of the truck bed. The helicopter could be heard then seen coming in and picking his body up. As the helicopter vanished into the distance Travis shot back into the current reality. His sister gave him a look of being scared but also curious about what was going on in his mind.

"Are you okay?" Vinessa said trading looks between him and the road itself.

"Yes, I believe I am. I was having a flashback to when the helicopter brought me back to the base. It was when the truck crashed into the sand dunes. The only thing is, I was watching from the view of one of the injured men." Travis said as he cleared the sweat from above his brows.

As Vinessa pulled the car into the parking lot of the hotel she handed Travis a wet nap for his face. Travis exited the car and started to walk to his room. As he entered the room he saw once more the shadow crawl up the wall and take its position on the wall. The difference is that now it has developed a mouth. Its mouth was filled with sharp snow-white teeth that did nothing but chattered.

The noise it made sounded of crickets in the night. It sounded like thousands had entered his brain. Travis clasped his hands over his ears trying to make it stop. No matter how tight he clasped his hands the sound continued. When the sound ended, he removed his hands he had blood on his hands. Quickly he ran to his bathroom and looked into his mirror to find blood coming from his ears.

He ran water onto a cloth to clean the blood. He leaned down and began to wash his face. As he came back up the shadow was looming over him and again the chattering began again. The shadow then produced a claw that crept over his head. With the force of a body builder Travis was thrown into the wall.

As he fell to the ground his vision was being teased by the darkness of unconsciousness. As he looked around the room, he could see his blood slowly working down the wall. He tried to move his arm to check the back of his head, but his body would not move. He was able to talk but barely. He looked around the best he could and was able to see his phone.

"H-hey Sheri." Travis struggled to get the words out.

He could see his phone chime to life and the words came out. "How may I help you?"

"Emergency." Travis saw blood come out of his mouth along with the words.

"Dialing emergency services now." The phone then began to ring.

"911 what is your emergency?" The operator asked from the other end of the line.

"H-Help m-me." Travis said but with mostly blood gurgling over the words.

"We have an ambulance on its way sir please stay with me." The operator spoke with haste realizing the need of emergency help.

Travis began to lose consciousness as time went by. He was only awakened by The slamming of his front door being kicked open. The same was done with the bathroom door as firefighters and paramedics came in. They yelled but it was muffled as his body lost its energy. Before he blacked out, he was being carried into the ambulance.

Chapter 4: Lifelines

Travis was put in a room on the floor with the intensive care unit. He had a breathing tube in his mouth to assist him and, was hooked up to every machine you could think of. In the background you could hear the vitals beeping on the machine up and down. He was unable to breath on his own, but his brain was still working. He could still faintly catch the smells of a cleaner on the air.

He was trapped in his own mind now. Travis knew he was at the mercy of someone else's ability to do their job. He could hear the nurses and doctors yelling at each other about medication and surgery. The one thing he knows about is that in his mind he is stuck. What Travis sees is he is trapped in a white room. He is trapped in a white room with one door. He doesn't know how to open the door even if it has a door handle.

"I wonder why I am here." Travis said to himself while he sat in the only chair in the white room.

"You are here Travis because you can't save anyone. Not even yourself." Spooner's voice echoed from every corner of the room all at once.

"You're not SGT. Spooner! I don't know what or who you are!" Travis yelled jumping up out of the chair as his face turned red and sweat poured from his forehead as he became more frustrated.

"I am Spooner, I am everyone that you have failed to save. I am everything bad and or evil in this world. I am your fear. I am your trauma. I am your nightmares. I am you." The voice said again echoing from every corner of the room.

"I don't care what you are. Why did you decide to choose me of all people?" Travis asked, starting to become level-headed once more.

"I chose you because, all the pain you have feeds me." The voice followed up with a laugh.

As things fell silent the only thing, he could hear was the sound of his breathing. Loud stomps began to sound of around the room sending his heart into overdrive. They got followed by the formation of footprints being formed on the walls in flame. He followed them in silence with his eyes as they kept going and going, slowly getting louder and faster. Until finally it stomped right above the door. Loud banging came from the door. He got closer to the door with the intention to open it. He stopped in his tracks as he saw a dent slowly began to form. Slowly the door began to open from the force.

The door flew off the hinges revealing a long empty white hallway. Shadows began to dance around the room in which Travis sat and slowly started to close in on him. As they continued to close in Travis ran from the room as fast as he could his heart pounding in his chest. As he ran from the room the door shot back on to the hinges locking the shadows within the room.

"I have to find a way to get the fuck out of here." Travis said out loud to himself.

Vinessa walked into the hospital room and began to cry seeing Travis in the bed. She ran to his side and grabbed his hand. She pulled out her phone and dialed a number. This number belongs to the family friend and priest Father David of Montecule Church.

"Hello this is Father David?" The Father said on the other end of the line.

"Hello father this is Vinessa." She said quickly after the Father finished talking.

"Hello Vinessa, how may I help you today?" The Father asked with concern.

"It is my brother Travis he is in the hospital. They said that he is in a coma from head injuries. They said he had been attacked and thrown into a wall in his hotel room." Vinessa said, trying to hold back some tears.

"I will be on my way. I will catch the first flight out of Marrion. You two should come back home for a bit after this for a vacation. I have my house open down here." The Father said with care in his sentence.

"I will run it by him Father when he wakes up." Vinessa said followed by a small chuckle.

As she hung up the phone Vinessa held her brother's hand tight and prayed over him. She let her tears flow freely as they sat there in that cold room. Breathing in the air freshener and the cleaning products didn't bother her. She was just worried about her brother surviving his ordeal.

Travis ran for the end of the hall and saw it turning to the left. He took the turn too fast and slipped causing him to slide into the wall. Travis winced in pain but still got up and kept going. The thought of needing to get out. He needed to get out of his own head. A voice was coming from somewhere, but he couldn't tell where it was.

"Vinessa? Is that you?" Travis said looking around to see if he could find her.

When he couldn't find his sister, he kept running through the hall. Something told him to stop and as he looked around all of the turns began to bleed together. As he turned around, he saw a shadow trying to stay out of sight behind him.

"I see you, you bastard." Travis said spinning around.

The shadow, his shadow didn't move this time. It grew in size and shape. It took the shape of the monster that I saw in the corner of his hotel room. It took the form of the bag lady that was outside of the therapy office. This caused Travis to check his own body out of question if, he was still himself. He began to see it forming a mouth, and then its eyes. It was the same eyes that had burned themselves into his very soul.

It was the eyes he saw every time he went to sleep. The same eyes he thought he saw around every corner. He knew he will never forget them even if he put effort into it. It was the eyes that will haunt him till the day he died. Maybe they will follow him after as well.

When their eyes meet, he could feel his body freeze. He didn't expect to see the shadow in his mind. He didn't think he would see it ever again after blacking out. He tried to move, but found himself only able to stare, and shiver as fear moved through him in waves. This feeling was made worse as he saw its mouth begin to move.

"You will not make it out of here." The monster's voice echoed in a loud booming tone.

"I will find a way out of here and I swear it!" Travis yelled at this monster on the wall.

Travis turned and saw a door on the wall behind him. Cautiously he reached out and grabbed the knob. With a deep breath he turned the knob and walked through the door. As he came through the threshold of the door he was hit in the face with a bright sunlight and the laughing of young children. The smell of fresh apple pie was light in the air.

"I know this place." Travis whispered as he looked around the room.

As he walked around, he realized it was his childhood home. The children he had heard were him and his sister running around. He quietly walked around and went down the stairs to find his mom in the kitchen. He walked towards the kitchen mesmerized by seeing his mother for the first time in five years. As he walked into the kitchen, he saw her cutting up apples with a large knife.

"Oh, hello there Travis." She said as she spun around with an unnaturally large smile.

"Hello mom. How did you know it was me?" Travis asked slowly backing up.

"I know everything you little bastard!" She yelled as her voice deepened and her face melted away to a sharp toothed demon.

Travis ran into a wall that wasn't there before. The only way he had left was a window that was behind this demon pretending to be his mother. Before he could think of a way around it the thing already charged him with the giant knife. He rolled out of the way catching a cut on the back of his arm.

Travis ran and dropped sliding between its legs and made a jump for the window. It managed to catch his leg in time and shoved him into the oven after slamming his head against the wall. He awoke to being in the oven as it heated up. He could feel the heat and could smell his own flesh starting to cook. Even with all the pain he was feeling he began to kick the glass window on the door.

"Let me out of this goddamn oven damn it!" Travis yelled as he started to kick the glass harder but barely seeming to work.

After ten minutes the glass cracked and finally broke. Travis took a deep breath before sliding out of the oven. As he exited, he suffered cuts on his back and arms. Blood dripping from his arms and feeling weak Travis ran to the window. Slowly he slipped out the window.

Travis looked out into the horizon and found a wall of doors. Each door had been branded with a number one-twelve. Travis walked to the doors and carefully considered which one to open. He walked to the door with the number twelve and turned around. What he saw was his blood began to glow in front of the door branded with the number eight.

When he walked up to the door it had words inscribed on it. *"The number of dead is the number for out. You cannot pass on the souls you owe. The trials you take is to total your fall."* Travis began to get puzzled by the words not knowing what they could mean. The first thing that popped in his mind was that eight people died when he tried to get his squad out of the base in Afghanistan.

Travis took a deep breath as he opened the door. "I guess I am having to atone for the deaths of the guys I tried to save." The guys from the base.

Travis stepped through the door and was met with the desert. Already in his mind Travis knew all that was left to do was to walk. He started to walk and picked only one direction. While he walked, he had his hands in his pockets, and fell into deep thought as he locked his eyes on the horizon.

Father David entered the hospital, and speed walked his way to the front desk. He quickly signed the papers and got directed to the elevator. He hit the button to be taken to the intensive care unit on the tenth floor. As Father David got closer to the tenth floor his grip on his bible tightened. He felt a heavy dark presence as he got closer and closer to the floor.

"Hello Vinessa. I am sorry it took so long to get here." Father David said as he entered the hospital room.

"It is okay Father. It isn't like we are going anywhere." Vinessa forced out a fake laugh at the end of her sentence.

"I am sorry you children are having to go through this." Father David said as he pulled up a chair and took one of Travis's hands.

"I know you are a spiritual leader, but I am assuming you are going to tell me to trust God and the doctors, correct?" Vinessa asked Father David.

"Yes, my child God works through these doctors, and he put them here for a reason." Father David said with a smile on his face.

Father David took one of Vinessa's hands and one of Travis's hands. Father David and Vinessa both bowed their heads. As they began to pray Father David began to feel the dark presence get heavier around him, but he kept praying. He knew that prayer wouldn't be the thing that will save Travis on its own.

"Father David, do you think my brother will be okay?" Vinessa asked, looking at the Father with misty eyes more tears threatening to come forth.

"Yes, Vinessa I think he will be okay. This too will pass as will many trials ahead." Father David said trying to give Vinessa a reassuring look.

Travis found himself staring at a city built of sandstone and glass. A city void of life. A city void of anything really. As he walked into the city, he saw himself as the only living thing there. As Travis looked around the city began to look more and more familiar.

"I know this place." He said to himself as he walked into one of the buildings.

What he saw inside was a set of helmets lined up on a bench. Each one held a card that had the name of each soldier that had died in the attempted escape. Travis went to each and every card leaving a mark on it. Each mark was a version of his impression of them.

"I couldn't save you, but I do carry your memories with me. You all left an impression on me. You all left me with a memory that I cannot repay you for." Travis said as he sat across from them.

As he sat there a heavy presence wrapped its way around him. He was filled with dread and fear. The voices of the dead began to swirl around him. They gave him messages of his failure to save them that droned like angry bees. He could feel them attacking from all sides.

"You could have saved us."

"Why didn't you try harder?"

"I thought I was your brother?"

"Get the fuck out of my head!" Travis screamed holding his hands over his ears.

The voices repeatedly told him that all of the death was because of him. They told him lies about all of what he had done while in combat. The voices began to run together as he began to feel the weight on his shoulders. It got heavier before they caused him to break, filling his body with anger.

"Shut up! None of you are real! You speak nothing but lies!" Travis yelled while he secretly felt that they might be telling him the truth.

Travis out his hands over his ears and hummed to himself trying to drown out the voices. He kept getting louder and louder still trying. The only downside is the louder he got the more persistent and louder they got. It seemed as if they had begun to dig their way into his brain.

Travis soon got up and ran from the building and that is when he saw it. Shadows had been swirling around the building and when he got out of the building a face had formed on the swirling shadows. The face gave the shadows the look of a giant monster about to eat the building not caring what was inside of it. Travis then turned and started to run as fast as he could out of the town. As he did loud footsteps shook not only the ground but gravity itself seemed to tremble with each step.

"I must keep going. I must get away. I must get back to my sister." Travis said to himself as he tried to force himself to get faster.

Travis pumped his arms and legs as fast as he could. The sand made it harder for him to run. The surface being soft sucked his legs down more than it did when the surface would if he had been running on a road. The sweat poured heavily down his face as he pushed himself harder. The sweat stung his eyes as it began to flow down his face more.

As he kept running the desert slowly began to fade away into pavement and concrete. As Travis looked around, he found himself in a city. He also recognized this city. It is the city he was born in. He was in Marrion, North Carolina. His breathing was heavy. He felt like he was going to pass out. He was also thirsty.

"What is the point of bringing me to my hometown? No one died under my watch while I lived here." Travis said as his knees buckled, and he fell to the ground.

Chapter 5: The Father, The Son, and The Sister

Father David walked into the hospital chapel as soon as he could. The place was a little lackluster and tried to cater to more religions than space allowed. Even with those feelings to the side Father David felt it was good enough for the time being. He found himself sitting at the front nearest the collection of religious symbols.

"Please father receive my prayers. I would like to ask you to place your hands on Travis and heal his body. He is needed here with us but if you do feel the need to take him with you, I understand that also. His sister is extremely worried about him. Please give her hope as well. Amen." Father David prayed harder than he has ever prayed before.

Even after finishing his prayer he sat and looked upon the cross. He couldn't find what he was thinking exactly but at the same time he knew already. The thing he knew for sure was that even in the hospital chapel that darkness was present. Father David felt it was most strange to have that feeling in the one place that it wasn't supposed to be. He was supposed to feel safest in the chapel.

As he sat there another person entered the chapel behind him. The footsteps got closer and soon a hand was on the Fathers shoulder. He turned around to see a disheveled old man with oxygen hooked up around his nose. The old man bowed his head and began to pray. Father David got up and took a knee next to the old man.

"How can I help you my friend?" Father David asked looking into the old man's eyes.

"You can get away from the boy and his sister. They are mine!" The Old man yelled knocking over the father baring sharp teeth and red eyes.

Father David closed his eyes and tried to hide his face from the old man. All Father David could do at the time was pray. The old man let out a laugh before knocking out the Father and walking out of the chapel. Father David spent the time he was knocked out in his own mind trying to sort out his thoughts. He felt worthless as a priest with how things are going now.

"Father? Father are you okay?" A paramedic asked Father David as they broke a smelling salt under his nose.

"Y-yes I am." Father David said with a cough as he sat up holding his head.

"Thank goodness." The paramedic said as he stepped back to give the Father room.

"Did you see an old man walk out of this room?" Father David said as he supported himself into the seat next to him.

"No sir, but we can look for him. Right now, we need to get you seen by a doctor." The paramedic said checking the Fathers pulse and blood pressure.

"No, it is okay. I would like to go get to a doctor now." Father David said as he got into a wheelchair that was brought to him.

Father David was taken to a doctor and immediately was sent to get his head scanned for fractures. During the whole time even with the machine roaring around him his thoughts never wavered away from the old man. Why was the old man attacking him? What did the old man want with the Marvic children? It played on repeat in his mind.

He was taken back to his room and within two hours was given a clean bill of health. The very first thing Father David did was go to the local Catholic Church and pulled every book the archive had on demons. As he poured through the books, he found a demon that fed on people that suffered greatly on a mental level. As he read the information started piling up. He quickly got his hands on a notebook and started making a list.

The demon feeds off of trauma of men that are near the host female.

The name of the demon is Valieen Sparia

The demon appears in different forms depending on what would cause the most fear in the situation

The demon appears most in the older texts and seems to have faded away as each new revision was made to the books themselves.

"Need to get this information to these kids so that I can tell them that I can help them." Father David said as he got up and began to put the books back on the shelves.

As Father David began to exit the church rain began to fall. The Father thought it was a bit ironic that rain was coming down. He let out a bit of a chuckle from the thought of how it was. He started off to the street and waved down a taxi. As he got in, he let out a laugh louder than his small little chuckle.

"It seems just like a horror movie doesn't it?" Father David asked the driver as he got in.

"Yes, it does father." The driver let out a laugh just as thunder clapped above in a roar.

"Where am I taking you tonight Father?" The driver asked ready to enter the address into the GPS

"To the hospital please." Father David said while going over his notes again.

The driver typed in the address and the ride started. As the ride went on Father David kept an eye on the price as it went up. In the back of Father David's mind, he couldn't stop thinking of the demon fueled old man. Father David got his wallet out as they pulled into the hospital parking lot. He paid for the ride as he got out of the taxi and thanked the driver. As he entered the hotel Vinessa was sitting in the waiting room crying.

"Why are you down here my child?" Father David said, taking the seat beside Vinessa.

"They took Travis back for scans to see his brain activity and are going to use that to decide if he needs to be taken off support or not." Vinessa had to fight her tears to get her words out.

"We need to have faith that it will be okay and that he will wake up." Father David said in the most comforting voice Vinessa had ever heard.

"Don't you see that God has abandoned him!" Vinessa yelled, jumping out of her seat dragging the attention of security.

"God hasn't abandoned anyone, Vinessa. We have to give him time to work." Father David said, trying to get her to sit down.

The Father and Vinessa sat in silence for what seemed like hours. The doctor had stormed into the waiting room but to them it was in slow motion. It reminded the father of when Bay Watch was on TV. The doctor was the lifeguard, and they had gone out too far into the ocean.

"Your brother no longer needs to be on life support and has woken up." The words from the doctor came out in slow motion.

Vinessa jumped out of her seat in happiness. When the doctor turned to look at Father David his eyes had the same shade of red as the old man. The doctor began to get a grin that was too wide to be human but to Vinessa he looked like a normal doctor. The three of them went up to see Travis in his room but the whole ride up Father David couldn't put his trust in the doctor. Even after, considering this could be a trick the demon was playing on him his trust couldn't be placed.

As they entered the room Travis was sitting up with a tray in front of him. He sat there and just looked at the food with a grim look on his face. He poked it with his fork just moving it around, so it looked like he ate. He didn't even acknowledge they had entered the room. Father David touched Travis on the shoulder and to respond to that Travis jerked up locking eyes with the Father.

"Travis it's me, Father David. Your sister called me here. I was summoned because she was worried about you. I would like to pray with you." Father David spoke clear and with a smile on his face.

"Father, I have fallen from the path. I fell from the path while I was fighting the war. I got men killed that didn't need to die." Travis spoke with tears starting to come from his eyes.

"I know you didn't get your men killed. It is hard to stay the path during wartime. I was in the last war in the Middle East, and you know that." Father David bowed his head and touched his forehead to Travis's then began the prayer.

Travis began to melt away at the thought that Father David would understand what he was going through. All three of them traded looks between each other not knowing what to say. The doctor escorted himself out so that they could have time alone with each other. If no one saw him walk out the door no one would have even known, he had made his exit.

"Travis I would like you and your sister to come back to Marrion. I would like you two to come home." Father David said in a pleading voice.

"I have stuff to fix here before I can come back home. I will end up back home. I think I am ready for that." Travis said nodding in the Father's direction.

"I will help Travis get everything straightened out here, and then we will be on our way there." Vinessa said with a smile on her face.

Father David patted Travis on the shoulder and walked out of the room taking his notes with him. Father David went to his hotel room and packed everything he brought with him. The sound of claws scraping on the walls started to come from every direction. The Father couldn't help but straighten up his stance and start to pray. He wasn't scared of this demon, but he also knew that he had to fight back.

"I know your name." Father David said with his eyes remaining closed.

"Oh, you do?" The sound of clawed feet approached Father David from the front.

"Your name is-" Father David began to choke before he could get the words out.

"You know my name, do you?!" The voice speaking got louder and more aggressive.

All that came from Father David's mouth is gurgles as his throat continues to be cut off. The Father swung his feet trying to get down before his foot made contact with the thing holding him in the air. He pulled his foot back for a kick when the thing threw him against the dresser of his room.

"Y-your name is V-Valieen Sparia, and I cast you from this room." Father David said as he held his jaw out of pain.

"How dare you! You puny fucking insect!" The figure yelled as a large gust of wind moved through the room.

Father David let out a laugh that sounded like a mix of exhaustion and triumph as he finished packing and left to go to the airport. He didn't think that knowing the name of the demon would help him in any way. He got to the street and looked back up at the hotel and saw a dark figure standing in the window of the room that was next to his own. He waved down a cab not taking his eyes off the figure. All it did was wave at him with an inhuman white toothed smile.

As the cab pulled up beside him to pick him up, he quickly got in and handed the cab driver the money needed to get to the airport. The cab driver drove him to the airport fast. As he rode Father David couldn't help but look around for the figure. It drove him crazy because that face wouldn't leave his mind. He couldn't think of anything except for that face. Everything from the pupil less eyes that you could still feel trained on your soul, to the teeth that looked so sharp that they could tear your limb from limb like a professionally sharpened knife. He shuddered in his seat the more he thought about it.

"Are you okay Father?" The driver asked making eye contact with the rearview window.

"Y-Yes I am okay just thinking of something." Father David said trying to make himself look more relaxed.

"Okay father I wanted to make sure I don't have to take you to the hospital." The driver let out a small chuckle.

"Thank you for being such a kind person." Father David gave him a small smile.

They sat in silence after the exchange. Father David just stared out the window till the sound of the cab's engine starting to fall came to his ears. The cab driver started to curse and slam his fist on the wheel. He looked back and apologized to the father, but the father wasn't paying attention. Everything was slowed down for Father David. He knew what was happening because as he looked out the window, he saw it. He saw that awful face sitting behind him.

"I am sorry for cursing like that in front of you Father." The cab driver apologized again before getting out.

"It is okay my son." Father David said as he also got out of the cab.

The cab broke down on the bridge halfway between the airport and his hotel. He felt a tinge of worry enter his body with the current situation. He thought the demon from the hotel had found him looking for revenge. He decided he wanted to use his wait to think about something that tugged at his mind. The whole situation made him think back to a conversation he and Travis had when Travis was deployed to Afghanistan. Travis killed his first man that day. It was also the last time he had talked to Travis before today in a year and a half.

"Father David I killed someone today." Travis spoke in a solemn tone.

"You are over in a combat zone my son." Father David said in a reassuring voice.

"I know father, but I am having nightmares about it every night." Travis said with Father David.

"I know how it must feel. I have been in your shoes before. I once was a soldier when we started this war." Father David said himself thinking back to his time in the military.

"How did you get the nightmares to stop?" Travis asked, curious and needing an answer.

"I didn't get them to stop but I did train myself to know that they had been just dreams." Father David said, pulling out a paper for a therapist.

"Let me guess, Father you went to alcohol but that didn't work, and you went to therapy?" Travis said in a sort of mocking tone.

"You mock it, but therapy is the best option. Let me give you a name and you go to him when you get back." Father David said as the line went dead.

Chapter 6: Therapy Visit Two

"Welcome Travis. I didn't think you would come back after last time." Dr. Marron said, opening the door to his office.

"I am sorry for blowing up on you last time." Travis said, trying to laugh off the comment.

"I see you had sometime in the hospital." Dr. Marron said looking at his chart.

"Yes, I had an accident at my hotel and was unconscious for a bit." Travis said eyeballing the chart in the doctor's hands.

"I am glad to see you up and walking now." Dr. Marron said, sitting his chart down.

"I am glad to be up and walking sir." Travis said with a smile.

"Please don't be so modest with me. This is your safe place. Tell me how your PTSD has been." Dr. Marron said as he put one leg over the other and sat back locking his eyes with Travis's.

"If I am to be honest, I have been seeing things. I don't think it is just along the lines of normal things. It has been shadows and creatures. They feel like they mean to harm me. I have even had dreams that I see myself back in combat. The only strange thing is that no one has a face when I see them." Travis said while he tried to avoid making eye contact.

"I see what you are saying. Maybe these are just visual manifestations of your trauma. Have you tried interacting with these, things?" Dr. Marron took extreme interest in what Travis just said.

"No doctor, I have not tried to do anything with them. I have been trying to avoid the things for the most part." Travis said feeling the same frustration he did in their last session.

"Maybe they will go away if you show yourself as the one in control." Dr. Marron looked smug with his answer.

"How would I do that doctor?" Travis asked, genuinely wanting to know the doctor's answer.

"Well, I think if you show the things that manifest that you are not scared, they will go away. I also think that you are in no real danger from them." Dr. Marron grabbed his notepad and wrote down more notes.

Travis looked down and pulled out his phone to send a text to his sister. He felt that he was getting nowhere with Dr. Marron and couldn't tell him what had happened in his hotel room. When his phone screen came up his signal was gone, and he had just a small amount of battery.

"Is everything okay Mr. Marvic?" Dr. Marron asked before sitting his notepad down.

"Yes, doctor everything is okay." Travis said being careful not to let the doctor hear his concern.

"Well, I would like to know what happened when you had your accident in your hotel room." Dr. Marron gave Travis a serious look when he made this statement.

"Well, I was attacked. I didn't get a good look at the person or thing that attacked me. To be honest I thought I was going crazy cause it looked like it was just a shadow. It was there when it hit me but was gone when I hit the floor." Travis said feeling embarrassed that he had said anything at all.

"Do you think it may be possible to have injured yourself?" Dr. Marron asked, sounding very serious for the first time since they met.

"I would never hurt myself. I have a sister to look after. I can't afford to do something to myself." Travis was beginning to become more and more frustrated with the doctor.

"Your sister doesn't need you. No one needs you." Dr. Marron said, or was it Dr. Marron?

"What did you say?" Travis asked confused with what he just heard.

"I asked you if you could be sure you didn't hurt yourself. Accident or otherwise." Dr. Marron said like he had to clarify each word.

"I am sure that nothing could have happened to me." Travis said frantically as he was coming out of a distraction.

"I hope not Mr. Marvic because you seem like a good man and I want you to be well." Dr. Marron said with a Mona Lisa smile on his face.

"Well thank you doctor. I am glad I have this time to talk to someone. I don't think you could believe half of the stuff I have seen." Travis said with a small laugh.

"Lay it on me. I have heard many things." Dr. Marron gave another one of those no tell smiles that could hide itself if you didn't look for it.

"The first one I saw was a lady that wore a bag with a hole at her mouth. The only thing that was there was a broken and hanging bottom jaw. She had flies that came in and out of her windpipe. I could never look at her directly. After that was a hooded figure that had no features. I saw the hooded one first but didn't register it till after I saw the bag lady." Travis said, tears building in the corner of his eyes.

"I see. Could she be a reincarnation of someone that something could have been killed over in Afghanistan? Someone that you could have seen over there during a mission?" Dr. Marron asked with a look on his face genuinely trying to help with these questions.

"I didn't see anyone like her in Afghanistan. I did see a lot of bad stuff over there, but nothing like her. I did see a lot of my men get slaughtered the day I was brought back." Travis said thinking back to his time fighting.

As Travis sat and thought he had flashbacks. It was more than just seeing things. He had flashbacks of smells and sounds as well. He wanted to take a serious look back and make absolutely sure about not seeing her. Even with looking back all the way back to his first deployment she wasn't anywhere.

"What are you thinking Travis?" Dr. Marron asked leaning forwards playing he elbows on his legs and his chin on his hands.

"I was trying to see if I had ever seen her, and I can't find her anywhere." Travis shook his head as he spoke.

"That is fine, it was just a question, no need to stress yourself over it." Dr. Marron gave him a smile.

"You will never know your sins in full no matter how hard you tried." A voice spoke in the back of Travis's mind.

"Could this be a punishment for my sins Doctor?" Travis asked out of nowhere.

"That is something I cannot comment on from my point of view." Dr. Marron looked confused from the question.

"I didn't think I could get an answer for that now." Travis ended the sentence with a small chuckle.

"Why do you ask about your sins?" Dr. Marron asked, causing Travis to feel like he was actually doing his job for once.

"I keep hearing this voice and seeing these things. They keep telling me that all of my men died because of me. That my actions had not been enough." Travis said letting his head drop some.

"You know that you cannot control the actions of those that you had been fighting. It was a war zone and things happened out of your control. You can't put all of their deaths on yourself." Dr. Marron said, actually seeming to have a hint of caring on his face that showed it self in a smile and a light that appeared in his eyes.

"I guess it is where I wanted to protect everyone there." Travis said, finally letting his wall partially down.

"See we are making progress Travis. I need to know more about stuff like that." Dr. Marron said, pulling out his pen and paper.

"Well, I went into the military to try to protect people. I went with the full pride of my country and my men. I did learn while over there that no one can save everyone in the world. I still tried but failed over and over. It is like every time I start to care about anyone they are taken out of my life. I try to keep them close, but I always fall short and the toll on my mind is worse for it. I feel so useless. When I think about it, I put myself into a hole of thoughts that I can't dig my way out of." Travis said, feeling a little down about himself.

"Having an attitude like that is not a bad thing. It gives you the drive to do your job." Dr. Marron said, trying to cheer Travis up.

"I see what you are saying. I am sorry that this has been a bit of a downer of a session." Travis said in a low tone.

"It is my job to be here for you while you are going through what you are going through." Dr. Marron said, adjusting himself in his seat.

"*You are a good for nothing human. You are nothing but a waste of space. You will be going to hell and I will drag you there myself. That will be so unless you drag yourself there.*" The voice in the back of Travis's mind said again followed by the laugh of someone that has gone mad.

"Dr. Marron I can hear voices. They are the voices of the men that have fallen, but they are not the words they spoke before they had died." Travis said with concern in his voice.

"Your mind already knows those voices like the back of your hand. It is possible that all of these hallucinations are just your brain using the information you already have to create the creatures and voice you are seeing. The only reason they look different is the memory bank is using it but also using your trauma to fuel them." Dr. Marron said with a voice that made the information make sense.

"That makes sense. Thank you, doctor." Travis said with a smile creeping across his face.

"*We may live in your head, but we are not parts of your memories.*" The voice in the back Travis's mind got louder.

Travis dropped his head into his hands and gave a sharp inhale out of pain. The voice in his head was getting so loud that he had developed a migraine. Dr. Marron as a response went to his desk and got Travis so Migraine medicine. With a nod thanking the doctor Travis took the medicine and took a deep breath before he was ready to continue the session.

"I am guessing that you have voices in your brain getting louder? I can understand if you are. A lot of the people that I see have it happening." Dr. Marron said with a sympathetic look on his face.

"Yes, I am sir. It is like a voice that keeps nagging at the back of my brain. It tells me stuff that is the exact opposite of what you said. It tells me that I am deserving of all of this. It gets louder and louder each time you finish a statement." Travis said to him with his face lowered out of embarrassment.

"You don't need to feel embarrassed about this. It is normal for people to come back to the states with these symptoms. Many people report a lot of similar events. I can say that you are the first one with nearly every one of the symptoms at once." Dr. Marron said writing in his notebook.

"What do I need to do doctor?" Travis asked.

"I am going to write a prescription for more medication as much as you might not like that idea." Dr. Marron said feeling like he was giving too much medicine also.

Dr. Marron Pulled out his pad for prescriptions and wrote about three medications to add to the one Travis already had. Travis took it with a smile and put it in his pocket. As Travis stood, he didn't really want to end his session yet, but he knew that taking the prescription was the end of it.

"Thank you doctor I will go get these filled right away." Travis smiled and shook his doctor's hands, but the doctor didn't let go.

"Travis I would like to take you and pay for your medication myself." Dr. Marron said, grabbing his keys.

"You don't have to do that doctor." Travis said feeling like he made himself seem poor even with having money.

"Don't think I haven't seen that look before. You feel that I think you have no money. I just know that you have better use for that money you have. I want to pay for your medicine. I prescribed it anyway." Dr. Marron smiled leaving his office with Travis.

"Oh, thank you, Doctor." Travis said not knowing how to take his gesture of kindness.

They exited the building and with the doctor close behind Travis stopped cold in his tracks. She was there again. The lady who wore the bag over her head. She didn't do anything this time. She just stood there, her head limp to one side, bugs crawling out of her mouth.

"What are you seeing Travis?" Dr. Marron asked, putting a hand on Travis's shoulder.

"It is the bag wearing woman." Travis said his gaze was not wavering.

"She isn't real Travis. She is just a figment of your imagination." Dr. Marron said slowly, helping Travis walk to his car.

Even though the Doctor couldn't hear it, the bag wearing lady was laughing. She was laughing at the fact the Doctor said she wasn't real. She was pushing to show Travis she was very real. As he got to his car Travis and Dr. Marron both saw a mark appear out of nowhere on the side of his car. They exchanged looks to each other and the car both. Quickly Travis got in his car and left the parking lot meeting the Doctor at the nearby pharmacy.

"Maybe it was a bird we didn't hear or see fly by." Dr. Marron said not knowing what to say.

"We can only hope that, but I am fearing that it was not." Travis said as he and the doctor went in to get the Medication.

They both took seats to wait for the medication to get filled. They both sat trying to process what they had just seen. Travis had been attacked before but never seen something happen to an object around him. Travis was starting to see that this thing had more power than he had thought it did.

"Is it possible that we are having a shared hallucination from sharing information about what you are seeing?" Dr. Marron asked Travis, trying to figure out an answer.

"I have to make a call doctor; can you get my medication for me?" Travis asked standing up.

"Yes, I can. You go call who you need to call." Dr. Marron said, waving his hand.

Travis exited the building and pulled out his phone. He had one person that would understand what was going on. He scrolled down in his contact and made a call to Father David. It didn't even take two tones before the Father answered.

"Hello?" Father David asked.

"Father David, we have a major problem." Travis said.

Chapter 7: Welcome, Home

Travis started taking his medicine after it sat in his briefcase for three days. It was something that sat in the back of his mind after he got them. He was never a big fan of having the medication. When he did take it, he didn't feel like himself and he didn't like that. He learned that as a child. The hardest thing he did was having to tell his therapist that he would have to start remote visits. He had his mind set on moving back to his hometown. In his mind it would help him by getting a change of surroundings.

"I am going back to my hometown, but I want to keep you as my therapist. Is it possible for you and I to have remote visits?" Travis asked Dr. Marron

"Yes, I would be Glad to continue that way. I will continue to keep your sessions at zero even though you won't live nearby anymore. " Dr. Marron spoke with truth and a smile.

"Thank you, doctor. I feel after what happened when you and I went to get my medicine. It would be best if you stayed as my therapist." Travis said before taking his medicine.

"I agree with that statement. I do have a unique view into your situation. " Dr. Marron said, nodding to Travis's statement.

After he had settled the situation with his therapy the next move was talking to his sister. When he got to her house, she was already packing up her bags. She closed her trunk ready to leave right as Travis put his car in park. She gave him a smile as she got in her car ready to begin the long drive back to Marrion. Marrion was a town they never thought they would have to go back to.

It was a small town that sat in the north west of North Carolina. It used to be a logging town before factories began to move in. Within a year of factories moving in the town moved to making textile products. It became a town you grew up and died in. You died as a factory worker.

The only thing the town had that Travis and his sister missed was the nature. Even with the factories the town had a large amount of nature. The streets had been lined with trees and flowers. Bright colors during the spring surrounded everything from buildings to trees. Rolling hills of blues, yellows and reds.

Travis loved the fall when he was at home. It was the perfect weather to him. He was never cold but also never hot. He also loved looking at all of the colors that had been new to him at the time. The oranges and the yellows appealed to him the most. They quickly rose to being his favorite colors just as fast as the season rose to being his favorite.

As the thoughts of his childhood came a smile crept across his face. Him, and his sister had a great childhood in his opinion. They played nearly every evening until night teased the sky. The downside of his childhood was seeing men exchange in place of his father during his deployments. Eventually his father just never came home. That was the darkest day. His father got an early ride home to surprise his mother but when he got there she was already being preoccupied.

He watched his father scream about how much he loved our mother and in response she threw things at him. She was yelling about how if he loved his family he would have stayed home. Travis knew why his father fought. He also knew his mother's pain as well.

His stepfather came to be four months after his father left. After his stepfather moved in Travis no longer saw days of playing late into the evening. He spent his day defending his sister from the abuse of his stepfather. Travis was beaten every day by his stepfather when his mother worked late. When she worked late his stepfather tried to take advantage of his sister, which got worse as she rose in age. The day Travis was working late at work he came home to his sister running out of the front door with torn rags of what was left of her clothes.

Travis blacked out and went into the house. All he saw was rage. He tore apart the house till he saw his stepfather in his sisters' room upstairs. He locked the door behind him when he heard his mother pull into the driveway. His stepfather threw the first punch. Though his memory was spotty he could remember the fight. He could remember the blood coming from a cut above his eye and from his busted lip. He could remember his mom screaming when she found her husband thrown through a window and landing on the picket fence below.

That was the last time he saw his mother. It was the day he walked into the back of a cop car without being cuffed. He also sat silently through the court process without fighting the charges. His sister was the last family he had left because she was the only one to visit him in prison. He only got out of prison when he was recruited into the military.

He regretted nothing he did that night. He knew what the man was and that he needed to be stopped. He learned that shortly after that night that his sister was removed from his mother's care. That made him feel that what he did was not a waste of effort. It made him lose his mother, but he didn't care. If she was going to allow people like that be around then he had no mother. His only family was his sister and at this point Father David. He had been there through everything. Even if he didn't agree with how he handled it, he saw Travis in the correct side of the situation.

Travis was sent a video of his stepfather's funeral even though he said he wouldn't accept it. The more he thinks about it the more it brings up a conversation between Father David and himself. It was one that made a huge impact on Travis. He even still uses the advice to this day when he finds something he can't stand.

"Travis even if you had done something with righteous motivations today. It does not mean you will not do it in the wrong tomorrow." Father David said from behind the security glass.

"Yes, I understand Father, but I hope God does not look down upon me for this action." Travis said, holding his head in his hands.

"Travis, he will forgive you because you did it to protect your sister. If you would not have done what you did who knows what could have happened to her." Father David said while putting his hand on the glass.

"Yes, Father I understand what you are saying. You have always been here for me. Can you tell me why it is you have come?" Travis asked remembering that the guard said the Father came with business.

"Yes, I have a way for you to get out of here early." Father David pressed a brochure to the window. *"The military is in need of soldiers and are giving prisoners that offer no threat to the public a chance to join."* Father David spoke with a smile on his face about this chance.

"I will take this chance and hope after my time I can return to my sister." Travis said as a guard began to dial a number into the prison's phone.

After that meeting Travis remembers three visits from military personnel. In three short months he was in the deserts of Afghanistan fighting terrorists and military alike. He remembered the rush he got from the fire fights. The only downside was he came back to a town filled with the darkness set in place by the events before he was arrested. Every thought of the town brought darkness throughout the years. It was the home to his darkest actions. It was also the place where his—in his mind—humanity died.

He hated this town to the lowest pit of his soul. He never wanted to be here ever again. This place sent him to that hell overseas. He was grateful that it gave him the escape he needed to run from himself, but he was too tired to run anymore. He was ready to find his place to die. He was dead within; he was useless to the world. These prospects came through his mind faster the closer he got to Marrion.

His hometown came into view on the horizon bringing both joy and anger to him. His joy grew when he saw his church come into view rising high above the other buildings like a beacon of hope to those who come here lost. That was the first place he had gone while his sister went to the home Father David said they could use. He parked in the parking lot and sat for an hour starting at the front door remembering coming as a child while his mother fucked all those men within their home. Brought in that man that bruised his body and tried to take his sisters innocence that night.

"Father David are you here?" Travis asked his voice echoing through the main chamber.

"Yes, I am here Travis, How may I help you?" Father David asked, coming out of his office.

"I would like to talk about the thing that has been going on." Travis said going to the Fathers office.

"What is on your mind Travis?" Father David asked sitting down at his desk.

"Father it has gotten worse." Travis said not making eye contact with Father David.

"I have something to tell you as well Travis." Father David said.

"What is it Father?" Travis asked but when he made eye contact with the Father his face was twisting and contorting.

To Father David he saw the same thing. Neither of them made any moves or said any words to each other. They held true hoping it would pass. When it did not Father David was the only one to speak. As he spoke Travis didn't know he was talking.

"What was it you wanted to tell me Father?" Travis said but Father David didn't know if it was Travis or not.

"Travis we are dealing with what I believe is a demon." Father David said, pulling the notes out of his desk and laying them in front of Travis.

"Father, I have a question for you." Travis said, still seeming normal to Father David.

"What is that Travis?" Father David asked, starting to feel something was off.

"Have you seen the eyes of an angel Father?" Travis asked looking out the window as a storm started to build.

"Excuse me?" Father David asked, confused.

"Have you seen the eyes of an angel Father?" Travis asked, raising his voice as rain started to fall.

"No, my son I cannot say I have." Father David said, still confused leaning forward on his elbows.

"They are filled with lies and tricks so that blame for their actions gets put on other religions. We all fall for it and fall into these tricks repeatedly. We blame religions for the evils created by God himself brought to the earth by his angels." Travis said, turning to the Father revealing that the demon was sitting there.

It lunged at the father knocking him out of his chair. The fall hit his head hard against the ground knocking him out. As he came back to reality Travis stood above him shaking him. Travis had a worried look on his face when the Fathers eyes opened. Father David was confused as to why Travis was worried till, he saw the blood that painted the wall behind him.

"Father, you hit your head pretty hard. What happened?" Travis asked still with the worried look on his face.

"You had become a demon asking about angels and their eyes then you jumped after me. Which is how I have come to be on the floor." Father David said, trying to sit up.

"I will go get a cloth to clean up the back of your head while I call an ambulance." Travis said while he made an exit.

The Father took his notes and read over them again the best he could. He had some issues reading it as his vision bounced between double vision and normal vision. He put it back in his desk giving up halfway through reading them. He knew now that it was no normal demon since it had power within a church.

"Father I have a rag here for you." Travis said coming back into his office.

"Thank you, son." Father David said unable to hide the worries he had.

"What's wrong Father?" Travis asked seeing how worried Father David was.

"W-We are dealing with a demon that has more power than any demon I have ever seen." Father David said fear continuing to build in his eyes.

"Why do you say this Father David?" Travis asked before he realized how dumb of a question it was.

"It managed to have that much power while inside a church." Father David said as the paramedics came inside to take him to the hospital.

Travis followed the paramedics out the door and to his car. He pulled out right behind them but went to see his sister instead of following them to the hospital. He knew in the back of his mind the father would be okay. As he pulled into the driveway of the house, they would be staying in his sister met him outside.

"Hey, Travis, where did you go?" Vinessa asked as she came out of the house.

The house was a large ornate old looking building. It had large marble pillars standing outside leading to two large heavy doors. Vinessa looked like a princess exiting the building. She smiled as she came down the large, curved steps. Travis pulled his car to a stop and his sister was already unpacking her car. Travis got out of the car and began unpacking his car.

"I went to the church to talk to Father David." Travis said with a smile.

"Oh, How is he?" Vinessa asked.

"He was doing good till he fell in his office." Travis said with a grim look.

"Is he okay?" Vinessa asked with an urgency in her voice.

"The paramedic said he should be fine from looking at his head." Travis said with a slight smile on his face.

As they entered the main room it opened into a large marble room with a checkerboard floor. Our footsteps echoed through the empty room. Travis and Vinessa had been in awe of the architecture of the room. It seemed like no one had ever been there in a few years. It was the cleanest building they had ever been in.

"This place is beautiful!" Vinessa yelled just to hear it echo through the halls.

"Yes, it really is beautiful." Travis agreed with a smile.

They both walked through the house to find their rooms. Travis was really snooping around to find where the library would be. This house was provided by the church so it should have a library of church books. Books about demons and angels. Books about how to get rid of demons. *"I needed to learn as much as I could about what I am dealing with."* He thought to himself as he walked the halls.

"Hey brother I found my room!" Vinessa called from down the hall.

"I found mine also!" Travis yelled back.

Travis did find his room, but he was looking for the library still. As he continued to walk the halls, he found the library. He went back and sat down his briefcase in his room. Travis went to the library shortly after putting his stuff up. He sort of knew what books to look for and just searched.

Chapter 8: The World Of Demons

Travis walked into a room that had three floors worth of walls lined to the roof with books. It had an open center with all of the walls to the roof allowing the skylight to send a shaft of light down on the room. It was bordered with balcony after balcony. Each one connected by steps and had ladders so you could reach high up books.

Travis noted the smell of old book pages. One book he picked up had worn and yellowed pages. He picked up one book that was on a nearby shelf and it was crisp with white pages. He found it amazing that each and every one these books had a different age. He was looking at decades on decades of continued knowledge that continued even today.

"This is so amazing." Travis whispered to himself.

He saw one book that stood out to him on the second floor. The light hit it just right to make the gold trim and letters shine like they lit up on their own. He quickly made his way up the steps to the second floor. It felt like his feet didn't even touch the floor his entire way to the second floor. When his hand made contact with the book, he felt like it belonged in his hands. Not just for him touching it but like he was drawn to it.

"This is amazing." Travis said slowly, running his hand over the book's leather gold lined cover.

The book's cover was pure leather wrapped over cardboard from what Travis could guess. The lining and trim was gold along with the letters. It had no author that Travis could see but it had a large font title. It was called *"The Book of The Trauma Eater."* Travis took the book down to one of the desks. As he opened it up, he saw the pages had gold trim as well but with normal black words.

"Someone took great care in making you, didn't they?" Travis asked as if the book would answer him.

He began to read the page slowly and steadily. Right away he learned that the demon that the book was based on not only turned-on God but the devil also. The demon named *"Valieen Sparia"* had formed his own cult through using puppets to write and publish its ideals. Through the formation of its cult, it gained power and instigated murders and sacrifices.

"Good God. This thing started its own religious army." Travis said, trying to hide his surprise.

"God does not live within this book." The words came from a shadow that pulled out the chair in front of Travis, sending a feeling of fear through his body and freezing the air around him.

He could feel eyes staring into his soul even though he could see none. From the shadow came a pale cracked arm lined with black veins. The arm was attached to a large torso that had a black hole in the center in which the black veins branched from. At The top, the torso was a fanged skull that held bright red eyes. Travis could hear claws tapping on the marble floor under the table.

"I am guessing you are Valieen Sparia?" Travis asked.

A laugh came from within the skull and it soon burst into a thunderous echoing laugh. After the short laughing fight the red eyes locked with Travis's own eyes. While the two locked eyes Travis could feel his trauma being dragged from his brain. It was like the creature was forcing his fears and memories out by force. Travis struggled to try to stay out of his memories.

"Yes, I am Valieen Sparia, and I have been waiting to talk to you." Valieen got up and began to pace around the table. "That book you have started reading was written by a priest, but it was no priest of the church. It was written by one of my priests. I have no fear of you or your little church." Valieen said with a large amount of pride in his voice.

Travis tried to get up but with a point of his finger Valieen pushed him down. Valieen shook his head telling Travis not to move. He didn't say it with words, but Travis understood. Travis sat in silent watching as this demon circled like a vulture that found a dying animal.

"You know. You're a great source of sustenance to me. The largest source of trauma I have ever found. I always eat like a glutton. Stuffed on the cusp of exploding." Valieen let out a laugh like he just heard the funniest joke on the planet.

"So, you feed off of the trauma that humans get." Travis asked like he didn't already know the answer.

"Yes, I do and when the trauma starts to leave, I drag it back out. That's why when the father talked to you and tried to help you. I attacked him." Valieen let out another laugh.

Valieen walked with a purpose like he ruled the world. While Valieen had a lot of power within himself he is far from the most powerful. Valieen vanished before he came back into Travis's view and reappeared on the second-floor landing. He was looking through the books and pulled one off the shelf. He flipped through it acting like he was reading it and threw it to the floor.

"You know Travis you are the only person to escape the mind prison, but you didn't leave undamaged, did you?" With a puff of smoke, he was in Travis's face.

"I was hurt mentally yes." Travis said with a straight face.

"I knew it!" Valieen yelled as if he had just won some sort of contest.

"I will not fall to you. I hope you know that." Travis said with the most self-confidence he has ever had.

"I will drag you to hell and it will be of my design." Valieen leaned over and whispered in Travis's ear.

Valieen disappeared shortly after the conversation finished leaving Travis all alone. He was afraid to move but did after five minutes of silence. He couldn't believe that he just had a conversation with something that wanted to kill him. The image of Valieen will stick with Travis for the rest of his life.

Travis went to the kitchen to get water locking the library behind him. His sister was nowhere to be seen; he just assumed that she went to get food. His footsteps echoed as he entered the kitchen. The first thing he spotted was the gold trimmed book sitting on the coffee table. The big lettering on the front is still reading the same as before.

"Why is this book out here? I left it in the library." Travis said as he reached out to grab the book.

As he got close to the book his hand only made contact with the coffee table. He let out a long sigh then made his way to the sink and got some water. He took a seat at the table and could see Valieen watching him with a menacing stare from the fence that bordered the property. Travis knew he couldn't run away. He couldn't hide. This demon will be everywhere with him.

"I guess I am not going to get rid of you anytime soon." Travis took a drink of his water.

"Well, no I am your sister." Vinessa's voice rang happily from behind him.

Travis turned around and smiled at his sister who was carrying Chinese take-out bags. She gave him a smile, but Travis was focused on Valieen who continued to stalk outside from the fence. She sat across from Travis allowing him to hold eye contact even if he had to multitask while she was here.

"Are you okay brother?" Vinessa asked.

"Yes, I am sister." Travis's face began to glow as he looked at her.

"Okay, good." Vinessa said, handing Travis a plate of food.

"Yes, it is. Thank you for the food my dear sister." Travis said with a big smile.

They began to eat and when Travis looked back up Valieen was no longer at the fence but right behind Vinessa. Travis began shaking his head begging him to leave her alone. Valieen raised his hands to say okay and then kicked her chair out from under her. As she got back up, he vanished completely.

"Ouch, I guess I wasn't as set in the chair as I thought I was." She followed her statement up with a small chuckle. All Travis could think about was how close she came to being killed. Vinessa finished up her food and began cleaning while Travis returned to the library. All he could think about was trying to find a way to kill the demon. It was stuck in his head like a nagging thought. It pulled him further into a darkness he didn't think he could climb back out of. Travis began to search through the books and pulled down books on exorcism and demons.

He searched and searched, what he didn't see was that he searched all night without seeing it coming. He passed out in the middle of writing notes and awoke to sunlight surrounding him. As he looked around Valieen sat upon a balcony about laughing at Travis being surrounded by mountains of books and piles of papers.

"What are you laughing at?" Travis asked in a raspy voice.

"You are stressing yourself out looking for an answer that doesn't exist." Valieen continued to laugh after finishing his sentence.

"I will find a way." Travis yawned before falling back to sleep.

In his dreams he awoke in a fire ridden world surrounded by shadowed figures. They all had been unique to themselves. He looked around and saw Valieen upon a throne with a big smile across his face. As his arms raised fire came from the vents beside him and all the creatures bowed.

"Welcome to my world Travis. The world of my demons!" Valieen announced his voice booming through the air holding the same power as a thunderstorm.

Travis tried to speak but his vocal cords had been removed in his sleep. All that came out was a whistle. Valieen laughed at how powerless Travis was without his voice. Soon spikes rose from the ground pinning his feet and blades cut his knees. Valieen was around thirty feet tall here. He raised his foot and dropped it on Travis. When it was coming down the air pressure knocked Travis down before his foot actually crushed him. The shock caused Travis to awake in such a large pool of sweat that all of his notes had been ruined.

"I hope you enjoyed your short visit to my world." Valieen said as he vanished into a cloud of smoke.

"Travis, where are you?" Vinessa asked from down the hall.

"I am in here!" Travis yelled, throwing a piece of paper out the door.

"What is this room?" Vinessa asked looking around in awe.

"It is a library full of church research books. It has a book on every subject. Some of the books focus on certain creatures and demons while others are broader." Travis said as he started putting up the books.

"So, you found this place without me!" Vinessa yelled, acting playfully angry.

"Yes, I did!" Travis yelled doing the same.

Travis's phone pinged out causing them both to fall silent. Travis checked it and had a notification of a text. It was from his friend that hadn't talked to him since he left for Afghanistan. The name read *"Garett Randy "* he clicked to read the text. *"I hear you are back in town. Meet me at the pizza place downtown if you can. I will be there working on my novel anyway. "* Travis texted him back saying he could meet him.

"Vinessa I am heading out to meet someone." Travis said running by his sister grabbing the gold trimmed book.

"Okay, stay safe." Vinessa said walking out behind him.

Travis drove down the road with memories flooding back to him. He had not been in town long but had not been there in years. The pizza place had been moved but he found it. As he got out and walked in, he was flagged down. The man that flagged him down had milky white skin and amber brown hair.

"Hey there Travis. It's Garett." The man said with a smile while embracing Travis.

"It has been a long time Garett." Travis said, smiling.

The thing that kept Garett and Travis close was a secret. It was a secret that Garett didn't know and that he doesn't know is still true to this day. Travis has loved Garett since they started being friends. It was something that formed when Garett saved Travis when they had been strangers.

"Garett since we are older, I have something I need to tell you." Travis said, avoiding the gaze of Garett.

"What is it Travis?" Garett asked curious as to what Travis could say that he hasn't heard already.

"Can we go outside about this?" Travis asked standing up.

"Yeah sure." Garett said standing as well.

They both exited the building and Travis guided him to behind the building away from the windows. Travis's heartbeat faster and faster the closer he got to Garett. He had made up his mind on his way there that he would be fully honest with Garett. As they got away from the windows he turned around and took Garett by the hands.

"Garett I am sorry." Travis said kissing Garett out of nowhere. "I want you to be my boyfriend." Travis went back inside leaving Garett behind him stunned.

"Travis wait!" Garett yelled from behind Travis too late to catch him as he had gathered his stuff and left already.

Travis heard his phone ding for a text as he pulled to a stop sign. He checked it and it said *"Garett Randy."* Travis sat his phone back down as a line formed behind him. He drove and drove before he had to stop at a gas station. There against his thoughts he checked the text. It said *"Give me time to think about it. It had never been with a man, but I didn't hate the ambush kiss."*

Even though he didn't say no Travis is worried about kissing someone and that person being the first to know he was gay. He sent back his own text because he couldn't just leave him on read. *"I have had a crush on you for what seems like forever now. With everything going on in my life here lately I had to try. I am not suicidal or sick, but I don't know how long I have left. I hope that even if we don't become anything just know I am still here for you. It makes me so happy to have you in my life."* Travis sent the message just as a car went off the road and hit his car.

Chapter 9: Coming To Be

Travis is awakened by his phone ringing as the sun breaks the night. With a grunt he sits up blinking to clear his vision. He picks up his phone to read the display. The display reads *"Garett Randy"* this makes Travis feel tight in his stomach.

"Hello?" Travis asked, hitting the answer button.

"Hey, Travis. I talked to your sister. I didn't tell her what happened when you came to meet me. That is something for us to talk about with her together. I did ask her about how you have been lately. I am sorry your PTSD is so bad." Garett said before stopping so Travis could answer.

"Yes, my PTSD has been bad lately. If you would like, we could talk about it today over some coffee or some tea." Travis said smiling a little from getting a call from Garett.

"Yes, I would like to do that. Can I come over today?" Garett sounded excited as he spoke.

"Yes, you can come over today." Travis laughed a little bit.

"You sound nervous." Garett said with care in his voice.

"I am nervous. You are the only person that knows I am gay." Travis said with a small break in his voice.

"He isn't the only one less you forget I have been in your head." Valieen said from the shadow while he was in the form of the black blob with sharp teeth.

"I didn't know that you hadn't told her yet." Garett said, sounding surprised at the new development.

"Of course, you hadn't told her 'cause you know she will reject you!" Valieen continued getting louder as he talked.

"Yeah, I have kept it secret all this time that it has just become normal to keep it to myself." Travis let out a nervous chuckle.

"Don't worry I will be there to support you." Garett said, sounding happy about being able to be there.

Travis and Garett sat silent for a few moments before Garett said he had to head to work. They both hung up without saying another word about what Travis had done at the pizza place. Travis laid back down to go back to sleep now used to the chattering sound of teeth coming from the corner of the room. It still drove him crazy to hear but it was becoming the normal.

Travis woke up a few hours later to loud talking in the kitchen. As he got up, he decided to start his day by trying to figure out what it was. When he rounded the corner, he saw his sister and Garett talking. He turned around to walk away still in his pajamas as his sister caught him.

"Why didn't you tell me Garett was coming. I haven't seen him in a long time." Vinessa said squeezing Travis's shoulder.

"W-W-Well I was asleep for this long and it was really early when he called." Travis said, trying to get her to let go.

"I wanted to surprise you Vinessa." Garett said prying her hand off of Travis's shoulder.

"Oh!" Vinessa said, starting to clap cheering "How are you going to do that?" She continued.

"Like this!" Garett yelled, turning Travis around and kissing him.

As his sister gasped out of surprise Travis began to be less rigid and kissed Garett back. When they stopped Vinessa was shocked but with a smile on her face. Even with his sister in a very laughable look the color was drained from Travis as behind her stood Valieen. It cast a very dark shadow over the entire situation.

"Travis why didn't you tell me?" Vinessa asked playfully, punching him in the shoulder.

"Because we didn't grow up in that kind of life. Plus, I couldn't have anyone telling Father David because he would never help me or let me back into the church." Travis said looking at the floor.

"Travis you are like a son to me I could never drop you." The voice was accompanied by a hand on his shoulder.

Travis turned around to find Father David behind him with a smile on his face. Father David brought Travis into a hug. Travis saw Valieen in the corner staring once again casting a darkness on the situation. It felt nice to Travis hearing the Father calling him his son. It was the first time he had heard that since his father had left.

"You know that it would be against my stance as a priest to tell you that you are not allowed to be in the church." Father David made eye contact with Travis to make his point.

"Thank you, Father." Travis said with tears pouring out onto his face.

"You will always be welcome to my church no matter what any other church says." Father David gave him another hug.

"Thank you. I also need to show you something I found in the library." Travis said leaving the room to go get the book he found.

"Oh, you actually got in there?" Father David said following Travis.

Garett Followed behind them but it was mostly because he wanted to talk to Travis. As he entered the room Father David had an extreme look of shock on his face. He didn't get close enough to hear but he saw how shocked the pastor was because all Travis was doing was talking. The Father had never been so silent over something before.

"My first question is how did you get into the library. I never got a key to it when I got the house from the church." Father David spoke with fear.

"It was open when I got here. The door was unlocked at the least." Travis said.

"That is strange because when I got to the place, and the door was locked and before me the owner said the door was locked. Nevertheless, about the fact I have never seen or heard about this book." Father David said inspecting the gold lined book.

"Um, If I may interrupt." Garett said entering the room finally.

"What is it Garett?" Travis said but sounded more annoyed than he intended.

"That's not the tone to take with your new boyfriend but I saw this book being talked about on a forum. It popped up on radars out of nowhere and from what people had been saying it pops up in waves every twenty years. Shortly after a cult follows then at the ten-year mark, they commit mass suicide and repeat." Garett said it felt extremely useful.

"That's a lot of information." Travis said trying to act like he wasn't blushing.

"So, this book has a cult following, but they die and come back. I wonder why." Father David said, trying to understand.

"I think I know why. I have seen the land of Valieen Sparia in my dreams. When they die, he makes them his soldiers in hell?" Travis said hiding the fact he is scared out of his mind.

"When did you see it? Did you see the demon itself?" Father David asked.

"Y-Yes I saw the demon. I saw it three nights ago in my sleep." Travis said backing up.

Travis saw Valieen crawling down the wall taking his place behind Father David. Valieen put a hand around Father David's throat. He gave Travis a smile before throwing Father David into the wall and throwing the book to Travis. Father David gave a cry of pain as his shoulder and arm shattered with an audible sound.

"Congrats on coming out to everyone Travis. I will see you again soon." Valieen followed his statement up with a cackle before he vanished.

Travis ran and called an ambulance. The Father was crying out in pain while Travis ran in with an ice pack. Tears ran down Travis's face while he tried to figure out what he was supposed to be doing for the father. The situation made him feel useless. He had visible defeat on his face.

"D-Don't t-think this i-is your fault T-Travis. It is w-what demons do." Father David gave a smile before he blacked out from his pain.

"Father! Wake up! Please!" Travis kept yelling as the paramedics came and got the Father to take him to the hospital.

Travis ran down the steps and out to his car to follow the ambulance. The entire run he felt like he was floating, and the tears flooded his vision. As they had been on their way to the hospital the ambulance turned off their lights and sirens. It was like the whole world went silent for Travis. He knew what that meant and decided to pull off the road.

The whole world turned red, and he started to hit his steering wheel and screamed at the top of his lungs. He got out of his car and started to throw rocks into the river. He saw Valieen smiling from his car. His vision went red, and he picked up a huge rock and busted out his window. He collapsed out of breath and out of hope. His phone began to ring as he noticed he had been gone for hours now.

"Hello?" Travis asked, sounding exhausted.

"Hey baby." The voice he heard on the other end of the phone surprised him.

"Mother?" Travis asked full of shock and fear.

"You remember me then?" His mother said.

"I can't forget the one person who didn't defend me in court." Travis said, feeling his anger rising.

"You killed my husband you little bastard." His mother's voice was rising in volume.

"He tried to rape my goddamn sister and you didn't want to believe he could do anything wrong. Instead, you accused her of trying to court him into doing something illegal just because she was jealous!" Travis yelled before throwing his phone into the river and driving back home.

As he pulled in, he saw several people at the front door. It ranged from police to military chaplains. The police got sent out to look for me and the chaplains got sent because Father David died in the back of that ambulance. He went straight to the chaplains for the news and pretended he didn't already know.

Slowly rain moved in over them as everyone started to go their own ways in silence. Everyone except Garett who stayed with Travis as he stood out in the rain. He could remember the joke Father David always said when he was a kid when it rained. *"It looks just like a horror movie doesn't it."* Then would come his laugh. It was so full of life when the rest of the world wasn't, but he will carry on in our memories.

Travis ran to the bar and started to drink. He thought back to his first time there. He and Father David drank his first beer together. He could still see the father sitting beside him talking about how proud he was. As funny as it sounds Father David was like his actual father. More than just his priest from the church.

He drank Father David's favorite drink, a rum and coke over ice. He wanted to drink and drink until his mind was nothing but a fuzzy mess. The bartender kept giving Travis a look of concern as the drinks moved. Travis did know better than to get up and walk after his vision started to change. Father David kept showing up in his mind with each new drink.

"It is quite the storm out there isn't it?" The bartender asked Travis.

"It is just like a horror movie isn't it?" Travis asked in response with a laugh.

"The priest used to say that a lot, didn't he?" The bartender said knowing the pain Travis felt.

"Yes, he did. Every single time it would rain." Travis laughed, shaking his head.

The bartender raised a glass to make a toast with Travis. He never thought of cutting Travis off. To no surprise Valieen sat down beside Travis and started to drink as well. He just had a smile and licked his lips.

Chapter 10: Goodbye, Father

The church called us about arranging what will happen with the house. They told us we could keep it and the church will pay it off as we had been given everything in Father David's will. He told them he had adopted us and that is how we ended up with everything.

"Are you okay Travis?" Garett said sitting up in the bed beside Travis.

"Yeah, I am okay beside spending the past three days getting everything settled with his will." Travis said rubbing his eyes to try to wake up.

"Well babe, it will all be okay." Garett said kissing Travis on the cheek.

"You didn't have to be here. You could have gone home." Travis said looking down.

"*You are pushing people away. This means I am winning.*" Valieen Laughed from the corner of the room.

Travis got up to wash his face in the bathroom and when he looked in the mirror Valieen stood there with flesh hanging from his mouth. It was fresh, still dripping blood. A small cackle came from him before he vanished, and Garett walked through the door wrapping his arms around Travis. Garett made Travis smile when he did things like this. It was the most love he had felt in a long time.

The one thing that sat in the back of Travis's mind is that every time he looks in the mirror is, he sees his father. He asks himself if his father would be proud of him and where his father was. Garett played with Travis's hair seeing the sadness that was starting to write itself on Travis's face. Travis smiled a little bit knowing someone cares about him.

"What are you thinking Travis?" Garett asked, kissing Travis on the neck.

"I just wonder if my dad is proud of me." Travis said his face not picking up any.

"I am sure he would be extremely proud of you Travis. Look at the life you have built out of the darkness war brought to your life." Garett said, making a good point to Travis.

"Yes, I know that, but I just wish I could get to meet him again." Travis turned around and hugged Garett close to him.

Garett sat and thought about trying to find Travis's father for him. The only issue was how would he find him. That's when a note dropped at Garett's feet out of thin air. As he picked it up, he opened it right away. It read "*I know how to find his father but first you must find me. I lay in this house. I spend it within the bowls of knowledge and the bowls of the free spirit.*" This was a confusing message, but Garett loved a good puzzle.

"What is this then?" Garett asked himself.

"*It is a puzzle.*" A voice said from behind Garett.

Garett turned around but found no one behind him. The only thing he noticed was a smell of smoke and sulfur. Garett made his way to the kitchen following the sound of pots and pans rattling. When he got there, he saw Valieen in his true form for the first time. This caused Garett to freeze in his tracks.

"You must be Garett?" Valieen said with a hiss on his voice.

"Y-Y-Yes I-I-I am." Garett said falling over the words.

"So, you must be the one I have seen beside Travis all these nights." Valieen said walking towards Garett slowly with eye contact.

"Y-Yeah I have been." Garett said as he backed into the door that closed without him seeing it.

"Well then you will be my food source also then." Valieen said touching Garett on the forehead.

Memories began to flood back to Garett. All of the bad memories he had repressed into the back of his mind. As Garett started to scream Valieen punched his throat breaking his voice box. So, Garett began to suffer in silence as Valieen leaned over him and a black smoke went from Garett into Valieen's mouth. After about five minutes Travis yelled down the hall causing Valieen to fix Garett and throw him to the floor limp.

"You got lucky this time boy." Valieen said making the room look like Garett fell, and then he vanished.

"Garett!" Travis yelled, running to him and picking up his head.

"What happened?" Garett asked in a weak voice beginning to wake up.

"It looks like you fell Garett. You need to be more careful." Travis said kissing Garett on the forehead.

"I-I guess I fucked up then." Garett laughed.

Travis helped Garett to his feet and sat him in a chair. As Travis cleaned everything up and checked Garett for any injuries. When he had found no further injuries, he helped Garett to the bedroom and put him to sleep. He tapped the bed in a way of telling Garett he needed to stay.

"You need to rest Garett. You took a hard fall." Travis smiled as he went to the kitchen.

Garett wanted to say something, but he knew that Travis wouldn't change his mind on the subject. He wanted to make something special for Garett. The funeral was tomorrow but Travis has had Garett nearby this entire time for that he owes him. Travis sat in the kitchen and began to cook a meal when Garett's snores filled the hall. This made Travis smile knowing he was with someone that could make him feel this way.

"Hey brother." Vinessa said with a smile walking through the doorway.

"Hey Vinessa. Was your day well?" Travis asked, smiling to himself with a small laugh.

"Is that Garett snoring?" Vinessa asked, trying to keep back a laugh.

"Yes, he fell earlier, and I put him to bed after I made sure he wasn't hurt too bad." Travis said unable to keep himself from laughing.

The two of them shared a good amount of jokes and listened to Garett snoring. It helped them feel better knowing he was still breathing. Travis has never felt better around anyone. He made a plate for Vinessa and himself a plate sitting down at the table. Travis found himself having a small issue here and there throughout the day with Father David's funeral being tomorrow.

They sat in silence and ate before Travis started to cry a small amount. Vinessa took his hands and made eye contact to try to comfort him. He let a small smile creep through knowing what she was trying to do for him. He took a deep breath and began to pray. It was something that felt right but was also something he hadn't done in a long time. He felt a hand touch his shoulder, but he didn't look up because he could feel the hate burning a hole through him. He knew Valieen was there and was making fun of his actions.

"I should get to sleep so I can be bright-eyed for my yule tomorrow." Travis said standing up and stretching.

"Yes, I need to do the same." Vinessa said, giving him a small smile.

"Good night sister." Travis said walking out of the room.

"Good night!" Vinessa yelled after him.

Travis made his way to his room to find Garett spread out of the bed snoring, and with drool leaking down his face. Travis walked to the bed and began to change for bed with a big smile on his face. As he laid his head on his pillow Valieen took up his spot. This night was strange mostly for the fact Valieen made no sound on this night. He still had his smile. It was a smile that was large and sharp. It always did, and probably drill chills down his spine.

Travis still got his full night's sleep but as he awoke the next morning he felt like shit. He feels like he didn't sleep at all. He had to force himself from bed but as he did Garett had already gotten to the shower. With a pop of his joints one after another Travis made his way to the bathroom.

"Garett are you okay this morning?" Travis asked, pulling the curtain back some.

"Yes, I am but I do think that we should move forward with our relationship." Garett said from the shower.

"What do you mean?" Travis asked, his face becoming slightly flushed from this new request.

"Get in here and wash me." Garett said, smiling to himself.

"Oh!" Travis said with real surprise.

Travis got undressed and did exactly that. As Travis washed Garett it brought him true joy to do so. The only downside is that Travis knew that this feeling wouldn't last long. He knew that later in the day he would have to bury the only father figure he had. All of this is happening because he couldn't save the father. He wrapped his arms around Garett and just sat in silence allowing the warm water to melt away his sadness.

"Are you okay Travis?" Garett asked, kissing Travis on one of his hands.

"No, I feel like we wouldn't have to be having this funeral if I could have saved him." Travis said burying his face into the back of Garrett's neck.

They sat in the shower under the water to allow Travis to calm himself. As they got out Garett pushed Travis against the wall and kissed him. They sat staring into each other's eyes saying nothing. Even with saying nothing they said more to each other than they ever have before. They shared feelings instead of words. It was like reading each other's thoughts before they could think them.

"You can do this Travis. We will go through this together." Garett said with a smile on his face.

Later in the day Travis found himself in the front row of a church beside the others who had been selected to read. As he sat there all he could do was think of issues and ways to leave early. His suit was too tight, His shirt collar was choking him, Shoes are falling apart, The list he had made just went on forever.

"My turn already it seems." Travis said to himself as he stood up and walked up to speak.

He took in a deep breath and began to speak. "Father David has been in my life as long as I can remember. He had picked me up when I fell to my knees. He gave me the hope that no one else ever has. I remember that he was always there for everyone, but I never remember anyone checking in on him when he was outside of church.

As a child I remember getting a call from him every day of the week outside of the calls on Sundays when we had fallen ill. He would always say if we needed the money for medicine, he would give it to us. I even remember the stories he shared when I said I was interested in military work. He always said 'Remember Travis you wanted to hear these stories' Then would burst out in the biggest laugh when I would say something about the details.

He was there when I was sent to jail for defending my sister. My stepfather at the time tried to rape her and I pushed him out the window. He died after landing on a white picket fence. After a long year and a half, I was sent to prison. While I was in the prison Father David brought me a brochure to join the army in their new rehabilitation program. They took in convicts and trained them to be better humans. It was probably the best thing to ever happen to me.

He called me every night for my first deployment. After my second deployment started the calls came less and less. I fell off the wagon of my faith when Father David was no longer able to call me each day. The platoon pastor just wasn't doing it for me. I think it was from where Father David made it feel like I was really his son.

Father David brought the best out of all of us. He made us know that we had all been wanted. It was like he was the light on the earth. He was the thing that brought happiness to us. All I can do is cry every time he comes to my mind. He even came to sit with me when my emotions got me in the seats at the bar. He listened to every story I had.

We lost a true gem when Father David passed away. I don't feel he is gone because I don't think anyone ever truly leaves this earth. We keep walking beside the people that need us the most. I feel we are tasked to watch our loved ones and then help them and ourselves to heaven. Father David if you can hear me, I loved you as a father and looked up to you with every bit of my heart." Travis finished and broke down into tears following his speech.

After two more people spoke their piece, they carried the casket to the grave. Father David's student Father Marrion spoke of his teacher's last rights. Rain began to fall getting hard as his body was lowered. Father Marrion got a smile on his face and looked up to the crowd.

"I only have one thing to say for Father David now. It is like a horror movie isn't it?" Father Marrion said smiling down at Father David's casket.

"Father David would say that. For once I have an answer for it. It is like a horror movie and you know it. You old but caring fool. I love you Father. Thank you for everything." Travis said, finally giving a true smile.

Slowly as the rain cleared up, they started filling in Father David's grave. Travis was silent the entire way home with something on his mind. The bad part was he couldn't figure out what it was that he had started to think about. He would eventually think about it now that he could think about it.

Soon after arriving back at home his phone dinged. As he pulled up the phone it shocked him with the name on screen. It read *"Father David"* He quickly clicked on it and was shocked even further. He read the content within the message. *"The snow falls in the desert when a king shall fall to the earth. No one can stop the snow of the giants. They will roam again and soon the earth will know its true masters. "* The message sent a chill down Travis's spine. He knew what the message read but couldn't believe it was there.

Travis quickly put his phone away. He didn't want to worry anyone with the strange message he got. He went to his room and pulled out a pen along with paper. The only thing he could think about was to write it down.

Chapter 11: Therapy Session One

"Well Travis this is our first over the phone session." Dr. Marron said with a laugh.

"Yes, it is doctor." Travis laughed as well.

They both felt a little silly with the idea. They knew this would be hard to do without making eye contact but at the same time they couldn't lose each other. They had made a connection that drove them both. The therapist gained new data and Travis got to talk about his issues. Travis knew the therapist was using him, but he also knew his doctor shared something special with him. He has seen the demon in a way. That didn't change the feeling though he had. It seemed like the doctor had a bigger drive after seeing the demon to achieve what seemed like a goal out of healing Travis's mind.

"So, what has happened recently with you. I do also remember you asking for three days or more for you to settle. I hope you settled in nicely." Dr. Marron said with a cheer-filled tone in his voice.

"Well, the biggest one is that Father David has passed away recently." Travis said a sadness filling each word more and more.

"I am sorry for your loss Travis. I know he meant a lot to you From the tone of your voice. What was he to you?" Dr. Marron asked finding a subject to start the session on.

"He was the closest thing I have had to a father in my life. He gave me a way into the military when my Stepfather died." Travis said, trying to answer the question completely.

"I see. I am here all hours of the day every day for you Travis." Dr. Marron said to Travis's surprise.

"Thank you doctor but you don't have to do that for me." Travis said with a small smile on his face.

"I am doing it, because I understand how everything is affecting you." Dr. Marron said feeling actual care for Travis.

"I also got into my first relationship since I was in middle school. I also came out to my sister about the fact I was gay." Travis did feel a small amount better telling this information to Dr. Marron.

"Congratulations Travis. Thank you for telling that to me. It is a big step in our lives to let the world know who we truly are." Dr. Marron said, trying to seem wise beyond his years.

"Thank you, Doctor It was a large weight lifted off my chest when I told her." Travis said his joy was clearly heard by Dr. Marron.

"So has your issue gotten any better?" Dr. Marron asked with a grim tone following to the other side of the line with his voice.

"It has gotten worse, but I am working on solving the issue as we speak." Travis said, trying to sound secretive.

"You are doing nothing of the sort you stupid bastard. Why lie to him when you know that you are scared. Just tell him you are scared." Valieen said with his claws on Travis's shoulders.

"Oh, I see. Is he talking to you now?" Dr. Marron asked.

"Yes, he is Doctor." Travis said with a tinge of regret in his voice.

"Don't let him get the best of you Travis. You will make it out of this whole situation in one piece." Dr. Marron said with a sense of urgency in his voice for sending Travis his message.

"It is so sad that humans like you two lie to encourage one another. You all go to hell no matter what you try to do." Valieen got louder as he came to the finish of his sentence.

"I won't let him bring me down doctor. In fact, I have gotten used to his tricks recently. He doesn't really ever change them up." Travis lied as he said each word.

As Travis sat here exchanging lies with truths talking to the Doctor. He knew that it would only make more and more people worry if he said the truth. He couldn't afford to have more people being worried about him. He was also worried that if he kept telling the truth that Dr. Marron will send him to an asylum.

"Travis please tell me how your nightmares have been?" Dr. Marron asked with the faint sound of his pencil scribbling on paper in the background.

"I have had dreams that keep taking me back to those damn deserts in Afghanistan. I am not taken back to the fighting, but I am sent back, and I am wandering the deserts as a nomad walking upon the ocean of the dead." Travis said with the grim tone echoing clear.

"So, you keep going back every time you sleep?" Dr. Marron asked Travis processing his words.

"It is strange that you ask that Doctor. I figured you would have wanted me to tell you more about the ocean." Travis said with a small laugh.

"I want you to tell me more about it." Dr. Marron said, sounding embarrassed.

"As I stood at the edge of the desert it looked like all of the faces had been looking me in the eyes. I could hear echoes of chattering teeth piercing my ears. It was so heavy with how loud it was. I can still hear it sometimes out of the blue here in reality." Travis said now that he was thinking about it, he could hear it.

"Do you go back to the same place every time you go to sleep?" Dr. Marron asked again.

"No, I end up in a different place every time I dream. When I do dream, I don't only get visions, but I get sounds, feelings, tastes, smells. I don't understand what it is but used to, I never had dreams like this." Travis said in a serious and heavy tone.

"That is called lucid dreaming. It is a form of dreaming where everything feels so real that it is a shock when you wake up. I would like to have you go get a C.T. scan to see what your brain looks like." Dr. Marron said with the sound of keys clicking in the background.

"When do you want to have me go get the scan?" Travis asked, grabbing his pen and paper out of his desk.

"I think I will schedule it for a week from now." Dr. Marron said as his mouse clicked in the background.

"Okay, I can do that." Travis said, writing down the date on his paper.

"How do you think Father David's funeral affected you?" Dr. Marron asked, changing the subject of their session.

"I would say that it is probably the hardest hit I had ever taken in my life. He was the only father figure I had in my life. As dumb as it sounds, he was." Travis said sadness choking him as it came up.

"Can you elaborate on what you mean." Dr Marron urged Travis further.

"He was there at every point when I was at my lowest. He got me out of jail and into the military. He put me onto a path that brought me to a happier place. I feel that his death was my fault." Travis said, his voice beginning to break.

"Travis, you can't take the blame for his death. It was something you couldn't have controlled. He would probably say it was his time to go." Dr. Marron said, trying to sound serious.

"You know what is going on with me. I feel that the thing that is following me around killed him." Travis said after a minute of silence.

"We don't know if that is the reason he died. He was at the age of which we always have health issues." Dr. Marron tried to rationalize the statement.

Travis's mind began to race as the events started to flood back to him. It caused him to develop into a headache. He actually began to wince from the pain he had developed. He took several deep breaths to try to refocus on the task at hand. He knew that therapy was the only way to keep his sister around.

"I know Doctor, but I don't know if he was actually that age though. He had always been healthy from what I could remember." Travis let out an awkward chuckle after the words.

"I think you are putting too much on yourself than you actually are responsible for. You care about everyone, but you are trying to be responsible for stuff in their lives that you can't control. I think you need to take some time and relax away from the rest of the world." Dr. Marron said.

"I have not really ever thought of taking time to myself." Travis said turning his computer on.

"You will never relax. You are responsible for everyone's problems. You are a curse to anyone around you. You should go ahead and take yourself out of their lives so that they never have to suffer again." Valieen chattered from the corner of the room.

"Has anything else eventful happened lately?" Dr. Marron asked to break the silence that had fallen between the two.

"After Father David's funeral I got a message from his number. It freaked me out, but the strangest part was the message contained part of a story my father read to me when I was a kid. It was a story about the giant's winter. It was a legend behind why the winter was so bad. I loved the story as a kid and would beg my father to read it to me." Travis said with a scoff at the end of his sentence.

"Might I ask you to go further into detail about it?" Dr. Marron asked Travis in a question form but with the tone of a demand.

"When I read it, I felt curious, but it became an obsession. I have not told anyone else about it. I want to keep it to myself till I can figure out what happened and how I got it." Travis said as his eyes moved to the piece of paper, he wrote the message on.

"What do you think happened?" Dr. Marron said, sounding more interested than Travis.

"I think that his phone number was taken over by someone, and they just happened to know the story. I am hoping it is something that is harmless, but I can't get the message out of my head. It is like my mind got the message burned into it." Travis said as he became anxious.

Travis could hear Dr. Marron writing and typing on the other end of the line. He is hoping that the Doctor is not calling some place to pick him up and haul him away. Even though it was a light sound he could hear Dr. Marron pick up his phone. After a few more keys being pressed sounding out over the phone he could hear Dr. Marron take a deep breath.

"Have you ever wanted to go anywhere as a dream vacation?" Dr. Marron asked Travis out of the silence.

"I have always wanted to go to Alaska." Travis said, perking up with excitement.

"You should take your trip to Alaska. Take your time to see if you taking time away from the busy life here will help. At least take the time to think about going." Dr. Marron said with a sense of honesty and caring in his voice.

Travis felt that the honesty he felt in the Doctors last message was fake. He was starting to feel that the doctor was getting more out of this than he was letting on. Travis still needed him so that his sister knew he was trying to get help. He did enjoy the idea of going to Alaska but if he went, he wanted to take Garett with him.

"Yeah, I will give it some thought but I can't promise anything Doctor." Travis said with a smile creeping up his face.

Travis and Dr. Marron both hung up, ending their session. Immediately after they had hung up Travis picked up the paper and stared at the paper, he wrote the text message on. He doesn't know why it was important to him, but he knew it was. He sat there for hours in his chair staring at the message trying to figure out how he got the message. If it was a planned message set to go upon Father David's death how did he know about the story being important to Travis.

Travis called Vinessa and Garett to the living room to talk about the trip to Alaska. He had serious thoughts about going to Alaska. He still hadn't made his mind up which is why he wanted to run it by his family. If he did go, he wanted to bring at least Garett with him.

"Guys I wanted to run an idea by you guys." Travis said as he took a seat.

"What is it Travis?" Vinessa asked as she also took a seat.

"Yeah, What is on your mind?" Garett asked, grabbing a mug of steaming coffee.

"I want to take a trip to Alaska, but I am not sold on the idea yet." Travis said sitting back.

"A trip to Alaska could be fun but who would stay here to watch the house?" Garett asked.

"You two could make it a couple's vacation and I will stay here." Vinessa said with a big smile on her face.

"Well like I said I haven't decided for sure yet." Travis said with a smile.

Travis got up to get a drink from the kitchen when his phone rang. He looks at it, but the screen is blank. He opened it to the main screen and sees a phone number he hasn't saved on screen. He Answered it with caution in his voice.

"Hello?" Travis asked.

"Hello son. It has been a long time since we talked." An unknown voice said.

"Who is this?" Travis asked, already annoyed by having to ask.

"This is your father. I have been working and living up here in Alaska. I got remarried and I want you to come visit." The man claiming to be his father said.

"I need to know that you are my father. You're going to have to give me some sort of proof." Travis said while his grip got tighter on his phone.

"When you had been a child, I told you stories of giants and kings. I also left your mother after I came home and found her in bed with your teacher." The man said, still claiming to be his father.

"Ok, I believe you but why are you contacting me now?" Travis asked, starting to become frustrated with this new information.

"I have tossed it back and forth in my mind this entire time. I felt that if i texted you back then you wouldn't understand, but now I see I was wrong. I hope you do come to see me and give me a chance to explain myself to you. I do love you my son. I am sorry for everything I have done." Travis's father finished and hung up.

Chapter 12: Family Ties

After the phone call with his father Travis couldn't get the fact his father was alive out of his head. Now the only thoughts he had was why his father wouldn't call him before. This entire time Travis thought his father was dead. He and Garett spent the past three days going over the idea of going to Alaska.

"Garett, I don't know what I am going to do. I just found out that my father is alive and now he wants me to go to Alaska. I know that I said I wanted to go anyway, but this is different." Travis said as he tapped a pen against his desk.

"I know it is Travis and I get it. You could always go and knock out two birds with one stone. I will of course still go with you. I think it could be a lot of fun for us." Garett spoke with a big smile even though Travis didn't return the sentiment.

"That's true we could knock it all out at once. I don't know if you will have as much fun since you will be meeting my father. He is not one that will agree with us being together. He is an old school type of man." Travis said, placing down his pen making no words on his paper.

Valieen was nowhere to be seen which was strange for how things have been. Travis still had his nightmares but with Valieen being gone they had toned down. Travis pulled out his medicine bottle which he hasn't touched since Dr. Marron helped him get it. He didn't think about needing it till now.

"I guess I actually should think about using these now. Sometimes I feel like the nightmares are too powerful to be affected by the medicine, but I think it will work now." Travis said opening the bottle and dumping the pills out on the table.

"Travis, I have to tell you something." Garett said, pulling up another chair.

"What is it Garett?" Travis asked in response as he took one of his pills.

"I have been seeing this monster..." Garett said when Travis stopped him.

"Is it a demon?" Travis said looking into Garett's eyes with fear.

"It is something built of fear and has the look of death. It dug into the back of my mind and pulled out my deepest darkest memories. It grabbed what I tried to forget. I guess it was a demon, but I do not know what I could call it. I just didn't want to keep it secret from you. It knew you by name." Garett said with tears coming to his eyes.

"I know what it is because it has been coming for me ever since I got back from war. It didn't tell you because I thought I could fix it. I thought it would drive you away from me." Travis turned away from Garett after he finished his sentence.

"I would never turn from you. I understand why you kept it away now but now it is our problem. We will get through this as one." Garett said as he put a hand on Travis's shoulder and smiled.

Travis placed his hands over Garett's and smiled. When they made contact it was at that moment Travis understood he was no longer alone in this. He was able to understand that now someone fully understood him. He loved Garett more than anything else in his life now, but he knows that he has more to protect. He will protect him with everything he has in his soul. Garett has his heart and soul for as long as Travis may live.

"Garett I am glad you told me, and I will remain sorry for not telling you sooner. You mean more to me than many people I have met. I wanted to protect you and I guess I tried too hard when it came to protecting you." Travis said as he smiled through the tears that had fallen from his eyes.

To Travis these tears felt different. These tears held a warmer feeling. They had been tears of happiness carrying the warmth from his heart to the outside. His tears had always been cold till now. They had been cold like they carried the sadness from a frozen heart to the outside. He was happy and in love now. The tears he has now proves that to him.

"Let us go to Alaska Garett. We need to make sure we have everything settled here before we go." Travis said as he got up and grabbed a wet cloth to clean the tears from Garett's face.

Garett nodded and left the room. Garett had gone to his job to make sure they knew where he was going before the time to leave. Travis went to go find his mother. She was still within the town and Travis didn't even know if he wanted to meet her. He still went to find her because he knew it was something he had to fix. He could feel she still lived in his childhood home. He started at that damned house that was cloaked in a darkness. It was a darkness Travis felt as soon as he stepped onto the lawn.

As Travis walked up to the door everything began to feel heavier. It began to become suffocating, and he struggled to breathe. He powered through knowing that this is what he had to do, not for everyone else but for himself. He knocked but with every knock time seemed to slow down. He saw the door open in slow motion. As it opened it was like he could hear the sounds of singing rising in the background.

"Hello son I knew you would be here." Travis's mother said as she opened the door.

Travis's mother was an older lady in her late fifties to her early sixties. She had been married around four times and now lives under the name Susan Berlow. She used to be the one-person Travis trusted until the night he killed his stepfather. He doesn't know why she contacted him either, but he wants to give her a chance to explain herself. He entered the house and as he crossed the threshold of the front door the building began to peel away from dust and mold. It began to turn back to the time of that night he was hauled away.

As he continued, he could hear his sister screaming, witnessing himself running up the steps. Each step echoing with force as events replayed themselves in his mind. It all seemed to echo as he got drawn deeper and deeper into his memories. His mind seemed to detach from his body. Following the events that continued to replay. Travis continued to watch as he slammed into his sister's door over and over again.

"So why did you call me mother?" Travis could hear his own voice echoing in his head while the action unfolded.

As he heard the words echo through his mind it was like the replay slowed down. As his focus wavered it would slow down. His full attention needed to be on the events, or they would never end. As he focused back onto the scene in front of him it got back to normal speed. He looked around at the familiar scene of overturned furniture and broken blood covered glass.

"I wanted to explain myself to you, but I also want you to apologize for what you did." Susan's voice echoed in his head once again slowing the scene he saw.

As his focus came back, he watched his naked sister wrapped in a blood covered sheet run out of the room. He watched what used to be an innocent person run in fear from someone who was supposed to guide her in life. He watched the anger in his face run through his body and out of his fist. Each blow that landed caused what looked like an eruption of blood to come from his stepfather's mouth and nose. He looked like a crazed beast of a man even to himself.

"I cannot apologize after knowing what that monster had done to my sisters. You know, your daughter!" His voice boomed this time as he watched himself beat his stepfather in slow motion.

As the scene he watched the voiceless figures yell at each other. His stepfather begged for him to stop, but he could see now that he was driven by anger. He still wouldn't go back and change anything if he could. Even though he could see he went too far. He watched himself pick him up and slam him against the wall screaming. His stepfather struggled against his grip. Just as he threw him out the window his vision changed. He was now watching his stepfather fall in slow motion.

"I know what he did, but I couldn't stop him! Every time I tried to stop him; he would beat me for it! He kept saying it was for the good of the family! I want you to apologize for leaving me alone!" Susan's voice echoed like thunder and as her last word fizzled out of the air he hit.

He could feel his body shudder as his stepfather's blood splattered all over his mother's car. She got out of her car and ran to her husband who now impaled on a white fence that ran along their yard. Susan looked up making eye contact with Travis tears running down her face like rivers flowing from a freshly cracked dam.

He pulled up a chair and sat in the window as she came up the steps talking to the police the entire way. As she entered the room a mixture of anger and sadness could be read on her withering face. She spoke no words as she crossed the room landing a blow on the side of Travis's face. He could hear her heavy breathing as his vision became fuzzy.

"What do you mean left you? You called the police on me!" Travis's voice boomed through the room filled with pain.

He watched in slow motion as his mother collapsed into tears while the police put him in cuffs. The police took him out of the house with a single word or change of expression. His view changed once more to see the paramedics and fire crew cutting the fence in which his stepfather was impaled. It didn't faze him back then, but he couldn't remember feeling much that day. Looking back on it now he does feel something. His only issue is he can't identify what it is he is feeling.

His vision was reunited with his body as he was driven away. He could see his mother crying in front of him even more weathered than before. Stress and cigarettes have caused her to appear older than her age. He could always remember a cigarette in her hand. Now all he sees is a nicotine patch and medication that they give you through chemotherapy.

"Why didn't you tell me you had cancer?" Travis asked his mother with a grim tone floating on his voice.

"I figured after me allowing you to go to jail it was better to leave you be." Susan said allowing her sadness to flow on her words.

"That's not how things work. Even if I am mad you need to tell me." Travis began to feel upset.

"I figured I needed to tell you, but I didn't know how." Susan began to raise her voice while saying this.

"I don't like the fact you kept that from me hurts. I am your son and what if you had been gone and we didn't get to have this conversation!" Travis began to yell tears begging to roll down his face warm with his anger.

These tears he felt carried the overwhelming anger that was in his heart. It made them warm like a hot summer rain shower. He got up and slammed his hands on the chair. He stormed out of the door slamming it behind himself. Travis got into his car and sped off towards his house. He felt a pain he hadn't felt in years.

It was a pain that hit him directly in his heart. As he got faster rain began to fall overhead. It was heavy rain like you get with a huge thunderstorm. Even with his windshield wipers going full blast it didn't take the tears away from his eyes. Before Travis could think twice his car hit a puddle and spun out of control. It pulled off to the left full speed. It was at this moment he was happy the road was empty. The car started to tip and as he saw the road vanish, he blacked out falling into his own mind.

As his vision started to come back it was blurry. He took a good look around and saw his windows busted. Tree leaves littered the car around him and as he looked down, he saw a branch sticking out of his chest. A small laugh came from him followed by a small wave of blood from his mouth. He knew this day would come, but he didn't think it would be like this. A metallic thump came from in front of Travis grabbing his attention.

"Well, well what do we have here." The sentence ended with a laugh following it.

"Let me guess it is you Valieen?" Travis asked with more blood following it.

"Well, who the fuck else would it be Travis?" Valieen said crouching down showing the skull he had for a face.

"Are you going to take me to hell yet?" Travis said with his voice giving hints of him giving up.

"Oh no you are not ready yet. You have much, much more pain to go." Valieen let out a cackle before grabbing Travis's phone.

Travis passed out as Valieen left his sight. The sounds of sirens and people yelling began to echo through his head. Travis could barely open his eyes enough to see people pulling him out of his car. He closed his eyes again only to open them back up to the ambulance box. Father David sat in the back smiling. Travis knew it was just a ghost of his memories, but it made him feel so much better. "You will be okay sir." A paramedic said placing a hand on Travis's hands.

Travis could only bring himself to nod in response. It hurt him to talk but it hurt worse when he could feel every bump under the ambulance. Each one made him wince in pain. He thought the paramedic would have given him pain medication. The one thing Travis didn't know was his face didn't move when he was in pain. Before he knew it, he was being hauled out of the ambulance and sent straight into surgery. He had a mask put on him giving him a gas that put him to sleep.

Chapter 13: Here Comes The Snow

While Travis was in the hospital, he spent most of his time with pain medicine in his system. This meant he had a blurry view of the world around him. Every person that came and went was nothing much more than a blurry figure with no face on it. The only person he knew was there was Garett. This was because he held Travis's hand the entire time.

The entire process of recovery meant he had to relearn how to walk, eat, sit-up, run, and use the bathroom on his own. Valieen spent every day watching and laughing. It was hard to forget the smile on his face when he saved Travis from the wreckage of his car. It was a smile that cut into his memories. It will forever be seen when he sleeps or shuts his eyes to rest at any time. The chatter of teeth was louder than it has ever been. Valieen made sure that Travis was to suffer his entire recovery period.

"Travis, are you feeling any better?" Garett asked, holding Travis's hand tight.

Travis just was able to turn his head to look at Garett with a smile on his face. Travis gave Garett a weak but thankful nod. He soon fell asleep once again being embraced by the dreams that have plagued him all week. Visions of burning lands and falling buildings. He could hear people screaming, and he had the smell of burning flesh. He could see the apocalypse.

The night he feared came, the night he didn't wake with daybreak. When Travis opened his eyes and all he saw was the sun rising above the ravaged buildings. He stood and walked to the end of the building to see piles of bodies burning in the distance for miles. A tear formed in his eye. It was the only tear he could form since his body began to shut down from the shock of what he was seeing.

"Why am I here!" Travis yelled at the top of his lungs to the sky.

No answer came from anywhere around him; he didn't expect one the more he thought about it. He sat on the floor with his legs hanging off the end of the building. His breathing began to get heavy the more he took in the scene around him. He began to take deep breaths in and out to try to calm himself down before he passed out. He began to cheer up when he saw a human shaped figure walk across the street.

"Hey!" Travis yelled down to the figure as he raced to the steps.

No answer came from the figure as it vanished into the alleyway. He continued to call as he chased it. He found a dead end as the figure was nowhere to be found. He looked around to find the figure only to come out fruitless. As he walked out of the alleyway, he saw a hunched over figure sitting on the curbside covered in a sheet hiding its face from the rest of the world.

"Hey are you okay?" Travis said being cautious with his words reaching for the figure.

With extreme speed the figure became nothing more than a blur as it put itself on top of Travis forcing him to the ground. As he collected himself, he saw that his arm had ended up in the figure's mouth that he now saw was not human in the slightest. It was a creature with a melting face and fangs. As it growled and chewed on his arm spit covered his face as it salivated. He tried to punch it, but he lost all drive to live on. He just sat there as his arm was chewed down to just bone and tendons.

"Come on! You are just going to let this damn thing eat you?" Valieen came walking from around the corner as the world froze in its place.

"Yeah, I am." Travis said as defeat ran rampant through his words.

"Well, that's no good. I guess you can go back to earth now." Valieen said as he dug his finger into Travis's skull.

Travis screamed in pain as blood began to block his vision. His breath wavered as more blood pooled below him. Each breath became shallower and began to stutter. He fell to his knees as Valieen's laugh echoed in his head. He could hear his slow heartbeat in his ear and nothing else made noise around him. It seemed like everything was in slow motion as he fell face first to the ground.

"Travis?" Garett said as his voice echoed through the darkness.

"G-Garett I-I am here." Travis said with a small laugh.

The doctor slowly made his way into the room with a half-smile on his face. Everything within the outside world fell silent to Travis including the doctor's voice as he told them about what will be done for discharge. From just focusing on his lips Travis knew it was a list. A long list at that. He turned to see Garett smiling but at the same time he was still crying.

"What did he say, Garett?" Travis asked as the doctor walked out of the room.

"He said that you will be in a leg brace for a while but other than that you will be fine." Garett said, still smiling through all of his tears.

"Then why are you crying?" Travis asked, his voice still weak.

"Because at least you are still alive, and I get to still love you." Garett said, clearing his tears away with his shirt sleeve.

"Well, I am not going to die that easy." Travis said trying to laugh after but only letting out what sounded like a wheeze.

"Human you would have died if I didn't show up. Your species is so weak." Valieen said with a huff.

Travis shot a look at Valieen who was standing in the corner of the room staring. He seemed to put out a stronger feeling of dread than he normally did recently. He is afraid it will begin to affect everyone if he lets it go on. He looked to Garett and smiled placing his hands on Garett's.

"Well time to get out of here." Travis said as he took his seat in the wheelchair next to his bed discharge papers in hand.

"Yes, it is time to get out of here." Garett said, pushing the wheelchair out of the hospital.

Travis smiled as the musty hospital air was traded out for the smell of the fresh air of the outside. He held his new leg brace in his lap still worried about having to wear it. What worried him was if he was unable to save everyone with a leg being messed up like it is. Slowly his faith in himself vanished as he fastened each strap on the brace. As he fastened the last one, he let out a sigh that was laced with defeat.

Garett looked Travis up and down before opening his mouth to speak. "At least I am not bringing you home with a permanent wheelchair."

Garett put a smile on his face trying to make it seem like he was telling a joke. Travis gave him a smile to make it seem like he succeeded in lightening the mood of the situation. The only thing Travis couldn't tell him is that he felt defeated. He felt like the world had finally beaten him so bad he wanted to give up. He sat back in his seat while Garett drove him back home.

"Garett, I still want to go to Alaska as fast as possible." Travis said as he and Garett pulled into the driveway.

"Okay, but what about your leg?" Garett asked as he opened the door for Travis.

"I am not going to let that stop me. I must get rid of our issue Garett." Travis said as he struggled to get up from the passenger seat of the car.

"Well, I can call and get the tickets. Just go sit down and I will be in there after I get the tickets." Garett said, pulling out his phone.

"Okay but please don't be to-" Travis said, getting cut off by his phone ringing.

"Hello?" Travis asked, answering the phone.

"*Hey Travis, did you decide if you wanted to come to Alaska or not?*" Travis's father asked.

"Yes, we are coming." Travis said putting the phone on speaker.

"*Okay, well I have a private plane that is going to pick you up at the airport and take you to a new airport for another private plane.*" Travis's father hung up after finishing his sentence.

"Did you understand that Garett?" Travis asked, putting his phone away.

"Yes, I did, now let's get to the airport." Garett said with a smile taking Travis's hand.

Two hours after the phone call came to signal their time to leave. Travis already had loaded his car with bags of clothes. As they began their journey to the airport Travis's mind began to wander to his thoughts of how strange everything has been lately. His mind always fell back to how his dad knew to call and what questions to ask. These thoughts didn't last long as he fell asleep for the rest of the trip.

As he woke up at the airport, they quickly grabbed their bags and walked to their plane. It was a small four passenger propeller plane that they could see used to be used for skydiving. With a deep breath Travis and Garett boarded the plane. All that was around as they boarded was the plane and the pilot. What did they have to worry about?

What they didn't know is that this was the first of five flights they will have to make. Each one getting them closer and closer to Alaska. It is one flight after another getting them closer to destiny. As they flew this flight was to take them from Marrion, North Carolina to Chicago, Illinois. They won't be staying in the city long as they will be going from one plane directly to the other. They will repeat this process until they make it to Alaska.

As they got closer to the arctic circle, they could feel the very air around them becoming colder. They could see their breath freeze into a fine mist. It made them happy to see the air being as cold as it was. It always made them happy to know they will get to see snow covering the horizon.

Outside a storm started to brew. Lighting flashed as thunder shook the very plane itself.

"Is it safe for us to keep flying through this?" Travis asked the pilot.

"Yes, it should be fine." The pilot said focusing on the airspace ahead of him.

As the flight continued the small plane swayed with every strong gust of wind. It jerked hard when it was hit by an extra strong gust that nearly sent the plane into a mountain side. As the storm continued to rage outside of the plane Travis began to worry that they wouldn't make it in the air much longer. Shortly after the strong guest the storm slowly began to clear. Travis and Garett smiled at each other as sunlight teased them through the window.

"We made it out of the storm!" Garett and Travis cheered in tandem with each other.

"I told you we would be okay." The pilot said with a sound of victory in his voice.

Everyone was smiling and laughing for the rest of the trip as the pilot announced the descent into the last city of the trip. This time stuff was different as they landed on the airstrip a crowd of men surrounded the final plane. Each and every one of them stood uniform. They all chanted something as Travis and Garett boarded this plane. Half of the men boarded the plane with them and sat in silence as the plane made its accent into the sky.

Travis gave everyone that boarded with them a puzzled and suspicious look. In his mind something was off and gave him a horrible feeling in the pit of his stomach. As he looked around all he could see was his reflection in each and every pair of sunglasses that each one wore. The plane hit a few updrafts between the final city and the place they had ahead of them.

As they looked out the windows of their seaplane the world began to turn white with splashes of green fields. They stared out the window in awe as the landscape passed under them. The pilot called for everyone to be ready as they started their descent to the airstrip below. The plane started to shake as its boats touched the surface of the lake. As the plane slowed you could feel the surface tension of the water taking hold.

When the plane came to stop all that was left was the bouncing of the currents. Everyone began to stand as a knock came on the side of the plane. When Travis tried to stand one of the men pulled him back into his seat and another opened the stairs. As the stairs began to open, they opened to a half-frozen lake with men at the ready. Still, all the men wore the same uniform from expression to clothing. They began to exit the plane surrounded by the men that boarded with them. Travis began to feel more unease as they continued their journey.

"Hello my boy!" A man yelled in a booming voice as he got out of a vehicle.

A man stepped out of the side of the car close to Travis and Garett then cleared his voice. "Introducing the grand duke, Johnathon Marvic!" The man commanded attention with each word.

Johnathon Marvic was a rough looking older man that walked with a cane and wore a sharp suit. A suit definitely not fit for the colder weather. He was broad shouldered, and his face bore scars from his military past. His peppered beard was clean cut and well-kept which is a sign he lives nicely for being in the middle of nowhere Alaska.

"Please boys, let us proceed to the heat within the car. I am sure we have a lot to talk about." Johnathon ended his sentence with a sly off-putting smile.

"Well, I guess we should get started." Travis said as they proceeded to the car.

"Yes, I am cold anyway." Garett said with a nervous laugh.

They could feel the cold melt off their skin as they entered the warm atmosphere of the car. As they began to relax Johnathon looked both of the men up and down in assessment. He let out a slight chuckle as he realized that both his son and Garett finally sat in front of him. As the laughs continued it didn't make Travis feel any better.

Chapter 14: The Great Gathering

"How are you, Travis?" Johnathon asked, taking charge of the conversation.

"I am doing well dad, but I have to tell you something first." Travis said fidgeting nervously.

"Well don't keep me waiting boy." Johnathon gave a hearty laugh.

"This is Garett. He isn't just my friend. He is my significant other." Travis said as Garett reached to his hand trying to calm him down.

Johnathon looked at the two for several seconds with a puzzled look before speaking. "Well, I am glad someone bothered to be with this damn fool of a man." Johnathon laughed playfully punching Travis on the shoulder.

"I want to hear some of your war stories, my boy. We have a long trip back to my home." Johnathon continued.

As they traveled through miles of road that changed between snow and green fields the Johnathon listened to Travis spill stories with glee. Not only did the stories have Johnathon captured but Garett as well. Travis spoke but his attention was on the mountains that passed commanding the attention of people like the Gods in legends of days past. Each mountain formed a beautiful grey horizon topped with snow caps that ran down the sides mixing with lush green evergreens. Each one a dramatic breath-taking height that could dwarf a titan if they had stood side by side.

As they drove several holes rocked the car bringing on the laughs of everyone within the car. The guide car losing its wheel caused the caravan to come to a sudden halt as each car pulled to the side of the road. Everyone began to exit their vehicles to check the lead car like a mobile pit crew. Travis and Garett soon followed everyone out but instead of going to the lead car they just looked around at their surroundings. Around them mountains chomped at the horizon like teeth from a giant's jaws. It stunned the pair in place, jaws dropped from the beauty of such untouched nature.

"It's beautiful, isn't it?" Johnathon asked as he walked up behind the pair, placing an arm around the two.

"Yes, it is Mr. Marvic." Garett said, trying to not sound awe struck.

"I can agree with that dad." Travis said, not hiding his excitement.

"This is part of the reason I moved here. This place has always attracted my attention. It has ever since my deployment here." Johnathon laughed as he turned around to check on the car that was being repaired.

They didn't notice the cold moving in on their bodies as Travis and Garett went on a walk around the area. A nearby stream called to them while they explored. The more they looked around the better the world around them appeared. It soon became the reason they lost any suspicion about this entire situation. After Johnathon called out that the car was fixed, they made their way from the cleanest stream they had ever seen to the vehicle caravan.

"So, boys how do you like the area?" Johnathon asked as they got back in the car.

"This is probably the cleanest place that I have ever seen." Garett said with excitement overflowing from his words.

"I will agree with you there Garett." Johnathon said with a smile on his face.

"Dad why didn't you call when you got settled?" Travis asked with his words unmoved with seriousness.

"That answer will be a little more complicated and I will explain more on that when we get to our destination." Johnathon said sounding like his mood had been damaged.

As they continued the world around them continued to change. Large fields filled with large groups of reindeer feeding could be seen out the window catching Travis's attention. The view outside of the window caused a look of amazement crept across his face unnoticed as he continued to take in the view. Johnathon let out a laugh before signaling for the caravan to stop once more.

"Go take pictures if you would like." Johnathon said while he gestured at the field.

"I think I will." Travis said with a massive smile on his face.

He got out of the car and pulled out a camera that he had packed in his bag. As he took the pictures of the scene, he didn't notice the men creeping up behind him in silence. They had already drugged Garett who was passed out in the car. Before he knew it a rag had covered his mouth and a strange smell filled his nostrils. He was held for several moments trying to fight back before he passed out from the chloroform.

As he passed out, he found himself sitting at a table with a man in a suit across from him. He couldn't understand the man, but he could see he was yelling. As the man circled the table, he threw down a folder of blank papers. A partner walked into the room and started to play what Travis thinks is the good cop. Now that he took a close look at the situation, he was in the same questioning he was in after the death of his stepfather. They tried to pin him as a premeditated murderer who had been planning to kill his entire family, but he was stopped and killed by the man for it.

Travis was awakened by being slapped. When his eyes opened a hooded man stood in front of him. He looked down to find himself strapped to a chair at his chest and wrists. Across the room Garett was also tied to a chair. Garett was still out cold but alive. He took a look around the room he was in. The wall was lined with statues that had been so worn down that they no longer have features of their own. The center of the room had a line of unlit fire pits that have been staged to be ignited and some set up for cooking.

"Why am I here and where being my father?" Travis asked only to get silence in response.

"Is Garett okay?" Travis asked still only to get silence.

Finally, the man spoke and spoke with a voice so deep it shook your very skeleton. "We will release you, but you must not fight us. We are not your enemy. We only had to make sure you had not been marked. Welcome to Kallet."

The man cut the ropes from around his wrists and chest. As Travis stood, he was handed robes and escorted out of the room. In this room he was asked to change into the robes and as he did the man that escorted him to the room continued to check him for this "mark". When the man decided he was clear to leave the building he was escorted to an exit. As Travis exited, he was blinded by the light from the sun but as his eyes adjusted what he saw was amazing. He saw a sprawling town with shops and homes. People could be seen trading goods for a local currency. No outside food chains or stores could be seen anywhere, but this town had its own local stores and restaurants. Travis found himself exploring, amazed by the fact that he had never heard of the place before.

As Travis started to walk out into the town square, he could feel a massive pain in his leg. He looked down to see his leg brace had been taken from him. Frantically he flagged the closest person down and asked if the town had a doctor. To his relief they nodded and helped him walk to where the doctor worked. As they entered the office the doctor got a seat ready for Travis.

"What may I help you with visitor?" The doctor asked in a thick German accent.

"My leg needs a support brace. I had one when I got here but it was taken." Travis said, his face revealing the amount of pain he was in.

"I might have something we can use to remedy that." The doctor said while he started to dig through his cabinets.

The doctor pulled out an out of era looking full metal leg brace. It looks like the brace from the start of the era. He still took it happily. He would do anything to make his leg pain go away.

"How much do I owe you for the leg brace Doc?" Travis asked as he stood up with the help of a cane the doctor handed him.

"You are in no need of paying me. I do this out of the love I have in my heart." The doctor said with a smile on his face.

Travis began his journey back out of the building and sat in the town square again. He looked around as Garett came out of the building he came out of. Garett had the same amused look that Travis had only moments ago. Travis started to get up to hug Garett but before he could Garett ran to him.

"Travis you never have to stand up for me to come to you." Garett said while laughing.

"Garett I will always stand for you." Travis said smiling before he gave Garett a kiss.

A lady yelled in disgust seeing the pair kiss and started to publicly condemn them. As the lady continued to scream a crowd began to form around. The crowd began to join in with the ridicule and disgust of what they had just seen. Soon people began to throw rocks at the pair who started to run away from the crowd. As Travis ran the leg brace proved to be difficult to run with. He only made it what he assumed was a few blocks before the brace locked, and he fell to the ground. Garett turned to pick him off the ground when the crowd swarmed them.

The crowd began to kick and hit the pair. As the crowd beat him Travis began to fall back to a time when he was beat during public guard in Afghanistan. He could remember the crowd calling him evil while the sole of their shoes made their marks on him. He began to cry out for his commanding officer with tears running down his face. He slowly started to come out of his memories as he could hear his father yelling at the crowd.

"Get away from him!" Johnathan yelled as gunshots echoed through the air around the town.

The crowd began to disperse as more gunshots filled the air. They didn't hear or see anyone injured so Travis assumed that they had been fired into the air. He could feel arms picking him up as his vision came back to reality. His dad's smiling face came into view as he was carried to a house and far away from town square.

"Thank you, father." Travis said his voice still weak from his fears of what's to come.

When Travis took a look at his father, he didn't see his father, He saw Valieen. Valieen was smiling at him or as much of a smile as a skull could muster. Travis tried to retreat but his back hit a wall. He tried to scream but Valieen being that close without him knowing it put fear so deep into him so fast he froze. He felt hands on his shoulders trying to shake him free of his frozen state, but it didn't work. He slowly worked his way out of his fear as they started to back away from him.

"Travis are you okay?" Garett asked as he took Travis's hand.

"Yes, I am fine. It is just that I saw him." Travis said in a whispering voice.

"Who did you see my boy?" Johnathon asked with a strange amount of excitement in his voice.

"It is, no one dad." Travis said with suspicion in his voice.

"I won't judge you for whatever you tell me." Johnathon begged his son for information.

"It is a demon dad, but I am not going to say any more than that." Travis said shying away from his dad a small amount.

"Is this demon's name Valieen?" Johnathon's voice changed along with his posture as he spoke.

"Y-Y-Yes." Travis said, pulling Garett away from his father.

"He is not a bad guy son." Johnathon said as his skin cracked, and his eyes turned black.

"Run Garett!" Travis yelled shoving Garett out of the door.

Travis tried to run away as Johnathon jumped between him and the door. Johnathon grabbed his shirt and threw him to the wall. Every time something happened, he saw less and less of his father on his father's face. Valieen had in some way taken his father's body, or he had gotten into Travis's dream.

"I have to be still sleeping or something." Travis said with his voice shaking from fear.

"You're not sleeping boy." Johnathon said his voice in a growl.

Johnathon grabbed Travis by the shirt again and shoved against the wall. Travis was lifted from his feet till his head was touching the roof. It wasn't possible unless his father was floating now. His eyes had turned the deepest color of black that Travis had ever seen. The longer Travis looked into his eyes the darker they got. As they got darker, he could see his father chained up in the depths of those black eyes. His father was no longer in control.

He could see his father struggling in his own mind trying to fight the demon. He new his father had a strong will, but he doesn't think it will get him back into control before the demon could do damage. For every inch, his father got back in his mind the stronger the demon got. He could see his father was losing hope on getting back his mind.

"See you later buddy boy." Johnathon's voice growled as he threw Travis through the closet door.

As Travis struggled to get up his body shook, and his ears rang. He could tell that his equilibrium was fucked up because of his ears ringing. He coughed up blood and looked out the door to see his father passed out on the floor. Seeing this filled him with anger and even being as uneasy as he was still, he rose.

"F-F-Fuck you. Y-You son of a b-bitch." Travis said looking over Johnathon's body.

Travis slowly limped his way out the door. He was covered in blood and his brace was broken, but he made it out the door. Travis swore he would never give up and he still won't let himself. As he sat down on the ground outside of his father's house Valieen appeared in the crowd of people that surrounded the place. Even if Garett and Travis could hear him laugh it was affecting everyone. It affected them like everyone started to feel sick or uneasy but didn't want to show it. It was written on everyone's face. Only a chosen few can see him, but everyone could feel him.

"Are you okay Travis?" Garett asked sitting down beside Travis.

"Yes Garett, I am for the most part okay." Travis responded with a smile.

"Well, that is good enough for me." Garett said putting an arm around Travis.

Travis leaned on Garett and started to cry. His tears cut through his blood covered face like two rivers after a massacre. The two of them sat as rain slowly moved in above them. Soon Garett joined Travis in tears as footsteps sounded behind them. It was Johnathon coming from within the house. He limped over and sat in front of the two and started to speak as thunder sounded above them. Tears formed in his eyes as he opened his mouth again.

"I am sorry boys, but I can't stop this. Not anymore." Johnathon said as his tears continued.

Chapter 15: Kallet, a cult town

Travis began to keep a diary of everything that was happening while he was in Kallet. It was his way of explaining his dreams and feelings since he couldn't get in contact with Dr. Marron. It seems that they took all modern items as people entered the town. This made it harder for people to get any pictures or information about the town out in the world that lies beyond the town walls.

The town seemed to be stuck in a mid-1800s unlike the rest of the world that kept moving forward. The closest the town came to being modern was the wall around it. Travis knew something was off when they had gotten to Alaska but even if he could try to reach out to them and them about the truth he felt they wouldn't listen to him. Everyone has been giving him the side eye since they saw him and Garett kiss. The towns people even act like they have never known the world kept developing further.

As Travis walked around the town, he noticed that all of the buildings except for two had been made of wood with stone foundation, The only two that had been made from full stone is the big temple-like building he had exited from and the black smith. Still the thought nags at him about the fact this place was here and how it hasn't moved forward at all. The town wasn't on any maps he had ever seen either.

The bakery here still used wood stoves made from stone. He thought the bread and cake was better, but it still was strange to him. Most of his time was spent looking for answers to why and how this town exists and the events that had gotten them there. The biggest thing for him was the wall that surrounded the town was wood on the inside but unless the outside looked different a plane should have seen it.

To keep himself sane he wrote and wrote about what he sees around the town. It just brought suspicion upon himself among the townspeople. He has heard them talking about him and calling him names. They didn't make much of an effort to show they don't like new people being in the town. They hated it more that he was writing down things about their town.

"Hey Travis, what are you doing?" Garett said walking up and placing a hand on Travis's shoulder.

"I am trying to keep myself a bit sane since I have no way to talk to my therapist." Travis said as he kept writing.

"Well please don't drive yourself crazy by doing it." Garett said as he walked back to the house the two shared.

The events that transpired from when his father attacked along with the deep black of his eyes revolved in Travis's mind. It was something he wished would leave his mind, but to his despair it went around and around like a movie reel. Travis couldn't trust himself around his dad after all of that. His mind has been a mess since they got into this town and at the current moment Travis can't tell who to trust around him. With every face he saw came the thoughts that they could have been his enemy. He feels like everyone wants to harm him, even Garett.

"Well, well, well, how are you enjoying the town Travis? It is beautiful isn't it." Valieen said following it up with a laugh.

"What are you doing here you monster." Travis said, not taking his eyes off his paper.

"You will find out soon enough Travis. If you don't want to look at me then I will just leave you with a parting gift." Valieen said as he cut Travis's arm length wise.

As the blood flowed down Travis's arm he fell over in pain. The pain took a few seconds to register, and it was all at one time. Travis got up from the ground and slowly made his way back to the house he was staying in with Garett. Right away he started to wash his arm in the wash basin.

"Travis what happened to your arm?" Garett asked, looking at Travis's arm.

"I was paid a visit from our friend." Travis said a small amount of anger in his voice.

"Well, I can see that." Garett said, taking hold of Travis's arm.

What Garett saw was the word *"Beldam"* carved into his arm. It was only seen when the blood was cleared away but after that it was very pronounced from the rest of the scars on Travis's body. Garett grabbed their mirror to show it to Travis. As Travis saw it, he began to freak out about the word and that he knows what the word means.

"Travis do you know what that means?" Garett asked, fixated on the word carved into his boyfriend's arm.

"Yes, I do know." Travis said with irritation on his voice.

"What is it?" Garett asked, sounding worried.

"It means witch. That can only mean that we are in for a wild ride now." Travis said, letting out a pained laugh.

"Oh, great now they are going to think we are gay witches." Garett said, trying to lighten the mood of the situation.

"That was funny Garett, but I don't think this is the time. Thank you for trying." Travis forced himself to smile.

Travis sat down in the chair that the two kept in the corner of the room and went back to writing. Garett gave him a worried look before he had left to go to the store for food. All Travis has done is write and write. He still didn't know why yet, but he continued to do it.

"Travis, could you please put down the book and talk to me." Garett pleaded from across the room.

"Garett, I don't know what to do anymore! My brain has been overrun with memories and nightmares since we got here! I don't mean to yell, but damn!" Travis yelled his eyes going wild.

Travis felt like he was about to lose his mind as his memories swam around mixing his memories. Travis began to look around the room as reality began to become patchwork with his past memories. Everything began to fragment from what it was. He didn't know what would come next. Would it be his past? Would he snap back to reality? Would he get lost in his mind again?

As Travis continued to slip into his insanity Garett watched on scared for him. He knew he could help, but he sat to be there when he was needed. He knew that Travis was suffering, but he wanted to help more than he was able to in reality. All Garett could do while Travis's mind sorted itself out was sit and be there.

Garett began to cry later that night because of everything. He knew that Travis needed to leave, but he didn't know how they would get out because the town was on lock down. Soon Travis ran out of room in his notebook and just sat staring off into space. Garett stayed up as long as he could, but sleep took him still. When Garett awoke in the morning, he saw that Travis had been busy, Travis had written all over the wall. He wrote the same phrase over and over. *"You can't hide, and you can't run."* It was written all over the wall from floor to ceiling.

Garett only became more and more worried as he looked upon the wall. Seeing the words written all over the wall sent a chill down his spine that shook him to his very core. He looked around but Travis was nowhere to be found within the house. He slowly, still in shock walked out to the town center. There he found Travis standing and starting at the temple. Garett made every attempt to bring him out of it.

Travis slowly moved his hands out in a bowl shape without moving his eyes or any other part of himself. Garett kept trying to snap him out of his trance as his hands caught on fire. Everyone's eye snapped to Travis with a gasp. Garett jumped back as he was consumed by flames himself. As the fire climbed up his body like a rabid animal his vision began to fail him. When his senses shortly followed, he fell in a flaming heap onto the ground without another sound.

Travis snapped out of his trance to see a body burned on the ground and shocked faces surrounding him. He staggered from his position as people began to chant *"Witch"* as he ran through the crowd crying. When he got to his house and shut the door it was like the voices began bouncing off the walls themselves. He clasped his hands over his ears and fell to his knees. The voices didn't muffle but got louder, then he began to scream. He let out a scream so loud and so fierce that he could feel his very vocal cords ripping into pieces.

As the voices began to fade away, he couldn't hear anything, but he was still screaming, or he was trying. Travis soon let his head fall to the floor breathing deeply trying to calm himself. He was trying to become calm even if he was calm just for one moment. His heart was racing and a pool of sweat formed a thin layer between his head and the wood floor under it.

Travis sat on that floor for two hours before he was able to stand up. He looked around the room just now realizing how crazy he must have seemed to Garett with all of this. He began to stagger to his feet small drops of blood forming in the corners of his mouth. His breath was still far from being regulated as pain coursed through his body. He walked to his water basin and tried to wash the blood from his mouth. The blood just kept returning, not slowing even for a second.

"Look who it is. It is the wicked witch of Kallet. The one who killed his only lover." Valieen said, appearing on the bed behind Travis.

"Don't bother saying anything because I know that you can't. You tore your vocal cords trying to drown out the voices. I hope you do know that they will burn you at the stake for what you did. I won't let them kill you because I am having too much fun." Valieen followed the statement with a laugh.

Travis yelled with no voice trying to protest everything that has happened so far. He stormed up to Valieen still yelling with no voice. Valieen sat with a smile on his face before leaving Travis to his solitude. Travis laid upon his bed tears streaming down his face like a free-flowing river. He felt the pain of everything emotional and physical all at one time. He knew that his world was coming crashing down around him. Despite his terror, he managed to get sleep.

Travis was awakened to his door being knocked down and people screaming. People soon began to tie his hands behind him and drag him out of his door. The scene he saw was a large crowd of hooded people standing around a wooden pole surrounded by sticks and grass. In the back of his mind, he knew that this was the time. This was when he was going to be killed, and he was going to die at the stake.

He tried to protest as they continued to tie him to the stake. Travis took a good look around him seeing three men stood in front of each one holding a book in their hands and had their faces hidden. They began to chant but Travis couldn't understand the language that they had been using. He could only watch on in silence, unable to defend himself, unable to proclaim his innocence. His mind flickered back drowning him in the past where he watched his men die unable to save them. In slow motion he watched the man holding the torch light the sticks and grass under his feet.

The flames licked at his feet as if it were hungry. He tried to stomp it out, but it continued to consume. In his eyes as he looked at the fire, he thought it changed into the shape of a beast. A beast with a fiery appetite. It was looking to eat him and every inch of his body. He took one final deep breath, closed his eyes, and stood stoic as he burned.

What stood out was as he was consumed, he felt no burning, and he smelt no flesh burning. What did happen was that as he looked upon the crowd time was frozen in place. Valieen floated with wings outstretched above the crowd. He had a massive smile on his face looking upon Travis burning in the fire below. As his smile grew Travis started feeling the pain that came with the fire.

"Here is where I save you from this situation." Valieen could be heard saying in the back of Travis's mind.

Valieen descended in front of the crowd unseen to the others but very real to Travis. He walked slowly up to Travis with his skeletal arm outstretched ready to touch him. His smile got bigger the closer to Travis he got, and as his hand wrapped around Travis's head the flames exploded upward. Travis's vision began to vanish, and his skin began to hurt as his scream returned to him. The fire dissipated where nothing was left but the stake and ash.

Garett jerked awake slamming his head against some object above him. He began to touch anything and everything around him. Every sense was gone except for his sense of touch and from what he could tell was probably a coffin from what he could go off by feeling the area around him. He sat his head back trying to think of what he could do. As his mind began to rest, he could feel that the air around him was beginning to get cold. His body began to gain a mind of its own as it started to thrash against what he assumed was the roof of his tomb.

"Come the fuck on!" Garett yelled slamming his fists against the lid above him.

"Don't you start doing that now." Valieen could be heard in a muffled voice as claws dragged on the outside of the lid.

"Let me the fuck out of here you bastard!" Garett yelled, starting to feel his own face start to get hot from anger.

"I can't let you out. This game is just getting started. Don't use up all of your air before Travis gets here." Valieen said following it up with a laugh that shook Garett to his core.

Garett sighed and dropped his head back trying to calm himself down. The air began to chill again after his breath began to become steady. His thoughts began to bounce around from his early life being alone with no one to love and going to abusive parents. While the other thought it went to was the current life of having someone to love but having to go through what was happening. Garett sat hoping that he could keep his hopes up for Travis to be in time to save himself.

As Travis's vision came back, he saw flames disappearing revealing that he was out in the middle of nowhere. His breath was visible in the air in front of him. His body began to get cold as he saw no one around him anywhere. He started to walk towards a pile of snow that was in front of him.

"What is this?" Travis asked, clearing away the snow to reveal a coffin.

"Garett is in there big boy." Valieen said holding a key in his hand.

"Let him out!" Travis yelled as Valieen threw the key out into the middle of the snow and flew away.

Chapter 16: The Snow Tomb

Travis forced himself to make his steps through the mud and snow, taking two glances at the coffin behind him. He continued to walk the only thing keeping him going was the thought of needing to get Garett out of that coffin. Travis got to the area where he thought the key landed and started to look around on his hands and knees. As he dug through the mud Valieen was in the back of his mind laughing.

"I will get you out of there Garett. I will somehow get you out." Travis said as he began to hyperventilate.

He began to dig deeper and deeper into the dirt as he saw a metallic object in the ground. He got excited digging faster and faster but to his shock it was not the key. What he found was a sword. He took the sword to the coffin and wedged it in between the lid and body of the coffin and tried to get it open. He pushed the sword down, lifting the lid high enough for him to pull it the rest of the way off.

As the lid slowly began to come off, he saw Garett lying motionless. He grabs Garett by the shoulders and shook him. Garett slowly began to open his eyes with a weak smile. Travis smiled back at him while he helped Garett out of his snowy tomb. Travis took a look around trying to find the town but had no luck. His heartbeat raised as he continued to try to find his way home. With the town nowhere to be found Travis knew they still needed to be on the move.

Travis threw Garett over his shoulder and started his slow walk into the wilderness. He may have been heavy, but Travis was driven to get him to some sort of safety. He took heavy and powerful steps each one testing his body further. His breath ran heavy as they got further and further from what was to be Garett's tomb before Travis saved him. They came upon a cave as a snowstorm began to form above them. Wind kicked up snow sending it flying at them stinging their bodies as it went past them. It was almost blowing hard enough to knock them off their feet. Travis struggled to pull Garett into the cave as his legs began to give out as they reached their limit. The cold was taxing his body more than the heat of Afghanistan did when he pulled men out of firefights.

Without a fire the pair began to freeze from the cold that still filtered in from the snowstorm, but Travis tried his best to keep Garett warm with his own body heat. He hugged him close as they got enveloped by a blanket of cold. The cold had gotten so intense within the first few minutes of entering the cave. It became a cold that drove its fangs to their very bones. They began to shake as the cold set in deep to their core. Travis kissed Garett on the forehead before begging for his forgiveness.

A bright light came from the opening of the cave as Garett's breathing began to slow. Travis begged the Gods for them to get out of the situation they found themselves in, but he started to give up when the cold didn't let up. It was like Garett began to move in slow motion. It started with his breathing which slowed before his body began to shake from the cold that still feasted on their bodies. A figure came through the light as tears teased at his eyes. His body began to warm as the figure got closer to him but at the cost of feeling in his limbs.

The figure grew even closer as the light died out behind it, but the figure became no clearer. It put a hand on each of the pair's foreheads and slowly each one passed out. Travis grew cold his core and out. He smiled as his cold body fell limp over Garett's seemingly lifeless body. He saw nothing when his vision finally followed his body into nothingness. It was like his very spirit left his body as he was walking upon a plane filled with wandering humanoids that bridged a gap between normal and grotesque decomposing bodies that walked like men. Some of them screamed for help but others stood silent. He saw one or two that had collapsed onto them slamming their heads against the ground.

"Where am I?" Travis asked himself as his voice echoed through the air around him.

All of the figures turned to look at him, all eyes trained into his very soul. They all froze just staring like statues. Their mouths all fell open, and they emitted a sound that started out small. It began to get louder as they got closer to Travis causing him to start running away as fast as he could run. He continued to run without any end in sight until a small black hole appeared in the distance. It grew in size rapidly as he continued to run. He cleared his mind about everything except for the hole like it was drawing him in. When he got close enough, he jumped for it.

When he entered the hole, he felt like he was back in his body as he jerked, and he felt a pain where his head was supposed to be. He couldn't see anything, and he smelled nothing but a must. His body felt restrained as he tried to move. He kept struggling for what felt like hours before even just his hand started to feel free from his bonds. He slowly tried to work himself free when he could hear a stone slab opening above him. A light got brighter as someone continued to open what he assumed was his tomb.

"I see you are back." The person said as they began to remove the bandages from his body.

"You got lucky Travis, but I can't confirm the same for your boyfriend." Valieen said from his unseen position.

"I thought for sure you two would have died on the way back." The person said with a laugh following up their statement.

Travis could smell food on the air as he was helped out of his tomb. His stomach began to let out a loud growl when he got a large whiff of the food smell. He gave the person an embarrassed smile covering his stomach with his arms. The person gave him a smile and gestured for him to take a seat at the table.

"I cooked up some food for you boys." The person said finally coming into a good enough light to see his face.

He was an older male standing at about average height. On the larger size of a body build. His face holds the looks of happiness but seeming to have had his fair share of sorrows. He seems to understand a person who has been through pain. He gives off the feeling of love and caring for everyone. Travis sat down with a smile on his face as he saw Garett laying on a cot breathing.

"I thought he was dead." Travis said, his voice coming out hoarse and weak.

"Don't strain yourself friend. He will live and from the way you held him I take that you two are together." The stranger smiled as he finished speaking.

"Yes, we are, I tried to protect him the best that I could, but I failed." Travis said lowering his head in shame.

"If you wouldn't have done what you did then he would be dead right now." The stranger placed a hand on Travis's.

"That fact I guess kind of does help me feel better." Travis said with a smile.

It did help Travis feel better but didn't change that he felt responsible in the first place. To Travis him meeting with Garett back at the pizza place set in motion something that didn't need to be. If Garett died here Travis felt that it was on him and no one else. He didn't feel he could even hold the demon as responsible. He shook his head with a small, stressed chuckle.

"Can you tell me what you saw when you went to the other world?" The stranger asked curiously.

"The other world is filled with spirits suffering in limbo. They see the wrongs they had caused in this world, and they must watch them as they die all over again. Some of the spirits get driven insane having to watch their deeds all over again and their spirits decay where they stood. Some of them try to speed the process by slamming their heads on the ground knowing they couldn't attack the other spirits. If you achieve the ability to break your trance and you can start to find your way out, they will give chase to try to take your place. Many of them look and sound like walking dead. They have skin mid decay that falls off while they walk, and their airways shake as they take deep breaths trying to keep on moving. I was lucky to find my way out." Travis's face grew grim as he spoke.

The stranger was visibly shaken by the story and didn't have anything to say in response to him. They both knew it was a touchy subject. It was still a new memory that sat fresh but just as rotten in his mind. Travis sat in silence just looking at the stranger as the orange light from the fire licked at their faces and their surroundings. He couldn't put his finger on it, but the stranger seemed familiar to him. It was like he has known the stranger his whole life.

Window shutters began to slam against the outside of the building as wind picked up outside. The stranger got up and opened a window blind to show snow piling up outside of the house they called shelter for now. With a laugh the stranger came back to the table and sat down. Travis gave him a strange look as he took his seat.

"You can call me Gavel friend." He said, outstretching a hand.

"M-My name is Travis." Travis said, shaking Gavel's hand.

"The snow seems to be rising fast. I guess we might be stuck here until it lightens up. It is a bit strange at the amount we are getting today." Gavel said as he went and grabbed two shot glasses and some whiskey.

They sat, drank, and ate while waiting for Garett to wake. When he began to stir, they got excited, but he was not near waking yet. It was like he was trapped within his own mind and fighting for his way back to the world. The longer Travis watched the more that a fear Garett will never wake creeps into his heart.

"He will be okay Travis. He is very healthy." Gavel said, trying to make him feel better about the situation.

"I know and I have faith that he will." Travis said, refilling his glass.

"He will need time to recover but the way it is looking with the snow out there I don't think anyone can go anywhere." Gavel laughed after finishing his statement.

"That is true," Travis began to feel the whiskey kicking in causing him to laugh.

They sat and finished off a bottle and a half before their vision made it impossible to pour anymore. They laughed and ate for another two hours before they passed out where they sat. Early the next morning they awoke to a freezing room filled with the smell of cooked eggs and bacon. As Travis forced his eyes open, he saw Garett cooking over the fire with a smile on his face.

"Good morning Travis." Garett said turning around and giving him a kiss on his forehead.

"Good morning Garett." Travis smiled, rubbing his eyes.

It was a welcome sight to Travis to see Garett awake and it made him feel that for once something was going the way he wanted it to. Travis got up to find Gavel nowhere in sight. He looked out the window to find the snow had moved up to the tops of all of the windows. He inspected the rest of the house and found a ladder leading to a hatch on the roof. He hadn't seen the ladder until now but Garett being awake put him at ease for now.

"I am assuming our host went up to the roof?" Travis asked in a sly tone.

"Yes, he is, and his name is Gavel if you didn't remember." Garett said laughing, turning around to show he was wearing a kiss the cook apron.

"I will go to the roof to see what the world is looking like outside." Travis said, giving Garett a pet on the cheek before ascending the ladder to the roof.

He was hit with a wave of cold and heavy winds as he climbed through to the roof. He shielded his eyes from the early morning sun as he stood tall upon a house that was surrounded by a sea of snow and ice. He looked around to find Gavel sitting in a lawn chair eating looking out over the snow with a brooding expression. Travis walked up beside him and put a hand on his shoulder shaking him from the view.

"This is an unusual amount of snow for this time of the year Travis, and I don't know why it is here." Gavel said, looking confused now as he cast an eye on the snow.

"I would like to know how this much snow came last night as well." Travis said trying to sound like he knew the normal amount for Alaska.

"From as much as I know and that is nothing about you. You don't know shit for shit about Alaska boy." Gavel laughed at his own sentence.

"You would be right about that but it being spring season, and I am pretty sure this is too much snow." Travis said looking out at the white that swallowed the world.

"Listen here, it is called the break-up season. Most people would claw your guts out, but I will let this one-time slide." Gavel said with a big smile on his face like he had just won something.

"You have the smile of someone that looks like they have just gained a victory." Travis said as he pulled up a piece of wood to sit on.

"Well, I have lived here a long time but never had the chance to tell someone that. I have lived out here on my own mostly, so I don't get a lot of visitors. I do know why you are out here though. You did something to piss off what that cult calls a God." Gavel began to look grim after his statement.

"In a way yes but how did you know that?" Travis asked curiously.

"Because I am on a mission from God to stop the cult." Gavel said as a bright light came from his body and wings formed on his back.

Chapter 17: The Arch angel Gavel

Gavel stood as his body changed from his older looking human body to one of youth and beauty. It was like he had found a way to shed fifty years off of himself in mere seconds. Travis fell back in awe of the brilliant display of power that he had just seen from this one creature. He didn't know how to act after the light died down. The loss of the light didn't reveal a creature that looked of power, but instead gave off an energy that you felt in your soul itself.

"Y-Y-You changed so fast and so much." Travis said with his breath escaping his words.

"Yes, I did but that is by the grace of our God." Gavel said, gesturing to the sky with a smile on his face. After he finished speaking he knelt down to pray.

As Gavel went to his knees Travis saw a crazed Valieen standing behind Gavel wide-eyed. Valieen licked his lips as he ambushed Gavel and for the first time, he looked physical. The power of the two-clashing flung Travis off of the roof and into the snow below. He felt a pressure as he was sent off that made him feel like his soul was separated from his very body.

He hit the snow in such a way that it felt like arms wrapping themselves around him and pulling him down. It was like the snow wanted to pull him to the very depths of hell itself. He felt at peace with the idea that he may die when he felt the ground below him. He could hear Valieen and Gavel fighting even with being buried in the snow each of their blows causing the snow to shift above him. It churned like the sea as the battle raged overhead.

He found the drive to force his way up to the surface. He needed to help because Gavel saved Garett and himself from freezing to death. It was time for him to help pay him back for it. With all of his strength he began to dig and drag his way to the surface, the snow feeling more like it normally did, allowing his hand to grab hold. The sun began to come into view as he got closer to the surface causing his determination to grow larger within him.

As his hand broke to the surface of the snow his hand was met with the bitter air. He took a deep breath as he pulled himself out of the snow as if he had just surfaced out of the sea itself. He cast his eyes upon the fight between Valieen and Gavel as a sword of light was cast through Valieen's chest. Valieen he pulled it out, he laughed and fell over. A black fire covered his body causing it to vanish into thin air. Travis let out a sigh of relief letting himself fall to the snow out of exhaustion. His eyes shut, and he cast off to sleep where he laid.

"Travis wake up we need to get you inside." Gavel said, shaking Travis by his shoulders.

Travis opened his eyes to see Gavel standing above him grabbing his arms. He inspected his surroundings and saw that his skin began to turn blue again. Weakly he began to move closer to Gavel. He rose to his feet with Gavel to assist, and they slowly began back to the roof of the house. When they got to the wall of the house, Gavel lifted Travis onto the roof. Travis investigated Gavel as he climbed onto the roof his wings had cuts on them, taking away his ability to use them for flight. Gavel stood turning back into the man Travis had met when he had saved them.

It looked as if all his age and weight had come out of hiding. The familiar but still strange face helped Travis process what he had just witnessed. He gave a small smile before descending the ladder into the home. Garett was asleep and the food was laid out for everyone to eat. Travis took his place beside the one person he had come to love in his life. A smile came across both of their faces as sleep took everyone present within the house. Gavel gave the boys–unknowing they had been much younger–one last smile before he too went to sleep.

Not a single one of them had slept in peace. Each one had a nightmare all to their own, but they couldn't speak of the horrors they saw the next morning. They all had been shaken awake by the chanting of hundreds of people outside of the home the three shared. They got out of bed and walked to the window to see a world consumed in torchlight. Each light cast upon one to three people. Not a single face in view but eyes could be felt. Voices rang out as one but alone all the same.

"What the hell could that be?" Travis said in shock.

"It appears the entire cult is here." Gavel said looking around at what he could see.

Slowly the crowd closed in on their house. The chanting got louder with each step they took. Their voices began to turn into one force loud as thunder and their torches fused into one massive light almost as bright as the sun itself. All three of the men scrambled to blockade every entrance to the building out of fear that the crowd would break into the home. Panic began to set in when the smell of smoke began to fill the house and the air began to become thick with the swirling colors of grey and black.

"The fucking house is on fire!" Travis yelled as he began to climb the ladder.

"Do you think the best way out is up?" Garett asked, watching the action.

"Well, it is a lot better than heading straight into that crowd!" Travis said coughing from the smoke that started to fill the air around them.

"That is true Travis, I am sorry if I upset you." Garett said, lowering his head into his hands.

"Garett you didn't upset me. I love you." Travis said kissing Garett then went back to getting their way out cleared.

"I don't know how long we have!" Gavel yelled looking out the window.

Travis pushed the hatch on the roof open as quietly as he could before signaling that it was safe to exit. He helped both Garett and Gavel out of the hatch on the roof as the front of the house was consumed in flame. They all rushed off the back of the house which was a short distance from a cave system which they decided to enter. They had been greeted by a darkness that felt deeper than any darkness any of them had seen.

"Where are we going to go now?" Garett asked, looking at Gavel who took the lead of their small group.

"We need to move forward till we are deep enough for the crowd to not see us light a flame." Gavel said walking forward with confidence.

As the group walked Garett and Travis tried to stay close to Gavel. Travis knew that Gavel could help them because he had already the day before. Garett hugged himself as close to Travis as he could be. The cave began to feel like it was squeezing them in clawed hands that they couldn't see. Gavel took a look around and proceeded to pull out a sword of light after he felt they could be declared safe.

"How do you have a sword like that?" Garett asked, his jaw falling open in awe.

"It is because I am an angel of God." Gavel said his age falling away again.

"This year just keeps getting stranger and stranger." Garett said picking his jaw off the floor so to speak.

They had been able to get a good look at their surroundings around them guided by the light from the sword. Around them they saw skeletons lying around them, some impaled on the stalagmites. They found puddles of bodily fluids that stained the floor below the skeletons. It got into their minds to wonder how the ones on the stalagmites had gotten there.

"I wonder what has put them where they are now." Travis said pointing at one of the impaled skeletons.

"I think we should avoid thoughts like that so that we don't suffer the same fate." Gavel said, trying to keep moving forward.

Garett covered his eyes as they made their way through the chamber of the cave. Gavel had signaled that they would have to crawl through a tight area. As they squeezed through the area it felt like the cave sucked the breath out of their bodies. They gasped for air as each one came out on the other side in a new chamber of the cave system. In the center of the chamber Gavel knelt down and prayed for their ability to make it out of the cave alive. It made Garett and Travis think about the fact they had never been much on praying.

"Okay friends let's go this way." Gavel said guiding the other two into the next tunnel they needed to take.

"I am glad we are friends now." Travis said with a laugh taking hold of Garett's hand.

Travis could feel Garett's fear and couldn't blame him cause Travis was scared as well. He couldn't let Garett know because he felt it would cost him all of the love and trust Garett has given him. Knowing that Travis pushed himself on hoping that he would be able to keep the feelings by staying strong not only Garett, but himself as well. They continued on till they came to another chamber in the cave that had shafts of light raining down from above them.

"This place is beautiful." Travis said while he looked around at the shinning spires of rock around them.

"It looks like this place was used to worship some kind of God." Gavel said while inspecting one of the spires.

"I wonder who it was they worshipped?" Garett asked sitting down in the middle of the chamber.

Gavel let out a gasp as the inscriptions began to glow and traced all around them. They watched in awe as words and illustrations began to glow a deep blue color around them. It seemed as if the cave had begun to wake up before their very eyes. Demons and angels came to life in the blue light. The carving arts told stories of wars raged in worlds beyond the one in which they lived now. One world in which the dead walked in fields of fire and magma. The other world the dead flew free with angels and birds.

"These carvings describe a holy war that is only seen in the prophecies of demons and angels." Gavel said, running his fingers over the carvings.

"So, it is stuff that isn't even talked about in the bible?" Travis said watching with curiosity.

"The bible was made by man not by God or his angels. It is just stories made up by people that wanted to put people under their control." Gavel said absentmindedly.

"I didn't expect to hear that from an angel." Travis said his interest was being peaked even more.

"Well religion is not how many try to make it seem. All of the religions exist at one time, but we don't hate each other. Hate between religions has been created by humans themselves. The true bible doesn't condemn other religions. It is actually the exact opposite, and we encourage people to learn from other religions. We want the earth to be united and humans to teach each other about other religions." Gavel said with a smile on his face.

"I know that someone stands against that." Travis said as the lights finally start to come to a close at a carving of what looked like his face.

"Travis that looks like you." Garett said getting up to approach the carving.

As the lights met on the carving a sound was produced from the wall itself. Travis fell to his knees gripping the sides of his head while the other two remained unbothered. In Travis's mind he began to relive every bad event of his life on repeat. To him everything passed in slow motion blending together every voice echoing in his head. He took a look in Garett's direction, but Garett didn't have his own face instead it shuffled between the pained faces of anyone that he ever hurt. He began to scream out of both fear and the pain he felt. He turned to Gavel for help, but his face fused and twisted with Valieen's.

"I thought he killed you, you son of a bitch!" Travis yelled as he fell back crawling away.

"What are you talking about Travis?" What Travis heard was a twisted fusion of Gavel's voice and Valieen's hiss.

Travis began to run from the chamber when a torchlight flickered at the other end of the tunnel. His breath began to go faster as reality became more fragmented, and he found himself in the tunnels of Afghanistan but with the same fucked up versions of Gavel and Garett. He began to feel faint as he could hear Dari—a song used by a hidden village they found in Afghanistan when someone dies—coming from the tunnel. He looked down seeing he was in his military uniform. When he looked back up, he saw his friend's casket sitting open against the wall of the caves chamber. He walked up to it and Spooner shot up out of the casket then grabbed him by the throat. His breath began to slow down, and he couldn't stay conscious as he blacked out and the last thing, he saw was his friend's decaying face.

"Travis!" Garett yelled putting his arms under Travis's.

"We need to get out of here!" Gavel yelled, throwing Travis onto his shoulder.

They both began to run down the tunnel that began to open across the chamber from them. As they began to enter the chamber lights started to twist around them. It twisted into the shape of snakes that had a face of all consuming. At the end of the tunnel the light formed into a snake with its mouth opened ready to eat.

Chapter 18: The Viper Pit

As they approached something that looked like a snake with a gapping mouth and red jewels for eyes. It put fear in everyone except Gavel. Their hearts began to race the closer they got to the snake. Inside the mouth was a giant stone door and below it an inscription. The inscription said *"Those who enter the pit of vipers must fight the poison. Those who enter the pit of snakes must resist the lies. Those who enter the pit of serpents must know what is real and what is not."* The words made them shudder as a shiver ran down their spines. They knew Travis would suffer more if he was to wake, so everything was left to them if they wanted to make it out alive.

"Well, that is not scary at all." Garett said, staying close to Gavel.

"They are just words, my dear friend." Gavel said, as he pat Garett on the head.

"I guess I can say you are right about that." Garett said smiling at Travis's unconscious body.

They continued through the snake's mouth with their heads held high as they went. When they got into the chamber hidden by the snake a door closed behind them. As it slammed shut the light was sucked from Gavel's sword and the room became pitch black. Slowly around them came chants and slowly torches began to ignite in a circle around the room.

"I guess they had us trapped this entire time." Gavel said with a grim look on his face.

"We tried Gavel and that is what matters." Garett said hiding his fear with a smile but not hiding it well.

As more torches lit hooded figures could be seen lining the chamber around them. They chanted louder as the chamber became brighter. They felt more hopeless the more they could see of the hooded figures. The chants began to fuse together into one voice as a figure holding a dagger was illuminated at an altar in front of them. The light flashed off the polished gold metal.

"We might be screwed in this situation." Gavel said, putting Travis onto the floor.

"You can give up now or you can die with him." The figure said pointing the dagger at Travis.

"No one is dying here today." Gavel said standing between the figure and Travis.

The figure raised his hands and fire climbed the walls illuminating Valieen's likeness carved into the wall. It stared down at them with a look of hunger and vengeance. It made Garett shudder and freeze in his place. Gavel shot a look back at him. He gave him a look of hope and it helped Garett calm down, but he felt no hope. As the figure studied the three where they stood.

"You have chosen to die where you stand then. So be it." The figure said as he and four others closed in all holding gold daggers.

The closer they got it seemed like the carving of Valieen moved to look straight at them with an expanding smile. Gavel could feel the hunger driving down into his very soul. Garett felt the smile driving its way into his mind. It was the same smile that Valieen had given Garett when they first met. It was the same hunger that he had shown when he pulled the memories out of his mind by force.

Gavel took a long look around the chamber in which they stood. His hope began to fall lower and lower with the more figures he could identify. He started to back up to where he was standing over Travis so he could better defend him. He noticed the look on Garett's face. It was one of fear and it seemed like his soul left him hollow in that very moment.

"No matter what you do, you can't save him." The figures face was finally starting to come into the light and what they saw was Johnathon's face fused in perfect sight with Valieen's.

His eyes had been black as the sky at night without the moon. His teeth are as sharp as knives freshly made ready to carve meat. His words carried hate so deep that it shook you to your core. It was like the human soul that once used that body as a vessel was dead and gone. Johnathon seemed to no longer exist in this world, but they knew better than that. They knew he might still be in there somewhere.

"You have nowhere to go." The voice was a hiss combined with Johnathon's deep booming voice.

"We will not fall to your evil!" Gavel yelled his voice bouncing off the wall of the chamber.

"No evil lives here only truth and judgement." The combined voices continued to drive its fear into them.

It seemed like the figures continued to grow beyond what was seen as humanly possible. Gavel tripped over Travis's unconscious body backing away. As they still seemed to grow in size, it felt like they filled the cave from one side to the other. Gavel couldn't think of how they had achieved the size that they have.

"What kind of magic do you possess? Whatever it is then you are no longer human." Gavel said, failing to pull his sword of light out for the second time.

It was like the power of this cult is pulling their power out of the air itself. Gavel was quick to realize he had no way to save them from their situation. He got on his knees and started praying to be saved from this cult. Around him everyone began to laugh at Gavel for his prayer. He kept praying even with the cold steel of the blades from every direction.

"Your prayer has no power down here. Not even if you're an angel." The combined voice said with a laugh.

The power in his voice shook Gavel to his core even though he was trying to keep Garett inspired. He felt he was the only thing that kept Garett from giving up at this point. When he looked down, he saw that Travis had begun to stir. This sight gave Gavel a small amount of hope that they might still have a chance to get away. Travis began to open his eyes, and when they began to open, they saw the carving of Valieen get a bigger smile. Its eyes began to move to look at Travis and the smile began to stretch past the ears on the carving, seeming like it might form a full circle around his head.

"W-W-What i-is going on?" Travis struggled to say like he was exerting all his energy.

"Don't strain yourself. We will get out of here I promise." Gavel said, giving Travis a stern look.

Garett grabbed Travis by the arm and pulled him up to help him to get out of the cave. They began to go back through the tunnel they had come through. Gavel stayed behind to protect their retreat. They could hear Gavel yelling as the light began to disappear behind them into the distance. They feared for Gavel's safety as they kept running as fast as they could out of the cave system.

After they had been running for what seemed like hours and their legs started to give out, they made it out. The light carved at their eyes as the sky became visible again. They could see a pile of smoldering ash where the house used to stand and burned-out torches around it. The pattern of an inverted pentagram had been burned into the ground with the house serving as its center. Travis gave Garett a look that had shown fear. He was still weak, and Garett could see that, but neither one of them knew which way to go. Garett sat Travis against some rocks until he could figure out what to do, and as if sent by God a car sped to a stop. A man drenched in sweat as if he had been running for hours got out and pulled them into the car not speaking a word to either one.

"Who are you?" Garett asked only to get silence in return.

Travis was too weak to say anything, but he gave Garett a look that asked the same question. They decided that since the question didn't get an answer they would just sit back since they couldn't change anything. As they sat back, they saw the man speed onto a road and drive past the cult village. They looked at the walls and could see snakes lining the wall all around the gate that went into the village. The further away from the village and the caves they got the more Travis started to look like himself.

"Where are we going and who are you?" Garett asked again with his voice becoming stern and serious.

Still, he only got silence in return.

"Fine, don't answer me but please don't kill us either." Garett said before becoming silent.

They stayed silent as the car pulled up to an unmarked building that was near a small town but not actually in the town. It sat above the town and was sitting on the ridge just outside of its limits. The driver got out then came to the back and opened the door for Garett and Travis. They got out the man reaching under Travis's arm to help him walk to the building.

As they entered the building was lined with walls like you would see forming cubicles. It wasn't an office but like a command center. It brought unease to the two men as they walked through escorted by someone who has been silent since they met. They both gave him a look, but he didn't return the favor but instead continued to remain silent. This caused their unease to only rise higher. They entered the only room to have a door and actual wall to be greeted by a small man with a face that could tell a million stories.

"Hello Garett and Travis." The small main said in a voice that sounded of age.

"How do you know our names?" Garett asked the small man.

"I know many things, but that doesn't matter. What matters is that you are the only two I have seen survive that cult." The small man said, pouring himself a cup of coffee.

They spoke for hours about what had happened. Garett said that over the few days they had been in the village was strange. The old man would counter with a revelation that Garett and Travis had actually been in the village for months and provided proof through videos with time stamps. This shocked Garett and didn't seem to bother

Travis–not that he had the energy to do much of anything–who just stared at the old man. Garett was afraid of what else they don't remember from within the village.

"I can't believe that we have lost that much time from our memory." Garett said, doubling over in shock.

"I wish I could say this was a normal thing, but I had never known anyone to ever actually leave them alive." The old man said, pulling a book of notes out of a cubby beside him.

The whole situation was starting to feel unreal to Garett the more he learned. Travis finally started to have color return to his face slowly after being in the place for well over five hours as they went over everything the small man had collected about the cult. It was making Garett wonder about how much the small man was actually involved with the cult and if he could actually be trusted.

"I can see that you have some questions to ask me." The small man said as he handed Garett and Travis cups of tea.

"How long have you been watching the cult, and are you alone?" Garett said, taking a sip of the tea.

"I have been watching them for about a year and no I am not doing this alone. Before you ask, No, I am not with any form of law enforcement." The small man let a smile come across his face.

"So why are you watching them if you are not part of a bigger group?" Garett asked as Travis sat up more in his seat.

"Because my daughter had been taken in one of their 'recruitments' and I haven't seen her since." The small man said this making a point to use sarcasm.

"Do you plan on going to the police?" Garett asked leaning forward onto his elbow pushing them into his thighs.

"I plan on going to them, but I don't have the backing information to actually go to them. I tried going when my daughter vanished into their little village and never came back. They told me since she was seventeen that they couldn't go to get her." The small man began to cry as memories of his daughter flashed in his mind.

"I understand how you feel, my sister was kidnapped when we had been younger. It isn't perfectly the same, but it helps me understand I think." Garett said, pulling a handkerchief out of his pocket and giving it to the small man.

"Thank you and my name is Hank by the way." Hank said, putting his hand out to Garett.

"Well Hank I would introduce us, but you already know us." Garett said with a smile.

"Hank, I have to know if you can let us stay here for the night, and we go to the police in the morning." Travis said not in a way of asking, but he was saying to Hank.

"I can allow you to say here, but I will not sleep here myself. I have a family to care for at my home." Hank said to the pair with a smile.

"Thank you, sir." Travis said standing up and stretching.

"You're welcome boys. To me you are as welcome here as my closest family is in my own home." Hank said getting up and yawning.

"We should get rest. All of us." Garett said looking at each of the men who look like they haven't slept in days and wore it on their faces.

The small man escorted the two to a room that had beds lining the walls from one end to the other. The man who had still yet to say a word brought the two a change of clothes each and pointed to a sign that guided you to the bathrooms. It depicted two men one on the toilet and another scrubbing shampoo into his hair while water fell. Travis had a small giggle at how the sign depicted the two men. In response to this Garett let out a small "awe" which he didn't try to hide.

Travis went to lay down putting the thought of a shower off until the morning. He began to sit in his own thoughts when he felt a hand slowly and caringly wrap itself around him followed by a soft kiss on his neck. He sat smiling as he allowed the hand to explore his body. It had been a long time since he had been this close to someone and didn't want it to end. He rolled over returning the favor to the one person he felt he could love as more than a friend. They kissed each other over and over feeling themselves falling into euphoria. This allowed the world around them to fall away and for once it was just them.

"I love you." Travis whispered as his body became entangled with Garett's.

"I love you too." Garett whispered as their souls became one.

The two could tell that this was what they both have been waiting on. They became one in soul and passion even if it was just for the night. The troubles of the past year had melted away for them and all they had left was each other. After their time of passion ended, they held each other close drenched in sweat and sitting at the top of the world in their minds.

Chapter 19: Fangs And Venom

Garett and Travis lay fast asleep as Hank pulled up outside. Everything seemed fine from where Hank sat till lines of red liquid began to inch down over the door. The driver who never said a word even now got out to investigate. He could feel a pull in his mind to get closer to the liquid even with Hank protesting. The man got closer and as he did it seemed like the liquid itself began to reach out to him with millions of tiny arms.

His arm outstretched; he came close to coming in contact with the liquid when Hank jerked him back by his other arm. When he looked at Hank, he saw a face of pure fear. It was a fear that was usually reserved for children. Hank guided him by the arm back to the car while they thought of a plan of what to do. The liquid continued to expand on the front of the building.

"Martin you can't touch that liquid. I don't know what it is, but it has a strange evil about it." Hank said the look of worry still on his face.

Martin looked Hank in the eyes asking to be forgiven in his own way to be forgiven.

"It is okay my boy. I think it was trying to control you." Hank said looking at the liquid.

It fully covered the door and the began to writhe. It looked as if it was alive, and it seemed hungry. The one fact that went against the theory is it didn't go after Hank and Martin while they sat in the car. It was at this moment Hank wished he knew what Martin was thinking. He loved Martin like a son and couldn't bring himself to lose him. In the event of Hank's passing everything from his business to his home will go to Martin.

"I am sorry Hank. I don't know what happened. I wish I had the ability to tell you, but I know you can see it in my eyes." Martin told Hank in his mind hoping that Hank could understand.

"You stay here Martin." Hank said, pulling out his cellphone and hitting his speed dial.

The phone rang in the building. It echoed through the sparse halls and lightly furnished rooms. Travis stirred with each ring. It began its fourth set of rings when Travis pulled himself out of bed not bothering to get dressed. He picked up the phone. His mouth was dry as he began to speak.

"H-Hello?" Travis said, his voice scratchy.

"Travis we can't get in. Some kind of liquid has covered the door. Can you get out the back door?" Hank said with urgency.

"We can try to get out of the building out the back door." Travis said, starting to wake up.

Hank hung up his phone and saw that Martin was trying to exit his car. He got to the car in time to shut the door before Martin got even a leg out of the door. His heart was beating fast knowing that the person closest to him was in danger. At this current moment, his life no longer mattered. His focus was Martin and Martin alone. He got in the car and locked the doors and backed them down the road till Travis met them.

"Travis who was that?" Garett asked, rubbing his eyes.

"It was Hank he said we need to get out of here." Travis said, grabbing a robe for him and Garett.

Travis began to guide Garett out of the back of the building following emergency exit signs. The fact that they had only robes on never crossed their mind. As they reached the door an alarm started to go off in the building as smoke came from the front of the building. He shoved Garett out of the door following behind him shortly. He grabbed him by the hand and pulled him in tow towards the main road. The cold didn't bother him as they ran from the building.

"Geez you're both naked!" Hank yelled as they got in the car.

"Yes, but we needed to get out of there without dying." Travis said looking at himself.

"We apologize sir." Garett said, pulling his robe shut.

"It is fine. I am just glad you made it out alive." Hank said, pulling the car out onto the road.

They both watched as the liquid melted the building from the outside. As the building melted a putrid smell filled the air accompanied by white smoke. It made them sick not only from the smell, but the fact it could have brought the building down on them. The building collapsed when they got onto the highway. What they could tell from the attack was that it wasn't meant to kill. They saw a message being sent to them for the things that they know. It was kind of like a message some sort of mafia would have sent to someone back in the 60's. It shook them all, but none of them felt it more than Hank. Hank lost years of work in the attack. The building contained years of data he collected in an attempt to save his daughter from the cult and the look on his face said that he lost her forever.

"I am sorry Hank." Travis said, putting a hand on Hank's shoulder.

"It is fine. I can go forward." Hank said but his expression didn't change.

From what Travis could see the world for Hank was hanging by one thread now. The only person left that was family was Martin since his wife left months after his daughter never came home. Martin was the one person who has seen Hanks' true pain. Travis could understand because if he lost his sister or Garett, he would lose himself. He saw Hank as an older version of himself and wished he could trade himself to save Hank's daughter. A tear came to Travis's eyes the more he thought about the pain Hank felt watching the building being melted.

"Hank. I can see the pain in your eyes. I know that what happened back there had ripped your soul from your body and that you are crying inside. You don't have to hide it from us just to save yourself from looking weak. We are in pain also and I personally stand in your same boat. I am still sorry that I caused the building to be brought down." Travis spoke with a caring and steady voice.

"You don't know a goddamn thing about my fucking pain! You have not lost your fucking child to some cult that is harder to know than the government! I need her back! I failed her when it happened!" Hank yelled sweat and tears running down his face like he just stepped out of a fresh rain.

Travis fell silent knowing that the anger was from his pain which was something that happened he knew very well. The pain felt by Hank was building a fire within him. It was a fire that Travis had inside he used to drive himself forward. Travis could see the fire in Hank's eyes, and it brought as much fear as it did respect.

"Hank I can see the fire in your eyes." Travis said lightly.

"I am sorry for yelling." Hank said pulling the car over and breaking down in tears.

Hank sobbed harder than anyone Travis had ever seen that brought into tears. His sobs got broken up by screams of pain. His face became as red as a tomato as the pain forced itself out of his body. His veins popped out on his neck as he began to struggle against his staggered breathing. He fumbled as he tried to open the car door.

"I-I-I can't take this." Hank said as he started to get out of the car.

Travis saw in the mirror that Hank's eyes had glazed over showing his control being gone. His body was moving on its own. Hank continued to exit the car when Valieen appeared in the mirror with his vicious smile on his face. Travis doesn't understand why he is seeing that demon everywhere. That demon was killed by the angel, but he is still here in a way. He is in Travis's mind everywhere he looks.

"Hank get back in the car!" Travis yelled, grabbing at the tail over Hank's shirt.

A car drove by and took not only Hank but the door of the car with him. The impact caused the car forcefully into a guard rail. Travis lost his breath as he got slammed into Garett. Blood was sent into the air as the windows busted. He struggled to look at everyone as his head began to throb from the impact. Garett sat slumped over beside him, blood coming from his head. Martin laid against the airbag that went off just seconds earlier the powder from its ignition still floating.

"H-H-Hank." Travis struggled as he pulled himself out of the car, his legs not working.

He crawled the glass cutting into his skin as he pulled himself out of the car. His breath was staggered as he kept pulling himself towards Hank. He couldn't register Hanks breathing with his vision. He would have called the police if his phone were able to be found. He could faintly see a shadow–it was barely a shape but there–forming over Hank. The figure had no features to show anything defining. It reached into Hank causing him to jerk in pain and scream at the top of his lungs for it to stop.

"Let him go!" Travis said, trying to lift himself to his feet.

The shadow stopped and pulled its arm out of Hank. It began to walk over to Travis accompanied by the foul smell of sulfur. It—Travis assumed—had locked eyes with him. It leaned over and grabbed Travis by the neck making breathing harder. He was raised to where its face was supposed to be but when looked at it, he saw through it. He didn't see his world on the other side, but a world of death and destruction. Through it, he saw the road being cracked, Hank half decomposed, and the car burning with Garett and Martin still inside.

His body fell limp from his mind giving up. He felt all the hope and drive he had got sucked from his body. The shadow dropped his body limp to the ground. He laid there his eyes focused on Hank who pulled his phone from his pocket and hit the speed dial. Travis blacked out when the shadow picked up Hank by his neck. It lifted him to eye level as well. The difference this time was Travis could hear a voice, or he thought he could.

"It is time to die old man." It sounded like a female voice that wavered in and out of existence.

As Hank began to struggle in the shadow's clutches it let him down when behind it came an ambulance. He dropped him the moment the lights could be seen against buildings. The sound of the siren made it jerk in pain as it pulsed through the air. The men seemed to pour out of the vehicle before it even stopped. They ran in silence, but was it real silence? It still seemed like the world had fallen away from Travis. It no longer seemed to fit him as a place to live.

"Sir can you hear me?" The voice sounded far away and behind a filter.

"Sir can you hear me?" The voice came again but came with a touch.

"Travis!" He could hear Garett yelling a lot of sorrow and tears filling it.

Travis looked up to see the blurry features of Garett. He tried to smile, but he could feel that his face wasn't moving. This fact brought a tear to his eye that he felt was also not going to happen for him. He didn't look, but he felt himself being lifted onto a gurney and being rolled to the ambulance. Garett tried to get in, but they wouldn't let him as Travis got sent off lights and sirens.

He could see another ambulance flying behind them also with lights and sirens. He was surprised at the speeds that these vehicles could reach. He suffered as he looked around the box to see what the paramedics had been up to. His vision waved and he fell into unconsciousness. He saw a hooded figure sitting on a throne of bones and blades. The top of the throne above the figure was a set of skulls in various states of decay.

"It isn't your time Travis." The figure whispered.

"How do you know?" Travis asked, taking a step forward.

"I know many things and I know it isn't your time." The figure said again pointing a finger at Travis. "Now go!"

Travis felt a force throwing him back causing him to jerk awake on a gurney. He was gasping with beads of sweat dripping down his face. He looked around the room seeming to drag in his vision. It was beginning to make him sick as his vision focused on Garett reading a Golf mag. His eyes had been red from crying. He reached out to Garett and tried to speak but only a dry scratching sound coming from him.

Garett ran to Travis and grabbed him by the hand pouring more tears over his boyfriend. He kissed Travis on the hand and held him close. He hugged Garett close as the doctor came into the room and gave him a smile seeing Travis had come from his sleep. He took Garett to the side and showed him the data on his clipboard. Garett's mouth dropped open, and more tears appeared on his face.

"W-What is it Garett?" Travis said, his voice sounding worn as it came from him.

"Travis all it says is that you have strange scars on all of your organs." The doctor said putting an X-ray on display.

"Oh, my fucking God." Travis said his voice was still worn as he looked at the X-ray.

He saw the scars lined up to spell out a word and just one. The scars read out the word "Dreams." It made Travis's heart drop into his stomach. The word only brought one face to his mind. As he closed his eyes Valieen's smile came to his mind, but it was only his smile. He heard a laugh and his eyes snapped open to see a look of concern on the doctor's face. He followed the doctor's gaze to see a small puddle of blood and spit on his pillow.

"Travis are you okay?" The doctor asked, pulling out his flashlight.

"Yes, I am okay doc." Travis said sitting up in his gurney.

"Well, I am asking because this blood is just showing up." The doctor said leaving the room.

Travis sat thinking about the conversation he just had. He was also worried with the blood, but he didn't need anyone else worried about him. In his mind he could figure it out himself. He was just ready to leave the hospital. He could never sit easy while in a hospital, never has been able.

"I am back, here is your prescription." The doctor said entering the room.

Travis closed his eyes laying back as a hiss came. He opened his eyes and began looking around hearing another hiss from under him. A snap came from above him, snakes raining down on him. Travis began to scream as the snakes buried him.

Chapter 20: Snake Oil

The snakes wriggled and writhed over Travis's body, cutting off his breathing every so often. He tried to fight them, but their weight was too much for him to handle. He struggled against them and could feel his muscles burning as he moved. Anger filled him, and he put all of his power into throwing all of them to the ground.

The snakes fell to the ground in a living ball. He looked around to find the building in disarray and decay. Parts of the roof falling in and lights busted or hanging down. He got up stepping over the ball of the snakes. His breath has gotten heavy as dust kicked up around his feet. A skeleton fell from the roof causing him to cover his mouth out of shock. He knelt down and inspected the skeleton finding it was wrapped in the last thing he saw Garett in. He shuttered losing his foot trying to walk back. He fell back into a medicine shelf all of its contents falling on him.

"What happened here? Why is all of this happening?" Travis said, his voice breaking from his fear.

He staggered back to his feet and continued to a hallway across from him. Around him he could see the paint peeling from the walls creating a sense of doom. The rooms he passed had been vacant minus a few that housed skeletons. As he kept walking the building started to melt away from around him. A few more feet down the hallway he found himself in an empty black void. He could still hear his footsteps like the floor had never vanished. Whispers gathered around him as the hallway finished melting away.

"Hello?" Travis asked not seeing anyone around.

His voice echoed as the only answer he received to his question. He walked even knowing that no destination existed for him. Around him Travis thought he could see faces–to him they looked familiar–appearing and disappearing around him. Every so often he would stop and look at them only for them to vanish seconds later. One he caught to ask it a question, but only to get no answer.

Some of the faces as he kept walking seemed like they had been talking. They spoke in whispers, and the whispers came fast too fast to hear. It was like a drone of a city center filled with people talking all at one time. You can hear the words, but it would drive you mad to hear it. Travis continued to walk wanting to find his way out of all of the voices.

"These whispers are starting to get to me." Travis said as he cautiously sat down feeling to make sure the ground was there.

As he settled into his resting place, he noticed he was sweating and breathing hard. His body felt like it had just walked a marathon, but to his mind it doesn't feel like he walked far at all. His mind wavered in a confusion as his body began to shut down while his mind stayed strong. He felt tired the moment his body touched the ground. In a way he was feeling relief and wanted to sleep.

Garett was awakened from his sleep when the machine showing Travis's vitals began to scream out. He began to run for a doctor as a nurse ran in shortly followed by a crash cart. The nurse screamed for a doctor as they began to tear off Travis's shirt and cleaned with alcohol pads. One of the nurses began to push Garett out of the room and told him to go get food or something. He knew that she was going to add that a doctor would come to get him, so he went and for once in his life prayed.

Garett walked downstairs to the hospital chapel. At this point in his life, he assumed every hospital had one. He sat in one of the pews and bowed his head. To himself he felt silly for it all, but what else was he to do. He couldn't help Travis in any way that would be useful at the moment.

"God, I don't know if you are real, and I don't know if you will listen to someone with my preference in love, but I ask that you save Travis. He is the last thing I have in this world. He hasn't done anything to deserve this." Garett prayed with his head still bowed.

"Garett raise your head." A voice came from behind him as a hand landed on his shoulder.

"Who is that?" Garett said as he raised his head.

"Don't turn around." The voice repeated another hand taking his other shoulder.

"This is not okay unless you give me your name." Garett said as he tensed up.

"I am the one you asked to show." The voice said slightly squeezing his shoulders in a fatherly way.

"So, you are God?" Garett asked, starting to shake from his nerves.

"You can say that." God said, taking hands off of Garett's shoulders.

"Why can't I look at you if you are God?" Garett asked, trying to resist his curiosity.

"I don't want anyone to see what I look like." God said leaning closer to Garett's ear.

"I don't feel safe with what is going on here." Garett said, turning away from the voice that was close to his ear.

"Good you shouldn't." God said as a long tongue entered Garett's ear.

He jumped from the seat he was in and saw no one as he fell over the pew behind him. His heart was beating at a speed that felt like it was digging out of his chest. His limbs starting going numb just as he pushed over a glass cup to get someone's attention. He started to lose consciousness as his chest began to hurt more. Soon Garett was out cold on the floor of the hospital's small quiet chapel.

Doctors poured into the room as Garett looked at his own body. The hope he held is that he saw his body was still breathing, but how was he seeing himself but not dead. He walked around the hospital and could see the other people walking around the hospital. It wasn't like it was when he first got into the hospital. It was now packed but not with humans. The hospital was now filled with ghosts and living humans. He was in shock of the fact he could still see all of this, but his body was still alive.

He followed the doctors to an ICU room with his body. He felt the IV being put into his arm. He could feel the pressure as they performed CPR. It was a shock to him seeing and feeling their panic from a third person point of view. He walked close to one of his doctors, the sweat on his brow fell down his face in slow motion. He could see inside of the doctor's chest and could see his heart beginning to break the longer Garett laid silent on the table.

A hooded figure appeared in the doorway of the room, and as Garett looked at it the figure pointed at his body. Garett tried to get a good view of the hooded figure's face, but with each view it just ended up being an endless black void. It held steady pointing at Garett's body not even with a wavering look. His blood ran cold if he could say he still had blood.

"This is not your time. Now get back into your body!" The figure yelled.

The force pushed him back into his body. He jerked awake in shock. His eyes shot wide open and sweat covered his body. His pulse was racing, and his skin flushed. The doctor nearly fell back from the fright brought by Garett's sudden return to this world. He began taking deep breaths trying to calm himself.

"Are you okay sir?" The doctor asked putting a hand on Garett's back.

"I-I-I just met death." Garett said with his eyes wide open.

"Sir I am sure you did. Many people do when they get to where you are right now." The doctor said giving Garett water.

Garett got up dizzy but still standing. He tried to walk forward, but he felt like he had downed six shots. The world twisted around looking as they tried to swallow him. He could feel vomit rising in his throat. Garett forced himself to swallow it back down. The breaths he took became focused and deep. He could feel the color drain from his face being replaced with that sick pale green color. He could see the worried looks from the nurses as he walked by to the bathroom.

Garett stormed into the bathroom slamming the door against the wall puking into the toilet. His vision got wavy as his stomach's contents covered the floor. The water turned on by itself and paper towels poured from the holder. He staggered, rushing over, shutting both off and cleaned his face of the residue. As he inspected his face a shadow began to rise behind him in the mirror. A cracking noise came as a smile appeared on its face.

"Hello Garett." The words echoed around the bathroom.

"Back the fuck off." Garett growled slamming his fist into the mirror in front of him.

"Are you okay sir?" A nurse called as she knocked on the door.

"Yes, ma'am thank you." Garett called trying to sound level-headed.

Garett turned as the footsteps of the nurse left the door. The water turned on again by itself and when he turned around, he saw written in blood and steam was the word "dreams." He sat against the wall of the bathroom. He began to think back and see the X-ray that Travis had done to him earlier. He fumbled to open the bathroom door and walked his way back to the hospital room that Travis stayed in.

"Please wake up Travis. I need you here with me. I am struggling with this world." Garett cried to Travis as tears ran down his face.

When Travis didn't stir, Garett sat into the chair and sat at the wall. He started to doze off as two men came over wrapped in bandages. Garett sat up and looked at them thinking he could recognize the build of their bodies. He stood taking a fighting stance even knowing that he couldn't win a fight. His body hurt from his stress and his sickness.

"Garett you don't need to fight us." One of the men holding his hands up.

"Is that you Hank?" Garett asked, starting to relax.

"Yes, it is." Hank said laughing.

"I am assuming you are Martin." Garret asked, pointing at the other man.

Martin nodded to Garett as he and Hank sat down in the only two other chairs in the room. Garett and Hank talked for an hour about what had become of the group since the car crash, exchanging the different operations, they needed to have and how long their recovery time was.

"You look drained Garett." Hank said leaning forward in his seat.

"I feel so tired, but I had a heart attack downstairs in the chapel." Garett said, wavering in his seat.

"Aren't you a bit young to have a heart attack?" Hank said curiosity marked itself on his face.

"Yes, I am supposed to be, but I am assuming that nothing is unusual for the human body." Garett said.

"I am just glad to see that you are alive my friend." Hank said leaning his chair back against the wall.

They all sat waiting for Travis to wake up again resulting in them falling asleep in their places. A nurse popped in later and brought covers for them all. Garett caught a blurry look as the nurse exited the room. Garett fell back into his sleep as clouds formed in his mind. They cleared away showing a lush green field below him. As he looked around, he noticed he had wings and had been flying.

"I am flying!" Garett yelled to the sky.

As he flew above the land smoke started to rise around him and his body got hot. He let out a cough as he tried to fly out of it. When the smoke cleared, he found himself head straight at the side of a mountain and too close to turn away. He coughed again getting the smoke left in his lungs and smacked into the side of the mountain. He fell to a ledge below giving a headache.

"Goddamn." Garett said sitting up and rubbing his head.

"What the fuck happened?" Garett continued looking toward the smoke that continued to rise to the sky.

He began to fly towards the smoke. He was determined to figure out what was causing the flames, and he wanted to know what it was. He got close and saw giant shadow figures ripping up trees. In the center they piled them on a massive bonfire. He dropped on a nearby hill. He was afraid to get any closer to them. They gave off an aura that frightened him to his core. They wore skeletons as suits, but one caught his attention more than the others. It was wearing Travis's face stretched over its skull.

"That is so fucked up." Garett whispered to himself.

He tried to be careful to try to keep from getting their attention. He wanted to get out of the world he was trapped in right now. He saw this exact dream when Valieen had first made contact with him but didn't say anything to Travis about it. He has seen it off and on again. He sat down and eventually fell to his back. He stared at the sky trying to think what his dream could mean for the future. Does his dream spell doom for the love of his life? Does a way to fix it even exist?

"What the fuck am I going to fucking do about this?" Garett said out of frustration slamming his fist beside him.

He growled to himself as thick storm clouds formed overhead, dropping sheets of rain and sleet above him. Thunder and lightning sounded above with light shows in the sky. He was so angry and frustrated that the rain turned to steam upon contact with his body. The rage caused his veins and muscles to become more defined all over. He became ready for battle when lightning struck revealing the shadows surrounding him, smiles stretched over their faces. They looked at him filled with an anger that bordered on starvation.

"Bring it you son of a bitch!" He yelled flying right at the shadow wearing Travis's face.

He slammed into it with all of his force but got swatted like a fly. He was thrown through the forest bringing down many trees slowly coming to a stop. Pain coursed through his body making him scream in pain. He still got up when a shadow hand grabbed him and lifted him into the sky. He made eye contact with the shadow as it ate him alive.

"Damn it. Damn it all." Garett said as shadows closed around him. "Fuck."

Chapter 21: Dream Eating Viper

Travis got to his feet and continued down the dark path when a familiar voice echoed. The voice gave him the drive to continue on his path to a way out. It reignited his feeling of purpose. He felt exhausted and ready to give up but couldn't bring himself to do it. Even if he were to die, he will help this person in need. He saw a light starting to form as he walked forwards. The closer he got the more he could see a room.

He could see the red gleam of light reflecting off of blood. He slowly went into a jog into the room his legs hurt too much to run. As he got into the room the blood, he saw spelled out the word "dreams" over and over on the wall. He looked around and saw his sister tied to a chair, her head limp laying in Valieen's hand. The stare on Valieen's face cut into Travis's very soul and into its lowest reaches.

"Sometimes the most beautiful of things must suffer." Valieen said as he plunged his claws into Vinessa's stomach.

"No!" Travis screamed at the top of his lungs as he charged at Valieen with everything he had.

When he made contact with Valieen it was as if he had hit a brick wall. Valieen was able to throw him like a stuffed doll across the room. With a cry of pain Travis realized how dire the situation had become as Valieen made his way to Travis each footstep made louder with its echo. His vision wavering in and out of focus Travis watched Valieen grab his shirt collar. His breathing got heavy as a pain shot through his spin.

"It's time to wake up my dear prey." Valieen his pulling Travis's intestine out and dropping them to the floor with a wet splat.

Travis shot up in his gurney dripping with sweat, and his breath frantic. He could only hear his breath catching in his throat seeing everyone asleep around him. He jumped to his feet and dug through his belongings for his phone. Fumbling to open it with his shaky hands he dialed his sister. The phone rang four times before her voicemail picked up making his heart sink to his stomach and his anxiety to rise like a poison.

His mind began to get away from him with thoughts of what could have happened to his sister. His biggest fear was that she could have been killed. He couldn't let the dark thoughts flood his mind, but no matter how hard he tried they still got in his head. He closed his eyes and started to pray that she would call him. As he opened his eyes back up as his phone rang. He quickly opened it without looking at the display.

"Hello?" He said, his voice sounding broken up by tears.

"Travis? I didn't realize this was your new phone number. What happened to your old one?" Vinessa's voice came over the speaker as alive and warm as ever.

"Yes, my other one got lost on my way into town." Travis said with the words tasting sour on his tongue.

"How did you lose it?" She asked, sounding confused by his words.

"I lost it when we hit a pothole in the road. I was taking pictures while holding it out of the window." Travis said with a laugh.

"You have always been such a klutz. I am glad you finally called me. It has been boring around here." Vinessa laughed at him as she said it.

"I will be home soon, I hope. Our dad isn't who I thought he would be." Travis said with a look of sadness appearing on his face.

"What do you mean Travis?" Vinessa asked, sounding worried about the answer.

"He is a-" Travis was cut off with static and then two beeps.

He threw his phone across the room out of pure anger. The sound of the phone shattering on the wall woke everyone in the room. They inspected the room with a look of shock covering their faces. They seemed to relax seeing Travis standing all on his own with no sign of weakness. He was breathing heavy staring off into space.

"I don't know what is going on, but the cell signals are gone." Travis said through grinding teeth.

"Travis, you're awake!" Garett yelled wrapping his arms around Travis.

"Yes, love I am awake now." Travis said patting Garett on the arm.

The doctor slowly walked into the room holding a clipboard filled with papers. He looked around at everyone and gave a small smile. He sat the clipboard down and helped Travis back to his bed. Travis didn't argue with the doctor and sat down while trying to calm himself.

"Well Mr. Marvic. It appears that your tests came back, and you are okay to go back to your home." The doctor said, smiling.

"Please just call me Travis and I would like to have my discharge papers." Travis said aggressively.

"Yes, here are your papers." The doctor said handing Travis the papers off of his clipboard.

Travis took them and shook the doctor's hand before getting up to leave with the others in his room. As they walked out of the hospital their shoes squeaked against the floor and it sounded like a fifth person was following along with the group. Travis stopped and looked around to see if they had a person was walking with them, but no one was found.

"That was weird. I thought someone was walking with us." Travis said seeing the sentence made Garett shudder.

Travis gave a shrug and kept walking. Garett kept looking around and could feel a chill on the air like something was looming over him. Travis could catch Garett's looks of being uncomfortable in the corner of his eye. Travis pulled Garett to the side as they exited the hospital feeling the need to check on him out of nowhere.

"Garett are you okay?" Travis asked with his eyes filled with care and concern.

"Yes, Travis I am okay, but I feel like something was following us while we left the hospital." Garett said, trying to hide his face.

"Garett, have you seen things recently?" Travis asked looking deep into Garett's eyes.

Garett just nodded and began to break down into tears trying to apologize. He felt that seeing the demon recently had somehow hurt Travis. All Travis could do was hold him and help him slowly to the ground. He could feel the world beginning to become heavy on his shoulders, and he knew that Garett could feel the pressure as well.

"Garett, I know that everything that is going on is hurting you as well." Travis said holding Garett as close as he could.

"I am sorry Travis." Garett mumbled through his tears with a breaking voice.

"Hush, you don't need to apologize." Travis said as the air got colder around him.

Travis pulled Garett closer to him and scanned the area for any threats that might be around them. A faint shadow could be seen moving across the tinted windows of the hospital ER. He tried to urge Garett to get up, but his legs couldn't carry him. Travis decided to hook Garett under his arms and started pulling him to their ride. His focus remained on the shadow that has seemed to multiply on the windows.

He managed to get Garett into their ride and the shadows seemed to stop and stare at him. Travis could hear a low hum starting in his ears, and as he listened close, he could tell it was his name. The shadows seemed to have grown an outline of a mouth, but he could hear it right behind him. He turned to see Garett was joined in with his mouth seeming to say his name at inhuman speeds. He begged Garett to wake up over and over. When it all stopped Garett's, eyes opened to reveal just white pupil less sockets.

"*Did you miss me Travvy boy!*" The voice that came from Garett was not his own, but the one of Valieen.

"Why are you doing this to him?" Travis said his voice filled with anger and his fist clenched so tight his skin began to turn white.

"Because it hurts you so deep that I can taste it from here." Valieen said with Garett's mouth.

"Get out of him and get out of him now!" Travis said now with his face as red as a circus balloon.

"Or what you'll kill him? You can't stop me, and you know!" Even if it wasn't Garett saying it, this was the first time Travis has heard Garett's voice raise.

"Please, please just give him back to me." Travis said tears forming in his eyes as his knees began to shake.

"So now you are begging me for mercy?" Valieen said with a laugh, but still with Garett's voice.

"I am not begging. I am demanding." Travis said, still unable to hold back his tears.

"I think I want to keep him for a little bit." Valieen said forcing Garett's body to get out of the vehicle it was sitting in.

"You can't do this to him!" Travis yelled not caring who thought he was crazy.

"You can't stop me. No one cares about your problems!" Valieen said as he used Garett to throw a punch sending Travis into the vehicle behind him.

Travis laid against the car seeing Garett walk away under the control of Valieen. He tried to get up to stop him, but every time that he moved the shadows moved from the hospital windows and grabbed hold of his arms to hold him down. The more he struggled the tighter their grip got. He got to where his body no longer wanted to move and gave up. He didn't want to, but he couldn't fight the shadows anymore. His body was spent, and his energy was at the maximum of its uses.

"I will find you and I will get him back!" Travis yelled after Valieen only to get a middle finger in response.

Travis could only watch as Garett vanished around the corner of the building. All hope Travis had sunk to his stomach and made him feel sick as it rotted inside him. The shadows let Travis go as soon as Garett was out of sight. When shadows had gone Travis slumped over to the ground his will to live had left with the person he loved. He laid on the pavement ready to give up on his life until a nurse pulled him up and took him back inside the place that took his life.

He watched as his mostly lifeless body was pushed in a wheelchair to an examination room in the psych ward of the hospital. He sat doing nothing but staring off into the distance. In his eyes Garett was on repeat being forced to leave by a monster that had taken over his body. Doctor after doctor asked Travis questions but he couldn't bring himself to answer them. He was lost now and felt that he had lost himself when Valieen took Garett.

Travis could still see the smile on Valieen's face as he walked away. It wasn't the smile he saw on Garett's face but the one underneath. The real face the Valieen had. It was contorted and broken. It was filled with pain and sorrow, but still held anger fuelled power. He knew Valieen was nowhere near done with him. He didn't know what Valieen had planned but it couldn't be good.

A doctor had told Travis that they had to keep him there until he decided to talk to them. As the days went by, and he kept refusing to talk to them he got handed a piece of paper with a pen. They told him to write down a name of someone he would talk to because their staff couldn't get him to talk. The only name they revolved in his mind was

"Father David" the only thing was that the Father was dead. He thought about his sister, but she didn't need to be brought into the situation. That only left one name for him to have them contact. He picked up his pen and moved for the first time in days. He wrote the name "Dr. Joseph Marron."

The nurse walked over to him and smiled picking up the paper. She thanked him and walked away handing the paper to his doctor. Travis went back to his starting and lifeless stature. He saw the doctor take one more look at him before disappearing into his office. Travis gave him a side glance as the doctor picked up his phone and started to dial a number. Travis watched as the doctor started and finished his call-in hopes that it was the person, he wanted them to call.

"Travis, we called Dr. Marron and he said that he will be here as soon as he could be here, but until then he requested that you stay in our care only for your safety." The doctor said before walking back to his office.

Travis gave no response with his words or his body. He just felt that it was nice he would be able to see Dr. Marron after being in Alaska for so long. Travis did not smile, and he did not speak. He refused to talk to anyone except for Dr. Marron because he did not trust the doctors that worked in the hospital. He hoped that it would not take long for Dr. Marron to arrive to the hospital. His hopes never leave his mind. He feels that since it was the only thing left for him to have then he will hold onto it with every ounce of strength he has.

Every night since then Travis barely ate or drank. Sleep couldn't come to him because every time he slept; he could only see Valieen. He could only see that fucking smile on the demon's face. If he closed his eyes, he saw all of his hope being ripped away from him. His dreams played on rotation between three things: his death, his sister being cut open, Garett walking away. He would see it over and over again.

Sometimes when he couldn't sleep, he could see the ghosts. They hadn't been the ghosts of the hospital. He wasn't sure what kinds of ghost they had been, but he knew where they had come from. They came from everyone that he had met dead or alive. He saw them over and over every night nonstop. He would cower in silent fear as the ghosts grew in number around him. Their laughter surrounded him as they mocked his situation.

One month on the dot an orderly came into Travis's room passing a glance at him as he sat silent staring off into space.. The orderly found a skinny pale man in his early twenties with a beard to his mid-chest area. He escorted Travis out of his room and into a private room containing Dr. Marron. Now more fit than fat but still balding from age.

Chapter 22: Welcome Back Doctor

"Travis, they tell me that you haven't talked in over a month since you got put in here." Dr. Marron said in a professional tone.

"Doctor, I-He-He took him Doctor. He took my Garett." Travis said in a dry and strained voice.

"Who took Garett Travis?" Dr. Marron asked, trying to stay professional in tone.

Travis looked at Dr. Marron with tears in his eyes. He was afraid to say because the rest of the hospital may be listening. He knew he would sound crazy to others, but Dr. Marron would know what he is talking about. He had been there when the demon had marked his car. Dr. Marron knew he wasn't crazy. Travis took a deep breath before answering.

"You know who it is Dr. Marron. The men that had followed me from Afghanistan. The ones that I have the nightmares about. I could swear that they came for me, but I guess now I realize that they didn't. I am sorry to drag you out here and to waste these people's time. I just want to go home." Travis said trying to make a point of hinting a major problem to the Doctor.

"Travis I can try to get you out of here, but you will be in my care for about a month." Dr. Marron held his tone steady with his words.

"I will agree to that Dr. Marron." Travis said with a smile on his face for the first time in a month.

"You need to sign over into my guardianship so that way we are official." Dr. Marron said, sliding a piece of paper over to Travis.

Travis signed the paper without thinking about it he slid the paper back to Dr. Marron and then he watched the Doctor exit the room. Dr. Marron went into an office with a nurse who processed the paper then he came back with a smile on his face. He handed Travis a bag of clothes and guided him to the bathroom to get changed out of his gown.

"Let's get out of here." Dr. Marron said, helping Travis out of the hospital's psych ward.

"Dr. Marron I couldn't say it in front of the doctors in there, but Valieen is within Garett's body, and they walked off." Travis said as he entered Dr. Marron's SUV.

"I understand that. I was there when it had attacked your car and put a scratch on it. They are too closed in their mind to understand what it is you are dealing with." Dr. Marron said before turning the key.

"I don't know how he is still able to hold this much power after an Arch angel had stabbed his through his heart." Travis spoke with a sense of panic in his voice.

"I think that he has the power to bring himself here, but he needs a vessel to be able to stay on the earth." Dr. Marron said as he pulled out of the parking lot.

"*You will never find me!!*" A voice yelled sharply in between the two of them causing Dr. Marron to swerve almost off of the road.

"What the fuck was that?" They both exclaimed looking at each other in confusion as the car slid to a stop.

Their breaths became heavy and slow as fear filled their eyes. They didn't know what the voice was till they thought about it. It sounded familiar in two different ways, but it was also unfamiliar in how it was combined. It sounded like Garett was speaking with Valieen's voice at the same time as his own. They had started to become one and the same. Now Garett and Valieen are no longer two people for the time being.

"I think that was Garett." Travis said not feeling that he could believe himself.

"It sounded like that demon. What was his name? Valieen!" Dr. Marron said feeling he found the answer.

"I guess given what had happened it could be both of them." Travis said, trying to find a conclusion to their questions.

"Yes, That sounds like it could be correct." Dr. Marron said before he started out at the road and sighed.

Dr. Marron pulled out onto the road and continued their journey. Travis didn't know where they had been going, but he felt like it was towards Garett. Travis slowly drifted to sleep. He felt that he was able to catch up on his sleep that was lost in that damn hospital. He had no dreams on this day. It was the first time in years that he had a peaceful sleep.

"Hey Travis wake up." Dr. Marron said, jabbing his elbow into Travis's side.

Travis slowly woke up to see that they sat outside of the wall of the cult town. He wondered why they had been outside of the town. He looked over to his therapist and friend for answers. When he got none, he sat up in his seat and cleared drool from his mouth.

"Why are we here?" Travis asked, trying to clear his throat.

"Well, I don't want to leave Alaska without Garett. That is even if I end up dying in the process." Dr. Marron said without looking up from the road itself.

"Well how are we going to do that with no weapons and no idea if we will remember anything after we get in there." Travis said with slight frustration in his voice.

"Well what else could we do?" Dr. Marron asked as his frustration started to reveal itself in his voice.

"Let me make some calls, and we will figure this out." Travis said, taking out his phone and calling the only people he could think of.

"Hello, this is Hank." The familiar was good to hear come through the phone.

"Hey Hank, this is Travis. We need your help. We need to rescue Garett from this cult." Travis said, trying to focus his words.

"You called me for help I am assuming?" Hank asked in a condescending tone.

"Well Yes. I think you are the only person with a personal army within miles." Travis said in a sarcastic tone.

"What makes you think that I have a personal army?" Hank asked with a real curiosity.

"Well, you had a compound." Travis said hoping Hank could hear him roll his eyes.

"I do know people that would be more than glad to help me get rid of this cult. I use that word lightly around the town. What do you need us to do?" Hank asked, his tone becoming more serious than sarcastic or condescending.

"I need a distraction so Dr. Marron and I can go in and get Garett." Travis said drumming the seat with his free hand.

"I will see you in twenty." Hank said hanging up before Travis could say anything else.

Travis got out of the car to stretch his legs. He sighed as the cold air touched his lungs cooling his frustrations some. Dr. Marron got out as well, lighting one of his cigarettes offering one to Travis who refused. Travis didn't hide his disapproval. He hadn't touched any tobacco since he left the military. The memories were the only thing he wanted to have to keep with him.

"I am guessing he is willing to help?" Dr. Marron asked after blowing smoke out of his nose.

"Yes, yes he was willing to help us get into the village." Travis said rubbing his hands together.

Garett entered the caves that lay behind the burned shelter. His body was no longer his own, but one that he still shared the feelings of. He felt fear filling his body, but he still didn't stop himself from going deeper into the cave. He just needed to go inside without resisting

Groans echoed from deep within the caves. As Garett walked, bones cracked under foot. Bodies at various stages of decay made a smile creep across his face as Valieen felt satisfaction from the death around him. It was a feeling he did not enjoy getting to know on a personal level like this.

"I bet this makes you happy doesn't it." Garett said within his mind.

"It does Mr. Randy. It makes me extremely happy." Valieen said, sending a feeling of pleasure through Garett's body.

Garett kept walking deeper into the cave as the groans got louder. They could be identified as groans of pain now. As they got closer Garett lost all control to Valieen. Garett felt his body and face change without control. He could feel pure evil being etched into his face and his heart. His body was no longer his and he knew it. As they got closer to the source of the pained sound Valieen started to grow hungry. Garett didn't know why he was hungry until he got to the source.

They came across Gavel, the arch angel that allowed Travis and Garett to escape the caves. Gavel looked at Garett with pain leaking out of his eyes. It was so powerful that Garett could feel his pain, but Valieen was feeding off of it. Garett got down on one knee and put a hand on Gavel's forehead. Gavel let out a scream of pain and his eyes began to glow red as his veins turned purple.

He jumped up in pain causing Garett fall back as he realized Gavel was fighting with Valieen in his mind. He jerked and writhed as his feathers started to fall off of his wings revealing the wings of a demon under the layer of feathers. His skin flaked as scales took its place. He clawed at his body leaving deep gashes and scars. His blood had a glow of purple and gold mixing with each other. Slowly it started to become more and more purple. His screams began to vanish as his vocal cords continued to pull themselves apart.

When his vocal cords finally snapped purple and gold blood poured from the corners of his mouth and his veins popped out on his neck. His eyes bled before he finally collapsed, falling limp to the ground. His eyes had turned soulless as Garett got up and tried to run. He was unable to escape as his leg was grabbed. He didn't know who to yell at as Valieen or Gavel could be living within that body, but he knew it couldn't be both. As he looked closer, he saw the final drop of gold fade away as it touched the ground. He knew Gavel was no more. The only thing left was Valieen within that body.

"I now have the powers of myself and the powers of an angel now Mr. Randy." Valieen said with his twisted now blood covered smile.

"Could you just call me Garett please?" Garett asked, trying to force a smile on his face.

"Well since you loaned me your body, I am trying to be polite, and I don't want to hurt you. Yet." Valieen said as his smile vanished.

"I would much rather take your polite side." Garett said realizing the situation he was currently in at the moment.

"Good, now let us go to the top of this mountain." Valieen said as a portal opened above them. The screams of tortured souls that got louder as it opened wider.

They got pulled through the portal by black hands that held them tight. As they went through their ears could hear the same sound you would hear if you held your head underwater near someone that was swimming. As they came out on the other side it too was just like if they came out of water. Garett let out several gasps as they came back into contact with the air but came to realize that he was lacking any.

He looked around to find the most beautiful view he had ever seen in his life. The air and seeing everything sitting below him took his mind off of his life being in danger. He took a deep breath and a large smile formed on his face. He chuckled a little bit, but it was all shortly ripped away by a large hand wrapping around him.

"You see that over there." Valieen pointed to a walled off village in the distance.

"Y-y-yes I do see it." Garett said, nervous to know the answer.

"That is where the change in this world has started. I don't want the man currently in charge to lead it. He couldn't take being a vessel. I want you Garett. The only one who has been able to endure my spirit." Valieen said with honesty in his voice.

It made Garett actually consider taking him up on this job, but that would mean betraying everything he knew and loved. He didn't know how long it would be before he was able to see the man he loved ever again. He felt breath on the back of his neck pulling him out of his thoughts and saw Valieen looking at him like a cat looks at a mouse.

"I can take you to him. I can take you to Travis. You just need to promise not to bring them to me. I don't care about that town just not to me." Valieen said truly being honest this time.

"I promise they will not come for you, but that cult has done so much to us. Hidden so much from us. I want them to burn in hell." Garett said with tears coming to his eyes from the memories.

"Let them die. Kill as many as you want. All I need is you." Valieen said his voice as even as Garett had ever heard.

"Please, please take me to Travis." Garett asked Valieen with his hanging low.

"As you wish, but I will come back for my answer." Valieen said, opening a portal that dropped him and Garett beside the village still out of sight of Travis.

Gunshots rang out just after Valieen vanished from the battle field. Garett ducked as some of the shots whizzed by his head. He could hear Travis yelling orders, but he was not close enough to understand what it was he yelled. Garett tripped over bodies trying to get closer to Travis. As Travis caught his eye, he could feel a warm sensation in his chest. He looked down to see a blood covered face that had a smile stretched across itself.

"Garett!" Travis yelled running to him as blood teased the corners of Garett's mouth.

Travis shot the man that had stabbed Garett and caught him as he fell. Garett placed a hand softly on Travis's face and forced a smile. Valieen walked up only to be seen or heard by Garett and tapped his wrist like he wore a watch. Garett knew this was his time to answer that question. He was frustrated by the fact he didn't get to enjoy Travis much longer.

"Yes." Garett said confusing Travis.

Valieen nodded with a smile on his face. Garett went on to live through his wounds. He tried to enjoy his time with Travis, but he knew what would happen soon. Travis sat holding his hand with a big smile on his face. Travis knew he never wanted to lose Garett. Travis's expression changed seeing the pain on Garett's mind.

"What's wrong Garett?" Travis asked, running his thumb over Garett's hand.

"It is nothing. I am just thinking about what happened yesterday." Garett spoke with a smile on his face.

Chapter 23: The Loss For Martin

Hank and Martin made their way from the car towards the hospital's front gates. Hank got halfway across the parking lot when a car sped around the round-about and hit him. Time went in slow motion as Martin turned around to see Hank's body coming down behind the car. A groan of pain came from him, his head starting to resembled a water balloon.

Martin ran to him with tears coming from his eyes. His knees buckled under him as he got to Hank. His cries of pain for the man that raised him became the first noises many people have ever heard him make. They echoed through the medical complex causing some people to tear up from feeling his pain. It took three doctors to pull Hank from Martin's arms even after giving him sedatives.

Martin went back to the car they had come in and sat in silence till the sedatives made him drift off to sleep. In his dreams he spoke perfect old English and fought crime as a privateer. The only thing was with recent events he saw him standing in the middle of black rain. It was rain poisoned by the ashes of buildings and burning bodies. They caused the earth around him to look as if the sky itself was dropping oil over him. He took a deep breath taking in the smells of flesh and fire while holding his arms out in the acceptance of his situation.

His dream self was filled with bullet holes and when his knees made contact with the ground Hank's face flashed in his mind. He shot awake and ran into the hospital looking for Hank. Every nurse he met was shown a piece of paper with Hank's name. Even if he couldn't talk, his written words expressed his desire to find his friend. In his words Hank was the only dad he had ever known his whole life. The tears once more came to him, but this time it was like an autumn rain. Heavy and cold as his tears pulled the sadness from his heart.

He cleared his eyes and got out to enter the hospital. He walked, but as he went, he could feel a bad feeling in his stomach as a shadow washed over him. His heart started to beat rapidly then he heard its voice. It was then he knew his fate.

"You're mine now."

It was then everything went black, and Martin could no longer feel anything. His body felt light and for once he felt good. He knew where he was, and it was no longer earth. It was no physical plane of existence. He was happy enough to know that Hank no longer had to be worried with a man that couldn't even speak about his needs.

Nurses and doctors that walk out of the hospital wouldn't even know that Martin had ever been in the parking lot. He was gone without a trace or without a trace that can be seen by a human. He could feel himself falling in a bottomless pit that was darker than any night he had ever seen in his life. He wasn't dead, but he felt like he was no longer alive at the same time. The silence didn't bother Martin since he spent every night sitting in silence on his own.

Hank lay on a cold metal table as a doctor works to keep him alive. He lives in his own mind while the doctors worked on him. He was still confused about the fact that he could no longer work his body, and why he couldn't see what was happening around him. In his mind–the that currently held his consciousness–contained his favorite chair, a TV, and his family on the chair beside him. He looked around and smiled at the situation he had. Even though making him happy it was clear it wasn't real.

The doctors got his head mostly put together and the bleeding almost stopped. Hank was taken to a room in hopes that he will recover from his injuries. It went well for a week and he was almost brought back to consciousness. With more and more time going by Hank got no better. He didn't get worse either causing the doctors grow more concerned as he lay unmoving for what seemed like days unending. They checked his vitals three times a day every day for that week only for them to show no change deciding he wouldn't get better. He was moved shortly to an ICU. With him even only in his mind he felt them putting the ventilator in his throat. Everything they have been doing he could feel.

He winced at the shots and the blood being drawn. He choked when they put in his ventilator. He could taste the food they put into his stomach. Hank felt trapped by the fact he was human now. He just wanted to die with every test he could feel them running on him. Soon Hank's mental home became more, and more detailed to him. He gained a house and a second floor. He walked up to that very balcony and looked out to what he could only see as a darkness. It was something maddening to him. It was like his world melted away from him and continues to fade from him. Even though he could feel the ventilator in his body giving him oxygen, He could feel his body losing the ability to breathe.

Hank came to accept that he would die soon, and it no longer scared him. He welcomed death at the point he was at with everything. He has grown tired of the back and forth that was caused with the hospital's care. He was done with them trying to save him and only making temporary progress with it. At this point Hank wished to at least be able to tell them to end it. A shadow crept over the end of the balcony claws leaving marks as it secured itself over the balcony side. It looked at Hank with deep red eyes and a smile that could freeze anyone that looked at it.

"You're mine now!"

Hank heard this in his head as the shadow threw itself at him. His vision left, and his body became light. He was in a darkness that was darker than any night he had ever seen. It felt like he was falling in a bottomless pit. He knew he couldn't be dead, but in his words he for damn sure didn't feel alive. He closed his eyes to see if he could hear anything, but nothing came to him. He didn't even get that strange ringing you would get when your house was quiet, and your ears wanted to find a sound.

He let out a huff before he saw a figure next to him. He turned his head which took effort to do the force he was falling. When he saw who it was it made him feel a slight bit better. He now knew that Martin was here in the pit with him, but it still had put a ting of sadness to know that they both had been out into this hell. What will happen when they finally die in this pit? Will their bodies be allowed to exit? Will they decay and fall until they become nothingness? How will it happen? These are the thoughts that flipped through Hank's mind as they continued to fall.

Soon Martin and Hank began to fall faster. They fell so fast that their air was being pulled from their lungs. They gasped and choked, grabbing at their throats as a light appeared below them. It got brighter and brighter as they got closer to it. It began to blind them even as darkness closed at the edges of their vision as their air left them. Soon they slammed into something solid stinging like an inferno on their skin. They checked each other seeing no major injuries.

They stood up to see a world of fire and suffering stretching out around them. They saw creatures that flew around made of nothing but muscles with bone rising like spikes out of their bodies. Their vision was bad due to the heat around them but with that they could see the creatures. They walked through trying to find shelter finding it hard to stay hidden from the things he knew watched them. They finally found a cave to stay in, to their relief it seemed to be colder than the rest of the world they found themselves in.

They could hear something approaching from behind them. When they turned around it was a monster made of skeletons that seemed to fuse together. It had eight heads and four arms. The arms had been so large it took five adult rib cages linked together to wrap around them. It carried a weapon that looked as if it could split a city in half with one swing. They turned and tried to run but were stopped short of the mouth of the cave by a net, and they found themselves dragged further into the darkness.

The two had been reported missing by the hospital four hours after they vanished.

Chapter 24: Final Act Of Wellness

Travis spent every day in the hospital with Garett until he was healed from his knife wound. He was told that Garett would fully recover, but he would have to visit the doctor every three months for the rest of his life. They made their way out of the hospital slowly since Garett now walked with a limp.

"Travis, can we go out to eat?" Garett asked, giving a weak smile.

"Yes, we can go out to a place to eat." Travis gave a smile as he opened the door to the rental he found on his phone.

They pulled out slowly admiring the trees gleaming with water from spring's thaw. Garett tried to enjoy every view he got to see. He tried to enjoy his last moments alongside the love of his life. He tried to hide the tears that got brought by the thoughts of the fact he will be gone tomorrow. The last moments he spends on this day will be spent in happiness. Garett found himself in a trance until they found themselves in a restaurant parking lot.

"Are you okay Garett?" Travis asked, noticing that Garett was in a trance.

"Yes, yes I am okay. I was just in deep thought about something." Garett said with another one of his weak smiles on his face.

"Might I ask if it was that has you in a bind?" Travis asked.

"Well, I had to do something rash to stay alive." Garett said, hiding his face from Travis.

"What did you do Garett?" Travis asked confused.

"I made a deal with that demon so that I could see you again." Garett said, putting a hand on the door handle ready to exit at a moment's notice.

"What did you just fucking say Garett? You made a deal with the demon that has been trying to kill us for so long?" Travis asked with his voice rising to a borderline yell.

"I am sorry! I did it so that I would be able to see you again even if it were just one day! I don't know what you expect me to do now!" Garett yelled his veins showing and tears following down his cheeks.

"What you did is make it to where I can no longer hold you after today! I just wanted to have a future with you! I saw us going so much further than this!" Travis yelled so loud people started looking at the pair.

"I just wanted to stay alive. I just wanted to stay with you one day longer. I feel like I will die either way." Garett said before breaking down into tears.

Travis just sat back and stared at the roof of his car. His memories took him back to his past. They flew by him like flashes of videos. Sounds surrounded him as reality seemed to fade away leaving him in his past. He relived every fight and every breath he had taken. Every smell he had ever smelt re-entered his nostrils. He kept going back over and over. He was trapped in his own life until Garett shook him free.

"I loved you Garett, and you betrayed me by taking that deal." Travis said with a grim look on his face.

"What are you saying Travis?" Garett continued to cry and to him somehow it seemed like he was crying more than he already was.

"I am saying that if I am losing you tomorrow then what would be the point in having you today." Travis said it as more of a statement then a question.

"Please don't send me away Travis." Garett begged as his eyes puffed from his tears.

"I am going to lose you anyway. I can't think of any reason to keep you here if you won't be in my arms when I awake tomorrow." Travis said his knuckles turned white from his grip on the steering wheel.

"You just keep repeating yourself. Why can't you make a proper fucking argument?" Garett said as his tears became far and in between.

"Because we have nothing to argue about if we have no way to stop it." Travis said releasing his grip on the steering wheel and letting his head fall against it.

"Well, I still want to have one last good day with you till I am gone." Garett said, trying to take hold of Travis's hand.

Travis pulled his hand away without looking at Garett. His tears rain down the steering wheel brought on by the thought of what has been lost to him. He felt like his life has spiraled out of control. No, it was spiraling out of control. He had lost everything and lost control of the memories in his mind. The demon had finally brought an end to everything he had ever had for himself.

"Travis!" Garett yelled from outside of his mind.

When Travis opened his eyes, they sat within a restaurant holding menus. He looked up to see the shadow hanging over Garett staring into Travis's eyes with a smile on its face. It knew it had beaten him. Travis and Garett ordered their food without a word of conversation. They didn't even lock eyes once and spent more time trying to avoid having anything to do with each other.

As they left the restaurant Travis took Garett's hands, and gently placed the keys to the car in them. In silence Travis walked away from Garett. In that moment Valieen appeared in front of Garett. Valieen wore a big smile and opened his arms to Garett who sunk himself into them. They had sunk back into one of the portals and came out from the other side inside of the village. Valieen and Garett took themselves to the temple where Garett died. The old Garett was no more. The one that lived in his place was one with no love for anything living due to the action of Travis leaving him.

All the life had left his eyes in one instant. As he finished his change the very air around him lost all of its life. It was like he caused everything to die just from being in proximity. Travis driving him away cost Garett his mind and now it has cost him his very soul. Without his soul Garett was no longer a human, but something, wrong.

Travis huffed as the air got to him. He made his way back to the hospital. He knew that he could find a phone at the hospital to call himself a way back home. He wanted to get back to a place that he found familiar. He started to think that Alaska was a mistake to have come to. Everything was lost to him in this place. He continued to walk as his breathing got harder as the cold air pulled his breathe away. It was a cold he wasn't used to being in.

Travis found a bench and sat down putting his head in his palms crying. He didn't want to leave Garett, but he couldn't take the fact that he would make a deal with Valieen. It was like the one sin of his list of sins that he couldn't forgive. No matter who it was that committed it, he would never forgive them. He was sure that he couldn't even forgive his own sister for it if she had done the same thing.

Garett took a deep breath as he looked into the mirror. He has black lines tracing his body stemming from his black eyes. He looked at his hands and they ended in claws. He looked back into the mirror to see a sharp toothed smile stretching across his face. He felt the power coursing its way through him. He was no longer that weak and useless man that used to be. He turned around to see Valieen standing in the corner of the room with a proud look on his face.

"You like your new power?" Valieen asked, while walking to Garett.

"I do enjoy this new power. I enjoy it quite a bit." Garett spoke with a smile on his face.

Travis sat on the bench crying for an hour before Dr. Marron found him and brought him back to the hotel he had booked. Travis went straight to the shower tears still coming from his eyes. Dr. Marron quietly shut and locked the door as he entered a few minutes later after a phone call. He heard the water running in the bathroom still feeling the pain that was left in the wake of where Travis had walked through the room.

"Hey Travis?" Dr. Marron said from the other side of the door.

"What?" Travis said, sounding in pain.

"I want to say I am sorry for what has happened to you and Garett." Dr. Marron said, trying to sound honest even if Travis didn't trust him.

"It is whatever he did that I could never forgive him for." Travis said letting his head fall against the wall.

"You say that, but do you really mean it?" Dr. Marron asked.

"I don't know anymore." Travis said his voice sounds tired and ready to stop.

"I think you should figure out what it is you do know. He is out there, and soon he will need you." Dr. Marron said in an assertive tone trying to drill the statements into Travis's head.

"I will, but I think I need to think about everything first."

Travis got out of the shower and got dressed hoping Dr. Marron had left the room. When he got out of the bathroom to his disappointment the doctor was sitting on his bed. Travis let out a groan of annoyance as he sat down on the other bed. He looked at the doctor then back down at his hands.

"What is it doctor?" Travis asked without trying to sound upset.

"It is just that I have never seen you so far down in the dumps about anything." Dr. Marron said, giving Travis a sympathetic look.

"Well, I loved him, he went and fucked us over!" Travis yelled and threw a book that was laying behind him.

"I just want you to talk to me sometimes." Dr. Marron said.

"I am sorry, I just feel that this is just not the situation to share very much about right now." Travis felt worse than before.

"That is fine, just don't keep me locked out when you feel it is a better time to share your feelings." Dr. Marron said, looking down at his feet.

Travis slipped under the covers that lay on his bed in an effort to separate from the world around him. He just wanted everything to disappear. Being alone felt like the only option he had left for himself. He pulled it over his head and tried to block out all of the outside light. Before he knew it, he had drifted off into a fitful night's rest.

"You know you can't run away from everything that has happened right?" Dr. Marron said, climbing into his own bed.

Dr. Marron slept hoping Travis heard what he said right before he went to bed himself. Travis needed to know that everything could be forgiven, and that is the point Dr. Marron set out to make. Soon the room fell quiet aside from the few fitful moves in his sleep. His dreams flashed of battles he had during his time in Afghanistan. Mainly the battle when he used his knife to kill someone for the first time.

"Doctor, I didn't sleep for shit last night. How well did you sleep?" Travis asked as he stretched.

He looked over to see nothing but the decayed body of the Doctor. He jumped back screaming. He ducked himself back under the cover hoping to see that it was all just part of his dreams. He started to pray and didn't stop until the doctor; the living doctor pulled the covers from over Travis's face.

"Are we going to sit here or are we going to get Breakfast?" Dr. Marron asked.

"I just thought you had died, and I had imagined you being alive this whole time." Travis said, trying to laugh it off.

"Well as far as I can tell I am still alive and kicking Travis." Dr. Marron added a laugh at the end.

The two of them got up and walked to the car. The morning's crisp air revealed every time they took a breath and froze their insides. To Travis it was a morning worth savoring. They both let out a sigh of relief as the seat warmers and the car's heated air grabbed hold of them. Seeing each other look so relieved lightened the mood, and they both gave a hearty laugh.

"Well, what are we waiting on? I am starving." Travis said, giving the doctor a bump on the arm.

"I am not as young as I used to be Travis. Let me warm up." Dr. Marron said, giving an exaggerated shiver.

"Yeah, yeah we all know you are old." Travis said, giving a deep gutted laugh.

"We who?" Dr. Marron said as a joke, turning over the car's ignition.

"I will figure that out at some point doctor." Travis said putting his hands on the vents.

They made their way to a local coffee shop where they found themselves among coffee and pancakes. Travis had a conversation with the doctor not really listening completely. His attention was on what the doctor had said earlier. It flew through his head over and over again "You know you can't run away from everything." It was like the doctor knew what everyone has always wanted to say. Travis could see it written on everyone's face that he passed.

"Why am I like this?" Travis asked out of nowhere.

"What do you mean Travis?" Dr. Marron said, confused by the question.

"I seem to get everyone around me in some sort of trouble, and every time I sleep, I am killing someone." Travis said, moving his gaze to meet the doctor's.

"That has not ever been your fault. With that demon following you around. You can't control his actions." Dr. Marron said before taking a sip of his coffee.

"I know, but I have failed to protect them. Just like I failed to save the ones I dream about over and over at night." Travis said, finishing off his first cup of coffee.

"Well, you see. Not being able to protect someone is just something that happens in this life. I am assuming it will happen in the next as well." Dr. Marron said with a sly smile.

"You know I could get behind that theory, but I just worry about Garett and where he is." Travis said as a waitress refilled his cup.

Garett stepped out onto a balcony looking out over the crowd that stood below him. He raised his hands and they all cheered. He stood and studied the crowd below. He was studying his army. Garett smiled at all of the soldiers he now had command over. With his new life he was going to start it with a new name.

"I am now longer Garett Randy. I am now High Priest Garton. I am your commander. I tell you when to attack, when not to attack, when to eat, when to drink, and when to breathe." Garett yelled out over the crowd.

Chapter 25: Alaska Is Now Behind

The pair—Travis and Dr. Marron—began to pack their bags after staying for the week that was paid for at the hotel. Travis began to take out his bags when a figure flashed in the corner of his eye. He turned to look at it, but it was gone before he could see it. He became more cautious after the sight. They knew until they left Alaska it would be dangerous.

"So, how are we getting out of the situation we are in." Travis asked Dr. Marron.

"Well, I thought about taking a plane. It was my main idea until I thought about the amount of things that could be done to the plane, and with all of these cult members we can't trust the flight crew. That being said we are driving." Dr. Marron shrugged after he finished talking.

"Well, I hope you have our passports." Travis said with a laugh following it.

"I do have them right here." Dr. Marron held up two blue folds that contained their information.

"Good, then let's get food and start our journey." Travis had a smile on his face.

Garton stood on the building next to a drab run-down hotel watching two men load a car. He saw a familiar face that he used to have feelings for, but he no longer cared. His heart was dead now. He watched the car pull off before opening a portal where he could see the village on the other side. He waited till the car was gone over the horizon before leaving. The spot where the portal stood now only held an out-of-place pile of snow.

"They are leaving this place." Garton said, passing by Valieen.

"Then everything is going just as well as we planned it." Valieen spoke with a bloodlust.

"We need to make sure we don't underestimate the strings of fate." Garton stated as he sat on his throne.

"Well yes, but sometimes the strings of fate can be moved." Valieen made the movements of playing an air harp.

"I want to peel the skin off of his body and roast it." Garton said, making the motions as he spoke.

"You will get your chance don't you worry. We just need to make sure everything is in place for it to happen." A smile crept across both of their faces at this statement.

Valieen had a growing sense of victory as each day passed. He finally put the final straw on the camel's back. Garton has seen this rising in Valieen and feels it will be the thing that will bring him down. If they are to win, he will need to keep Valieen in check for the time being.

"Valieen you know that he is the one that is meant to be your true vessel. Even if me taking my place here at the throne brought his mind to its end you have work to do." Garton said looking into the fire pit.

He lifted his hand and looked at it. The more he focused on his hand the more a small, detailed version of the world formed. After it had formed fully, he slowly began to crush it with his hand. As it cracked and broke apart his smile got bigger. He didn't stop until all that left in his hand was dirt.

"This world will be turned into dust before I allow it to return to the way it was." This statement was followed by High Priest Garton's signature laughs.

It was one of those laughs that sent chills down the spine of anyone that has heard it. Garton was the one that now lived while the old Garett has died off. His heart was now filled with darkness that will consume everything around him. He held the darkness to create demons of his own. Valieen saw a chance to teach someone that could take his place if he were to die before he could take Travis as his vessel.

"We should get some rest, Garton." Valieen said walking back to the beds.

"I will get some rest later. I have planning to do in the morning." Garton said, standing to leave the room.

Valieen shrugged and went to bed while Garton went out to the balcony. The cold air met him right away at the doorway. He took a deep breath before walking out. He looked out over the place he now controlled. His mind ran wild with every possible outcome from the actions his people will have to make in the near future. He was in such deep thought which he was pulled out of by the golden light of the morning sun.

"Valieen we are off to Marrion." He said just as Valieen opened the door.

"Do we have a specific goal there?" Valieen asked joining at Garett's side.

"Yes, we do." Garton gave a sinister smile and opened a portal behind the pair.

They entered through the portal and came out in the kitchen of Marvic house. One person stood in the room and that person was Vinessa Marvic. Garton walked up and stabbed Vinessa in the spine while covering her mouth. Before she blacked out Vinessa saw his new horrendous face. It was the face of someone so evil they held no regard for anyone. He had eyes so absent of a soul that it felt like they could steal another person's and not be filled.

"Wake up Vinessa. Your brother is on his way home. He will be here in a week." Garton followed this with an evil cackle.

Vinessa shivered as he laughed. It brought out a fear in her that she thought could have never of been caused within her body. She wanted to move, but thanks to his knife she couldn't even feel her legs. She assumed that he crippled her. She wanted to scream out, but she was gagged. Garton sat on a chair five feet away from her with a hunger in his eyes and a predatorial smile on his face. This was no longer the Garett she once knew before. This thing that sat in front of her–in her opinion–was nothing, but pure evil.

"You used to be a pretty woman Vinessa." Garton said as he ran a blood covered knife over his forked tongue.

"I believe I smell fear, Garton." Valieen said, licking the sweat off of her neck.

Vinessa grimaced as Valieen's rough tongue glided over her skin. She threw a sharp look at both of them as the front door burst open. As wind poured through the house the lights flickered. When they finally went out leagues of shadows darker than the night itself poured through and filled the house. Vinessa squirmed trying to get away as they got closer to her. Their hands wrapped around her slowly until their fingers began to enter her mouth.

"Look at her squirm!" Garton couldn't contain the amusement he felt.

Shadows started to consume as Vinessa blacked out from fear. Her cell began to ring displaying *"Big Brother :-)"*

Garton looked at it and sighed dropping the phone in the sink. He as it turned in the water watching the display flash from the incoming call get deeper under the water. He turned back to Vinessa with hunger and revenge coloring his face.

"I am going to have fun with this one." Garton's face grew dark as he lightly drew the blade's tip over Vinessa's thigh as he spoke.

Travis and Dr. Marron stopped at a local dinner just across the northern border of America. They stopped to eat spotting a pair of people watching them from across the street in a parked car. They tried to make it not so obvious that they had spotted them so the pair across the street wouldn't run. They communicated through a small notebook they passed under the table.

"I couldn't get a hold of my sister over the phone." Travis said breaking the silence.

"What do you think is going on with her?" Dr. Marron asked, a look of concern on his face.

"I am hoping it isn't anything bad." Travis said lowering his face to avoid eye contact.

The dark feeling of fear that Travis had settled in his stomach the entire time they sat eating. No matter where the conversation went his mind stayed on his sister. Even after they grew up, he always dwelt on her safety. It was what he called his big brother instinct. They checked out the window to see the pair that was watching them had vanished from sight,

"I think it is safe to go out now that they have gone." Dr. Marron said as he called for the check.

"I can't help but be worried about my sister doctor." Travis said getting up from the table.

"Well, we are on our way home. Keep trying to get her on the phone." Dr. Marron said, turning over the car's ignition.

"I will." Travis said, pulling out his phone.

Vinessa's phone vibrated under the water refusing to die. Garton growled, dropping the blood covered knife to turn on the garbage disposal unit, finally finishing off the cellphone. Vinessa sat shaking from blood loss her body covered in cuts and burns. He nodded for Valieen to cauterize her wounds. She screamed as a heated knife was pressed on her skin closing the wounds with burnt skin.

Valieen and Garton fell into a fit of laughter simultaneously from the sight of her pain. She began to wish she could die as they continued to torture her into the early morning. When she blacked out, they waited for her to recover before starting again. Her pain fed the monsters that found their way into her home, and she could see it in their eyes. She could see a hunger never to be satisfied.

"Come on, give me a smile you bitch." Garton growled through his teeth.

All he got in response was a shake of her head. This got under his skin worse than anything causing him to lose his temper. He gave her a heavy-handed punch to the back of her head. She got knocked out from the punch causing her day of torture to end early. Garton went and collapsed on the couch trying to focus himself.

"I lost my temper." Garton said, shaking his head.

"I can see that you did Garton, and we can't have you killing her." Valieen said leaning against the wall.

Garton let out a loud sigh and laid down to get rest. He could feel that Travis was not close to being home, but he didn't feel that having spies to follow them didn't hurt either. He was willing to do anything to make sure the cult could achieve their goal. This was war to him. It was a war that no other could see unless they were involved. It was still not a cold war because it was highly active in its fighting.

"Doctor, do you think I can save her if she was in trouble?" Travis asked his breath fogging up the cold window he leaned against.

"I am hoping she isn't, but if she is, I believe you may be the only one that can save her." Dr. Marron said, hoping that was what Travis wanted to hear.

Travis became entranced by the lights seeming to fly by them as they drove past fields of crops. Farmers put up lights to see people who started to use their fields for food or to play within. He began to feel like it is hard to trust human nature anymore. He couldn't even trust the people he loved anymore. Travis was to his breaking point mentally, and he could feel himself slipping closer and closer to it. It was so bad he could feel it physically. He could see Dr. Marron gaining a more, and more concerned look every time he looked at him.

"You know you don't have to worry about me, right?" Travis said to the doctor sitting next to him.

"I know that I don't, but I have moved past being the therapist. I am your friend, and, in that position, I worry about you." Dr. Marron said, staying focused on the road, but putting the same amount of power behind his words.

They drove until the sun licked the darkness from the sky. It was their signal to pull over and get rest. Every day Travis felt like he got less and less sleep. He woke up exhausted and his heart beating so fast he thought it would come out of his chest. One of the days he woke up and for ten minutes he couldn't move and saw the sky pulling apart to reveal a sky filled with fire.

"Are your dreams getting worse?" Dr. Marron asked early the next morning while rubbing the sleep from his eyes.

"I would say that they have gotten a little worse, but mostly still the same." Travis ended his words with a sigh before rolling back over and went back to sleep.

Dr. Marron gave a worried look to Travis before he also went back to sleep. Travis dreamt of a world under the torture of flames and steel as people fought each other to the death. Men screaming as they tried to hold back monsters that rose from the ground already carrying a bloodlust for human flesh. Things that made nightmares seem like a movie meant for children. He began to think it was a prediction of the future the more he had the dream.

"We are still days away from getting to Marrion. I think that we may take longer to get to your home." Dr. Marron said, stretching behind the wheel of his car.

"As long as we get there in one piece, I think we will be okay." Travis said, handing the doctor a cup of coffee.

"Yes, we wouldn't be useful if we died." Dr. Marron took a sip of his coffee, and they headed on their way.

Garton slowly pulled off one fingernail after another from Vinessa's hand. He laughed as shadows entered and exited her body keeping her screams of pain muffled. From her blood shot eyes she could see it looked like they had become more revitalized, and more, human in a way. It seemed the more they fed into her pain it brought them closer to a disguise in this world. It broke her mind to see the normal version of Garett with that sickening and ravenous look on his face. She didn't know what their plan was, but it felt like the shadows wanted to take over her body.

"Come on, don't black out like that." Garton said before backhanding Vinessa.

"Yes, you need to stay awake." Valieen said looming over top of her.

"Fuck off." Vinessa managed to get out despite the shadows choking her.

She could hear the shadows inside of her head. She could hear them talking about how bad they wanted to have her body. They sounded, so hungry. She didn't want to give up her body. She wanted to fight, to live.

"Help me brother." Vinessa yelled at the top of her lungs.

Chapter 26: Shadow Of The Past

Travis awoke to his phone ringing the display saying *"Mother"* he answered the phone. On the other end of the line his mother was in tears, her words making no sense. He tried to calm her down, but nothing was working. He gestured for Dr. Marron to pull over and he got out.

"Mom what is wrong?" Travis asked as soon as he shut the door.

"The doctor told me I don't have much time." She said on the other end of the line.

"How long exactly is that?" Travis asked, his face becoming grim from the conversation.

"I have around a week left, and I want you to bring your sister. I have a lot I have to say before I go." She said her voice sounded ready to give up.

"Yeah, we will come to see you." Travis said a single tear forming and rolling down his cheek.

"Son, I lo-" The line dropped the call as a thunderstorm formed above the pair in the car.

"Damn cell service." Travis said getting back into the car.

"Is your mom okay?" Dr. Marron said already knowing what the answer would be.

"She said that she only has a week left." Travis said leaning his head against the window beside him.

"I will get you to her before that can happen." Dr. Marron flashed a smile that contained both happiness and sorrow.

The both of them got back on the road this time planning to drive nonstop. Every three hours they switched who was behind the wheel at the time. They got right across the state line into North Carolina when Travis's phone rang. The display showed that he had a text from an unknown number. He opened it thinking it was a spam number, but he was wrong. What he saw was a message with no subject. It had an image attached to it. He opened it to find his sister tied to a chair with her head thrown back in a scream. Hands wrapped around her lips pulling themselves out. Some of the hands reached out to thin air like they had been asking for help.

"What the fuck is this?" Travis said his eyes wide with shock.

"What do you mean?" Dr. Marron asked pulling the car into a nearby gas station.

Travis handed Dr. Marron the phone to let him see the picture. His eyes couldn't hide the amount of fear he felt looking at the picture. His hands began to shake as he slowly put the phone back in Travis's hands. Neither of them found the power to move much less utter a word. It was like both of them got struck with one of those stares where they looked off into space.

"I can't believe what I am seeing." Travis said his breath catching with each word.

"I think it may be a fake photo." Dr. Marron said his words betraying him.

"Doctor it doesn't look fake and who would do something like this?" Travis asked, his voice rising in volume.

"We live in a world of sick people, but you do have a point on this one." Dr. Marron sighed.

Travis had to get out of the car for air. Everything around him started to feel like it was closing in on him. A panic attack started to creep up on him, and he could feel it. He went into the gas station hoping to find something that will take his mind off of the picture he just saw. While he searched the aisles, he could hear his sister yelling for him in the back of his mind.

"Travis!" A voice yelled from behind him.

He turned around to see his sister, but something was wrong with her. She gave off a dark energy that he could almost see radiating from her. He started to walk after her when she vanished behind a shelf. When he got around, he saw her on the floor crying. She had loud sobs of pain with a puddle of blood around her.

"Why didn't you come for me?" She asked.

"Vinessa, I am almost to you." Travis said, his breath escaping me.

He touched her shoulder causing her to fall forward onto the floor. Her body began to jerk on the ground. When her body finally rolled over and shadows started to leak from her nose. He leaned down to inspect her nose when a hand reached out of her mouth. He recoiled in disgust as it shot after him. He fell back knocking over a small display shelf.

"Hey man are you okay?" The cashier asked running over to check on Travis.

"Y-y-yes, I am okay." Travis said unable to take his eyes off the spot where his sister used to be.

Travis helped to clean up the merchandise he knocked over. He stood up to apologize to the cashier as a hand shot within an inch of his face before vanishing. The color drained from his face and his body grew cold. He saw his sister was hanging from the roof by a rope made of hands. He turned and walked out of the gas station without another word. Travis stumbled back to their car fear etched all over his face.

"Are you okay?" Dr. Marron asked with a look of worry on his face.

"I-I-I-I just saw Vinessa." Travis stumbled over his words with sweat forming on his forehead.

"I have been watching you this whole time. The only people in there were you and that cashier." Dr. Marron said, putting a hand on Travis's shoulder.

"Are you sure about that?" Travis asked, his eyes looking crazed.

"Yes I am." Dr. Marron nodded after his words.

Travis just nodded before dropping his head against the dash in front of him. Dr. Marron started the car before pulling back onto the road. As they drove another car pulled out behind them. Travis was watching in the rearview mirror as they got closer behind them. Dr. Marron sped up, but then they felt a force hit the back of their car. Their tires screeched as their car went off into a ditch breaking the axel and causing it to slide to a stop.

"Fuck!" Dr. Marron yelled, holding his forehead.

"What the hell was that?" Travis said as his vision turned red.

Two men got out of the car that had run them off of the road. They carried themselves with a pride like they could be untouchable. A sharp metallic sound came starting at the rear of the car and went nonstop. Travis looked out the mirror on his side to see a blade in one of their hands. When he got to the window blade in hand the light glinting off of its tip as he started to punch the window. Before they knew it both figures had started to pound away at the windows. Even as the blood started to ooze from their knuckles they kept going.

"We gotta figure out how we are going to get out of this." Dr. Marron said stealing looks at both windows as small cracks started to appear.

"We gotta fight our way-out doctor." Travis said with his eyes trained on the man hitting his window.

They used their blade hilts, and the cracks grew larger with each hit. The window busted followed by the mans arm reaching in and was quickly grabbed by Travis. The struggle was bad, but Travis got the upper hand throwing the man's arm into a piece of broken window. The man dropped his blade screaming in pain. Travis looked over to see the doctor was being held by a man who's arm had broken through and he was struggling to save himself.

"Move doctor!" Travis yelled, trusting the blade at the man on the driver side of the car.

"Shit!" Dr. Marron pulled the lever on the side of his chair and laid back as far as he could.

Travis thrusted the knife causing the man to lean back in pain. Both of their attackers ran back to the vehicle they arrived in and drove off. As they sped off Travis got out of the car. Dr. Marron didn't get out right away and Travis walked over to the driver side of the car. He opened the door and drug the doctor out and found a clean wound going into his arm. He ripped his shirt and tied off his arm to stop the bleeding.

"Doctor if you don't be more careful, I won't be able to tie off all of your wounds." This statement made them both chuckle a little bit.

"You are a smart-ass Travis." Dr. Marron laughed at his own words.

He went to the car and pulled his phone out of the floor and dialed 911. The pair traded jokes and stories while they waited on the ambulance to arrive. When it finally pulled up alongside them Travis helped the doctor to his feet. The ambulance pulled away leaving Travis to search for anything usable in the car. His phone went off to show he had another text message same as the last containing only a picture. This picture had his sister tied to a cross in a Jesus mocking pose as shadows wrapped around her body again entering her body through her mouth.

"This makes me fucking sick." Travis cursed putting his phone back into his pocket.

After Travis got all he could out of the car he called a tow truck. As he waited for the tow truck, he could see his breath forming as the air around him began to chill. A car stopped in front of him. He tried to ask the men inside a question, but they sat in silence and just stared at him with eyes that seemed soulless to him. Silently they pulled away as the tow truck pulled up behind the car.

"Did you see that car?" Travis asked walking up to the vehicle.

"I did, what did they want?" The driver asked in a heavy southern drawl before spitting out his tobacco.

"They just stopped and stared at me." Travis shrugged after he spoke.

"That is the oddest damned thing I have ever heard. I wouldn't say I'd put it past anyone 'round here though." The tow driver said hooking up the car.

Travis managed to get a ride to the hospital from the tow driver who spouted out stories of the "Good 'ol days." Travis had forgotten that North Carolina had such accents among the people that live there. As he entered the hospital, he found the doctor sitting waiting for someone to take him to his room. The moment he sat down he showed him the newest text message he got from the unknown number.

"Holy shit. This stuff is getting worse. You need to go to your sister." Dr. Marron said, lowering his head.

"I can't leave you here." Travis said shaking his head knowing he will need Dr. Marron's help.

The pair sat in the waiting room for three hours before anyone saw Dr. Marron. He ended up getting stitches on his arm and put on pain medication. Travis drove on towards his hometown. He was fueled by the anger that came from seeing those messages. He felt a drive to go save his sister. Even as his vision wavered, he didn't stop driving. Dr. Marron tried to help keep him awake with stories, but Travis just drowned them out with his own thoughts. His phone rang out once again, but this time it was a call from the number that sent him those photos.

"Who are you, you son of a bitch!" Travis yelled answering the call.

"Travis please help me!" His sister yelled from the other end of the line followed by the nonstop sound of her choking.

He hung up the phone when the sounds didn't stop. His eyes began to fill with more tears forcing him to pull over.

Dr. Marron took over with no words exchanged. They exchanged one look which said everything that needed to be. Travis sat back with the light in his eyes being gone. He was sunk back into his mind again.

He was transported back to a time he was sent to a small village during his time in the military. It was a hostage rescue mission. They entered their target building after a short gun fight to find women and children alike killed. Their corpses had been posed in ways to mock the Christian faith. What stuck with him the most is a woman that had been crucified was still alive and tried to talk to him. No matter how hard she tried to talk all that came out was blood and air. Some of it turned into foam that when the bubbles popped it sent blood onto him and his fellow soldiers.

They didn't realize when they tried to save her that a bomb was set to start countdown when she was pulled off the cross. He saved as many as he could, but the explosion was just too fast. He remembers it so well because that was the first time he was injured. He can see her body all the time and hears her trying to talk when the room is too quiet. It gets to him every single night. Sometimes her face gets to him so bad that he sees her on his sister's very own face.

"Hey Travis come back to us." Dr. Marron said tapping Travis on the shoulder.

"I am still here. I just had something on my mind." Travis said trying to play it off with an awkward smile.

"It was your PTSD wasn't it?" Dr. Marron asked

"Yes, I think the pictures set it off." Travis said watching his phone flash the low battery before dying.

"I would say that it would have been a big contributor to it." Dr. Marron said, pulling over at a restaurant.

"We have somewhere to be doc." Travis said, his voice barely rising above a whisper.

"Well, you're going to be goddamn useless if you don't put some fucking food in your stomach!" Dr. Marron yelled only to make his point.

Travis just nodded and they both went inside. He didn't feel like arguing with the doctor. He wanted to, but he would be wrong. They ordered a large meal each even knowing Travis wouldn't eat all of his. He could only bring himself to sigh and take small bites of his food. The image of his sister being tortured kept revolving in his mind.

"Why don't we call the cops?" Dr. Marron broke the silence with his question.

"Do you think they will believe us about what those pictures showed?" Travis said without looking up from his plate of food.

"You make a good point with that." Dr. Marron went back to eating.

"I know." Travis said sharply.

Travis got up and went to the restroom. He was just unable to face the world right now. As he looked in the mirror, he saw himself in his sister's place. He just felt useless where he was. He just kept thinking of how he was going to help her.

Chapter 27: Home Of Darkness

Vinessa sat tied to a chair with shadows crawling over her body. Some of them moved in and out of her mouth causing her to choke. She could feel them as they got into her stomach before twisting to come back up out of her mouth. She wanted to vomit the entire time. Every time she tried it only showed that she had nothing in her stomach to vomit.

Her vision was blurry, and she could barely keep her eyes open. Her breathing was heavy from exhaustion. She wanted all of this to end. A figure moved from left to right in her vision. She tried to turn to look at it, but her body didn't have enough strength to move her head. Her breaths became staggered as she could feel someone walking up behind her. Her breaths stopped as she could feel fingers running through her hair. They stopped halfway up the back of her head and gave a sharp pull snapping her head back with enough force to hurt.

"Your nothing to us, but we keep you here because he will come for you." The voice growled behind her.

"F-F-F-Fuck you." She managed to get out with effort.

The hand let go and her head fell down her hair falling in front of her face. Below her she saw a crazed maniacal face that was acting like it was biting at her. When it saw her fear, it laughed before vanishing. She no longer felt like living will be worth it with everything that has happened this week. Her mind, body, and soul has been broken by the recent events. Vinessa could hear a pair of laughs every time she begged for them to kill her. She so desperately wanted that sweet release of death.

"You don't get to die. Not by our hands, and not before your brother gets here." A deep voice said from behind her.

"Do you remember where you are and who we are?" Another voice said from beside her.

"N-N-No." She said with a weak defeated voice.

"You are within your home. You're being held here by Valieen and Garton." One of the voices said.

In her mind Vinessa has died and been replaced with emptiness. She had been driven mad by the constant sight of shadows surrounding her, closing in on her. She began to feel like the house was falling in on her. It caused her to start having a panic attack. It caused her body to shake, her breath to quicken, sweat poured down her face. She almost fell over till one of them kept the chair from falling over. She let out a sigh that she didn't know if it was out of annoyance or relief. She wanted to feel something, be it pain or otherwise, but at the same time she didn't want to be laying on the floor. The floor was dirty with the dark spirits that had entered.

"What's wrong Vinessa?" Garton asked, leaning over to look her in the eyes.

"Y-Y-You, never mind." Vinessa felt no point in saying anything because it won't change anything.

Garton let her head drop back down. They decided to feed her for the first time in two days. The way they did it was with a blender and a tube. She felt the most disrespected she had in her whole life with the way they treated her. She spent the entire time she was forced food and water begging her mom to forgive her for being the position she is in.

She felt they took all of the control she had in her life from her. Valieen walked up to her after the tube was taken from her mouth and gave her an off-putting smile while clearing any leftover food from her face. She spit food in his face. He locked eyes with her then laughed. When he did that it made her feel small. She felt smaller than she has ever in her life. She dropped her head and let out a sigh of defeat.

"You won't piss me off with that same shit that pisses off Garton. I already know you're broken." Valieen said sitting in front of her again.

Vinessa just nodded in response. She could feel that Valieen was watching her along with the hundreds of eyes that the shadows brought into the house. She could feel the hunger that came from every corner of the house. They wanted her soul. That would be saying that she still had a soul for them to take.

She fell back into her mind allowing her body to rest in a way. She kept thinking of her happy place. When she got there, she found herself in an ice cream shop. She was with her brother back when got his first job. He always told her when he started a new job, he would always take her to get ice cream with every first paycheck. He kept that promise up until he joined the military. When that happened, he would take her to get ice cream every time he came home. Her happy place was with her brother, he was the only one that ever cared about her.

It brought her comfort through all of this to be able to go back on these memories. She didn't feel okay with the real world anymore. She only wanted to live in her memories. It was her closest sense of heaven. Garton grabbed a large handful of her hair pulling her back to reality. She saw a blade in his hand that was dripping with water. He dragged the blade against her scalp. It pulled at her skin as he cut her hair with it. When he was done, she could feel patches of hair still sitting on her head. Blood began to run down her face as Valieen threw a bucket of ice water on her. She shot up straight gasping for warm air.

Vinessa sat with an angry look on her face as she shivered. She could feel the shadows moving in on her as Garton pulled out a cell phone. She could feel claws digging into her skin and pulling up her body. She could feel her skin tearing apart as they did. Garton smiled as he recorded the whole event. When he put the phone away her wounds repaired themselves slowly, and painfully.

"Come on bitch." Garton said as a hood went over Vinessa's head.

"What is going on?" Vinessa begged for information.

"It doesn't matter!" Valieen growled before hitting her across the just with his arm.

"Get her in the van." Garton said as a door slides open.

The ride to wherever they were going was bumpy with only two stops. She could hear the buzz of gas station florescent lights with each stop. She tried several times to get the hood off of her face only to be met with a punishment. She could hear as the van went from pavement to gravel. As it slid to a stop Valieen grabbed her by the arm.

"Let's get her out of here." Garton said, opening the door.

Valieen jerked her out of the van causing her to land hard on the gravel. She could feel it cut into her skin from the impact. She let out a grunt of pain as she could feel dirt and liquid go down her arm. Her arm shook from the pain she felt in it as tears started to flow from her arm. They forced her to her feet and started escorting her to what she hopes was a shelter and not a grave.

"Put her in her room!" Garton yelled as voices started to chatter around them.

She could tell from the sounds of birds around them that they are out in the countryside. The same heavy feeling from her house had followed her to this new shelter. She got tied to another chair before they had finished moving her. She was left in her hood for two hours before they came to take it off of her head. She looked around in a panic inspecting the place she was in now. It was an old decrepit wooden home. It seemed clean to her, but it needed some repairs. It creaked with the wind as it blew.

"Welcome to your new home." A voice echoed in the empty room.

Vinessa looked around to find no one around. She struggled against her bindings with what little strength she had. She continued when her arm started to get free footsteps echoed through the hall. She froze in fear as they stopped in front of the door and fists hammered at the other side of the door. She jumped back her heart starting to race. When the footsteps disappeared down the hallway, she started to try to free herself again. She felt a small amount of happiness when her arms got freed from her bindings. She ran to check out the door and when she found no one she cautiously made their way down the hall.

As she entered the main room no one was around. Vinessa stopped to listen, and no sounds came to her except the building sounds. She made her way outside to see the van and everything gone. They had left her out in the middle of nowhere. She sprinted off into the woods ignoring the sticks and rocks cutting into her feet. It made her panic as sticks broke and echoed through the wilderness around her.

"Fuck I need to get out of here. I hope I run into someone soon." She huffed as she kept running through the woods.

As she ran her vision began to become dark around the edges. She could see it was daytime around her, but her exhaustion was clearly catching up with her. Her legs started to give in as she came across a clearing. Her vision was getting darker and darker when she got to the clearing. The last thing she saw before blacking out was a shadow forming in the center of the clearing. It had no face, but she knew it was just as hungry for her soul.

"You shouldn't be here." The shadow said gliding towards her as her vision finally gave out.

Travis's phone dinged to life with a text notification. He knew who it was before he picked up his phone. He gave a groan of frustration as he opened his phone. Dr. Marron looked over his shoulder as Travis opened the video attached to the text message. They both recoiled in disgust as he watched Vinessa's body being ripped open by claws made of shadows. She tried to scream but some of the arms emerged from her mouth as they tore his skin. Travis dropped the phone and ran to the bathroom to vomit.

"This is sick. We need to get there now!" Travis spoke his breath still recovering.

"Yes, we do. I have a car on the way for us to drive." Dr. Marron said, trying to keep himself from vomiting as well.

"Good. Wake me when it gets here please." Travis laid his head down to rest for a moment.

Dr. Marron went out of the room pulling out a cigarette. He closed his door and pulled out his phone holding the cigarette between his lips. He hit a speed dial number on his phone and held it to his ear pulling out his lighter. The door shut behind him just as he blew out his first puff of smoke.

"What do you want, doctor?"

"We are going to be back in town tomorrow." Dr. Marron said in a low voice.

"Okay, and your point is?"

"We are clear to go ahead with our plan." Dr. Marron gave a smile.

The doctor spent two hours outside on the phone while waiting on the car. It was unknown who he was speaking with, but the car arrived just as he said. He crushed his cigarette under foot as the man brought him the papers to sign so he could drive it. He shook Travis awake shortly after smoking a second cigarette.

Travis drug himself out of the bed still looking sick. He went and took a sip out of the bathroom sink to wash out the sour taste in his mouth. He sighed and walked out to the car. He took his place as the "window" guy as he always called it. He was pretty sure the doctor was trying to talk to him, but he wasn't listening. He looked at the doctor who looked concerned while keeping his eyes on the road.

"Are the windows unlocked?" Travis asked the doctor without looking at him.

"Yes, Travis they are unlocked. I need to roll mine down as well." He said, pulling out his fourth cigarette of the day.

Travis rolled down his window and took a deep breath. He pulled out his phone looking at the background which was the last picture he and his sister took before he went to Afghanistan the last time. It was a trip to their favorite ice cream shop, and he splattered the ice cream all over her face. She laughed so hard she fell over. The memory made him smile before throwing the phone out of the car.

"Travis what the fuck?" Dr. Marron asked, sounding freaked out.

"I am tired." Was all Travis said before dropping his seat back?

Before Travis knew it the doctor was waking him up. He opened his eyes to see his house in front of him. He got out of the car and charged into the house. He looked around to find written in blood the words "Sometimes the most beautiful things must suffer." Below the words he saw a doll that was the perfect likeness of his sister. He searched around the house and found no sign of his sister. He did see things moving out of the corner of his eyes at every corner.

"I can't find any sign of her." Travis said walking down the stairs.

"I know." Dr. Marron said, holding the doll in one hand.

"What do you mean you know?" Travis asked confused.

"We needed to feed our God and you haven't stewed long enough." Dr. Marron said his face changed to an expression Travis had never seen.

"What do you mean?" Travis asked, starting to get aggressive.

"We need you to finish cooking." Dr. Marron said, pulling out a metallic object which was followed by a rush of air.

Travis looked down to see a dart sticking out of his leg. He exchanged looks between the doctor and the dart. His face twisted into a look of worry as his vision got dark. He let out a chuckle before passing out on the floor.

Chapter 28: Home Sweet Alone

Travis awoke in a dark room that was bare except for a single bulb hanging from the center of the roof. It swung in an eerie silence that could be felt. It couldn't be felt physically, but deep in your soul itself. He watched it swing back and forth without knowing why. It seemed to just pull him in. It was entrancing to him and seemed to call to him. Behind it two eyes started to form in the light.

As they formed the light seemed to drag leaving a trail that looked like it formed the mouth. He could feel the fear rising in him as the face slowly got bigger. He tried to get further away only to find a wall closely behind him. A growl came from the growing face. He wanted to scream out as it rushed at him. To his relief the face vanished inches from his face. It took all of his will to force himself to his feet.

"I must be inside my own head again." He said, feeling the walls for a door.

When he found the door, he opened it to find a hallway covered in blood. Beyond the hallway was an intersection for another hallway. A noticeable, but quick large shadow boomed down the hall. He took his time moving to the next room of the house. As he slowly opened the door the room had dolls nailed to the wall covering it from wall to wall. Every one of them looked like Vinessa. It looked as if they all bled from the nails that went through their chests.

"This whole situation has me fucked up." He shook his head at the room.

He wanted to walk away until the booming footsteps got closer. He quickly reentered the room he was originally in when this all started. He collapsed against the wall at the furthest end of the room in hoping it would keep him safe. A large beast with three heads opened the door and looked around for five minutes before leaving the way he came. It seemed to have no eyes but could still somehow see. It must see through sound or smell. He started to think of a way around both of these senses. The only thing is that to combat one you free yourself to the other one. He made his way out of the room to see the large creature disappear around the corner of the junction.

"Now is my chance." He whispered to himself heading into the next room.

He couldn't afford to take any chances with getting out of here. Once again, the creature made its way through to the other room. As he saw it disappear around the corner again, he moved on to the next room. This room had drawings on the walls of people being killed in various different ways. The air in the room carried a musty smell of rot that hung thick in it.

"This room fucking stinks." Travis said as he covered his nose.

He stood in the room waiting for the footsteps to come, but they never came. He peeked out the door to see if he was being tricked when a tap came on his shoulder. He turned to see what it was to find one of the stick figures standing in front of him. It pointed at him then pointed at its absence of a face. He was confused and asked what it wanted. It pulled off its arm causing an ooze to come from its body. The liquid didn't smell like blood but that didn't make him feel any more at ease. The stick figure used it to write on the wall the words "only you can give me my face." These words made his skin crawl, and it gave him a choice to make.

"You want me to give you a face?" Travis asked it, getting down to what should be eye level.

It nodded responding yes to his question.

"How do I give you a face?" Travis asked curious but still not sure if he wanted to give it a face.

The stick figure pointed to the goo that came out of where its arm was and then pointed at his finger. A sting came from his finger and blood slowly began to ooze from the tip of his finger. Looking at his finger bleeding it once again pointed to the area where the face should be. He could feel his body fighting itself between putting the face on the figure and knowing not to do it. He was losing the fight with himself but managed to keep himself from drawing its face.

"I am sorry, but I don't feel safe giving you the face." Travis tried to apologize.

The stick figure began to get more aggressive with him. It shoved him into the wall using its one arm to push him up the wall. He tried to get free, but its arm wasn't letting go. It threw him against the wall in the back. His body didn't want to move from the pain it was in. The stick figure grabbed hand and forced his finger against its face. It stepped back gaining more detail over time. It gained a face with an evil grin and bright red eyes that burned like fire. Spikes and wings formed down its back. A guttural growl came from its throat shaking Travis to his core. Travis froze as it charged at him.

"Fuck." It was the only word Travis could think of at the time.

Before he knew it the wall behind him gave out, and he fell for what felt like three floors. He hit the ground hard enough for his shoulder to feel like it broke. He rolled over onto his back and gasped as the creature looked down at his from the hole in the wall. It did a motion that looked like it waved goodbye to him. He could have sworn it laughed at him before vanishing back into the hole.

"You're welcome for your face." Travis groaned as he got to his feet.

He sighed as he explored the underground tunnel in which he found himself. All of the cave walls had been covered in stick figures. None of them moved for now, but he couldn't be too sure about his situation. He walked with caution when a flash came from deeper in the tunnel. When he saw this began to run as footsteps gave chase from behind him. When he turned, he caught a small glimpse of one stick figure sticking against the wall.

As he turned back around, he tripped. He inspected the area to find one of the stick figures painted on the floor where he tripped. He was confused due to it being flat against the floor, but he knew better than to get closer to the creature. It was just a disguise for the ones that lived within the void their faces held. When he looked at it the face lifted to look directly at him causing him to run as fast as he could to whatever was flashing in the distance. He could hear the army of feet running behind him. He had sweat stinging his eyes, but he knew he couldn't turn around. If he looked, they would likely drain him of his sanity to look at. A loud guttural growl emanated from behind him from the entire group.

"Fuck all of you!" Travis yelled as he forced himself to run faster.

The flashing light got brighter as he felt like he was getting closer to it. Soon he saw a small shape that the light was coming from. He stopped when he saw it was a flashlight. He picked it up and pointed it at the army of stick figures causing them all to freeze in place. He was catching his breath as he weighed his options. It was either sit here and keep the stick figures at bay or use the flashlight to light his way out of the tunnel. Never in his life did he think he would be chased by a child's drawing.

His breath shuddered as the air around him got cold. He felt an intimidating presence behind him. He knew if he turned around with the flashlight in hand the stick figures would be able to move, but if he didn't turn around, he wouldn't know what was behind him. He weighed his options before making a decision.

Vinessa woke up in a farmhouse, but not the one she had been taken to in the van. This farmhouse looked new and very much intact. When she sat up an older woman looked in the door at her before yelling for her husband. Her voice was one of experience and age. Her husband's voice that called back sounded of the same age. As the older woman entered the room, she was followed by her husband who carried a platter of food.

"Here young one eats up." The old woman spoke with a smile that showed enough lines to measure all of her years of laughter.

"Where am I?" Vinessa asked looking around at the room.

"You are on Merry Gold Farm young lady." The old man's voice was gruff and coarse with each word.

"Thank you." Vinessa said in a voice that was barely above a whisper.

"We found you passed out in the woods. The demon tried to take you, but my husband here saved you from it. That damn thing has been terrorizing us for years. We couldn't take you to the hospital, so we brought you here and called the doc to make a house call. He covered up some cuts you had on your feet." The old lady sat sitting in a chair near the door.

"We will open our home to you, but don't panic if you see or hear the ghosts at night. Our house has been haunted since we got it twenty years ago." The old man said.

Vinessa stopped eating long enough to nod her head in agreement. She hasn't felt kindness like this since her brother saved her from her stepfather and a couple of her exes. They left the room to let her finish eating, and she did that with glee. She ate for about an hour before sneaking down the stairs to bring her dishes to the sink. Remained silent enough for the old lady to not take her eyes off of the daytime show she was watching. She thought of the encounter she had before blacking out while she washed the dishes she had eaten off of. She looked down to see shadows swimming in the water. Falling back in fear it made a loud crashing noise.

"My dear is you okay?" The old lady asked moving with a mother's speed.

"Yes. I just thought I saw a spider." Vinessa tried to laugh it off.

"I will handle washing the dishes, you go rest in the living room." The old lady gave her a smile.

Vinessa looked on with a face of horror as black hands pulled themselves out of the sink. She tried to get the old lady to go watch TV with her, but she refused. No matter what Vinessa said she wouldn't listen. She intended on being a gracious hostess. Her heart was pounding as the hands tried to weakly reach for the old woman's neck. A ringing started in Vinessa's ear as the hands grew in number and slithered around each other.

"Go rest dear. I promise it is okay for me to wash these." The old lady gave her a smile then turned to now black and hand infested water.

Vinessa walked out to find the old man when she saw a trail of blood. She followed into the barn where she found the old man eating his own arm. Behind him was a pair of eyes. The only thing that existed at this point was the sounds of the old man tearing into his own flesh, and those fucking eyes. A laugh echoed around the barn, but it didn't come from the old man. It came from everywhere at one time. She turned to run back to the house when the old man's body was thrown past her, his head turned backwards.

"You have been a bad girl." A voice echoed in both of her ears at one time as she ran for the house.

She yelled for the old woman as she entered the door she was hit with a shock. The old woman struggled against the sink full of water as hands overlapped behind her head non-stop. Her screams only came as bubbles. When she stopped fighting and went blue, she was dropped to the floor. As her limp body came to rest Garton came from the top of the steps shaking his head.

"You made me do this. If you wouldn't have been such a bad girl, they could have lived." He said as he approached her.

He pulled out his phone and dialed 911. When she tried to stop him, he hit her so hard she fell to the ground. She saw his mouth move as he talked to someone on the other end of the line. When he vanished, she went still in shock and sat in the chair that once held the older woman. She turned on the TV and waited. Sitting for two hours when the blue lights from the police cars as they pulled in. All that could be heard was them yelling as the door was kicked in and all of the flashlights became trained on her.

"I am coming willingly, so you don't need the cuffs. I don't need a lawyer, just know the demons of this house did it." Vinessa said as she sat down in the car to the surprise of the police force.

She was driven to a mental hospital about twelve miles away from the farmhouse. When she got there the police committed her until her court hearing. Most of her time was spent doing nothing for about a week when they took her to the courthouse only to be taken back to the hospital. When she was told that she wouldn't get out even getting out of the hospital it would only lead to jail. She accepted the ruling because she knew no one believed her. She will just stick to her story to stay in the hospital. Prison was not a place she wanted to go after the stories she had heard.

"Do I make myself clear Ms. Marvic?" The judge asked her in a commanding voice.

"Yes, your Honor." Vinessa said just before being escorted out.

She was taken back to the hospital where she was given her permanent room.

Chapter 29: My Friend Dan

"Vinessa it is time for lunch." A lady said appearing in the door.

"Okay, I have to go Dan." Vinessa said to the stick figure drawn on the wall of her room.

Vinessa pranced into the lunchroom greeting anyone and everyone there. She was happy to be in a place where she wouldn't have to worry about Garton and Valieen. It was somewhere she felt safe. The only thing that worried her was thinking about what her brother was doing. She wanted him to be safe and hopefully come to see her. Her lunch was a cheeseburger and fries–her favorite meal–the moment it touched her plate she clapped.

"I wish Dan could see this beautiful meal." She took one bite and a huge smile stretched across her face.

"Who is Dan Vinessa?" The golden-haired girl beside her asked.

"He is my best friend that watches over me while I sleep." Her smile only got bigger the more she talked about him.

"I have one of those also, but he lives in the ground now." She smiled at the ground and broke out into a laugh rocking back then forward.

"You seem so happy for your friend." Vinessa smiled at the girl.

The girl just continued to rock back and forth till an orderly made her stop. When he got her to stop, he shot a glare at Vinessa who raised her hands to the sky. A bell rang to end their lunch time and Vinessa wasted no time going back to talk to her new friend. She ran into her room and did a baseball slide to the wall that her friend Dan was drawn on. It made her smile to see Dan each day.

"You missed it Dan. We had cheeseburgers and fries. I want to know how she knew that was my favorite meal?" The more she talked the more she began to glow with happiness.

"*I also wonder how as well Vinessa.*"

"We will figure it out one day Dan." She smiled pushing the thought to the back of her mind.

"*Yes, we will Vinessa. I hope you have been having fun today.*"

"Oh, yes Dan very much so. I have, I have." Vinessa clapped her hands to this statement.

"*Good I am so glad something could sweeten you.*"

"You know Dan I heard you say that before, but never asked why you say it that way." Vinessa looked at the drawing on the wall with a curiosity.

"*It just means something has made you happy.*"

"Oh, I just didn't understand what it was. Being the fact, I have only lived in two places I guess I just didn't get a chance to hear new things." Vinessa giggled a little.

"*Did anything else happen? I am assuming not cause you spend most of your time here with me.*"

Vinessa sat and pondered what Dan had just told her. It made her think back on how she has spent the past three days in her room talking to Dan. Did she spend too much time in her room? Sure, she talked to him most of the day, but it was something she enjoyed. She smiled knowing that he cared enough to make her think about it.

"Dan, I know I spend a lot of time talking to you, but it is my choice to talk to you that much." Vinessa crossed her arms and huffed at the drawing on her wall.

"I am just saying that you should make at the least one real friend."

"You're as real as I need." She put her arms out and pressed her chest against the wall in a way of hugging Dan.

"You know what I mean Vinessa."

"You have no eyes, but I know you are rolling them." Vinessa said, rolling her own eyes.

"Go, go make at the very least one other friend."

"Ugh fine I will go make one other friend." Vinessa said heading into the rec room.

She walked to the blonde girl playing chess by herself. She would play one move for one color switch sides and do it again. Vinessa watched on in curiosity. The girl saw her and approached.

"It is you, the girl with the friend that lives on the wall." The girl said getting close to Vinessa.

"Yes, it is me." Vinessa followed up with a laugh.

"Is your friend okay?" The girl asked the lights giving her blue eyes an extra layer of beauty.

"He is okay. Can I be your friend as well?" Vinessa asked.

"Yes, yes you can." The girl jumped up and down clapping.

Vinessa skipped back to her room with a smile on her face. She sat back down in front of Dan and just stared at him. She got a worried look on her face when he didn't talk to her right away. She tapped the stick figure on the wall. She tapped it a little harder, her face growing red.

"Yes Vinessa?"

"I thought you died on me." Vinessa let out a sigh of relief.

"I can't die."

"Oh yeah, I forgot you drank a potion that stops that from happening." She laughed.

"Yes, when you gave us that castle."

"Yes, we had a lot of fun that day." Vinessa laughed at the memories.

Vinessa let out a yawn and passed a look at her bed. She thought about laying down for the day till she looked at Dan. He sat in silence against the wall with knowing eyes. She wanted to know what he was looking at. She got up and went back to the rec room. When she got there everyone was gone, but it wasn't just the patients. The entire building was empty from room to room. She couldn't think clearly as she walked around. It was like the building was filled with fog, but only for her. She walked back to her room to find Dan sitting on her bed looking through the books she kept next to her bed.

"D-D-Dan how are you sitting on the bed like that?" Vinessa asked, hiding in her doorway.

"I am real, but only within your head. That is where we are right now."

Vinessa gave Dan a smile before skipping over to the bed beside her friend. She looked at him closely as she got closer. He went from being a simple drawing into being a knight in armor worthy of the kings themselves. The sight of him being in his "true" form made her smile. She couldn't see past his helmet to his face, she knew he was smiling.

"I knew something was strange about the building when I walked out there." Vinessa said, rubbing her chin.

"Yes, dear it is strange."

"Do you know why we are here?" Vinessa asked, perking up looking at Dan.

"Well, you fell asleep leaning against the wall. I do think it is time to wake up. You have work to do before your brother arrives."

"Oh, Travis is coming!" Vinessa began to cheer.

"You bet he is, and he will bring you ice cream like he normally does."

"I can't wait, I love ice cream!" Her voice had a shriek to it this time.

She got up and jumped around in excitement. It was a happiness she hadn't felt since she had gotten into the hospital a week ago. While she was jumping around, she tripped over her books. She let out a scream of pain while rolling around on the ground. She had gotten shaken out of her mind by orderlies that come to restrain her from hurting herself. It was like a storm of blues and whites as her vision came back to her. She felt a pain in her wrist as an orderly twisted what looked like a pen out of her hand. Many of them had been men yelling for her to *"Drop the fucking pen!"* When she did finally drop it everything began to settle down.

"I am sorry, I got excited because Dan said that my brother would come and bring me ice cream!" She yelled in her excited voice.

"Vinessa, Dan isn't real." One of the orderlies said in a soft voice.

"Yes, he is, he is right over there." Vinessa said, pointing at the wall.

What Vinessa didn't realize was that the stick man that was on the wall was no longer there. The orderlies tried to explain to her that he wasn't on the wall anymore. Vinessa fought with the orderlies with every word they spoke. Eventually they got her restrained to her bed and a nurse gave her a shot. It was a shot that she had gotten before, and she hated the shot. It made her feel sleepy and sick. She tried to fight it, but she lost and slipped into sleep.

"Honey, he may be real to you, but we can't see him." The nurse said right before Vinessa fell fully into sleep.

Chapter 30: No Ice cream

Travis decided to take a risk to turn and run around no matter what was behind him. When he turned he discovered nothing was behind him, so he ran. He ran as fast as he could hearing the stampede behind him. He kept running until he started running out of breath. He started to regain hope as the smell of fresh air hit his nose.

"I can't give up!" He yelled as he ran.

The air started to get a hint of blood to its smell as a light showed up. He kept running even as his hope began to run low. He could see the stick figures moving in around him, but he didn't stop. He jumped to the light, even without seeing what was on the other side. As he did, he shot up in his bed at home within his home. He looked around the room with his heart beating against the inside of his chest.

"How did I get into my bed?" Travis asked himself to look around.

He inspected the dust that had collected on everything when he spotted it. He saw a stick figure painted in the corner of his room. It wasn't big enough to be seen upon general inspection. It was like it was trying to hide in the corner of the room itself. He walked over to it and could feel its evil when he put his hand next to it. He didn't know why it appeared in his dream, but he also didn't know why he was afraid of it. It made him feel so silly to be scared of a stick figure.

"I don't know why, but you scare the shit out of me." Travis said chuckling at the very sentence.

"May be it is because I am already in your fucking head!"

The voice came out of nowhere as an invisible force shoved him into the wall. He scrambled to his feet and ran out the door hitting the wall hard as he did. He was breathing heavy as cracks formed on the wall accompanied by loud booming footsteps that shook the foundation of the house. He ran for a closet to hide in. He knew this thing wouldn't let him out of the house.

"Come out, Come out you little bastard. Come out and let me give you your medicine." The voice shook the very walls themselves.

To Travis it felt like the voice of a God. His heart could be felt in his ears from his fear. Backing as far from the door as he could get, fear crawled down his spine. He was hoping that this was just another layer to his dream, but this felt all too real. It probably wouldn't help but keep checking the things around him to make sure it was the real world. He saw a shelf filled with food, a broom, a mop, drinks. His mind began to race the more he realized it was all real and he was not dreaming. A breath escaped that he didn't realize he was holding when the loud footsteps had gone. Exiting the closet only after he heard the bedroom door shut.

He slowly walked toward the front door hoping his feet wouldn't land too heavy. He made it to the door only to find the door handle stuck. In his mind he was cursing himself for not being able to get out. He took several steps back, and then ran shoulder first through the door. He heard it crack, but it didn't break. He repeated the action, as it broke away, he felt a mix of satisfaction and pain. He watched the door hoping to see the thing that was chasing him, but all he saw was a small stick figure above the door. The sight of it made his body freeze.

"Fuck this shit." Travis said, running to his car.

As he got in the first thing, he did was search his car for a stick figure. When he didn't find one, he let out a sigh of relief. He started his car almost immediately a call came from the hospital. Before he answered it, he pulled over into a parking lot.

"*Is this Travis Marvic?*" A doctor asked on the other side of the call.

"Yes, this is Travis. May I ask what this is about?" Travis had a hint of suspicion in his voice.

"*It is your mother. She passed away this evening. She left a message for you.*"

"What was the message?" Travis said with tears being able to be heard in his voice.

"*It was a bit strange, but she said the shadows made her sick. I don't want to lie to you, but she was in severe pain when she died. It happened out of nowhere. I am sorry.*" The doctor sounded as if her death hit his soul.

Travis hit the end call button before collapsing against his steering wheel. Tears ran from his eyes like a day of nothing but rain. He started hitting his steering wheel throwing his tears against the window. He let out screams of primal pain. He could feel his heart breaking in his chest. In his mind he had failed her because he told her that he was coming to be with her.

"Fuck!" Travis's face turned red as tears and snot ran down his face.

He got out of his car to try to get air. As he tried to stand on his feet, they gave out on him. He hit the ground hard enough to knock the air out of him. He found himself on the ground with his tears dry and mind covered in shadows. His staggered breathing fell away into a laughter that was fueled by loss and madness. His head laid back against his car as his laughter got louder once again causing tears to flow.

"Why do I fuck up everything I come in contact with!" He yelled it to the skies hoping to get an answer, but only to get none.

He sat staring at the sky as rain began to fall upon him in a thick unending sheet. This caused him to laugh to himself. He didn't feel a need to put effort into getting out of the rain as he got to his feet. He shook his head as he got back into his car.

"I gave God my pain and all he had fucking given me was rain to hide the tears I shed." Travis said, laying his seat back to fall asleep.

Vinessa woke up to a padded room where a tray was slid under the door holding waffles and eggs. She licked her lips, but as she did it only showed her how thirsty she was. She wanted to yell out till she felt that it hurt to even breathe. She crawled over to the food still feeling the effects of the drugs the nurse gave her. The world around her felt hazy and seemed to swirl around her.

"Thank–You." Vinessa managed to croak the words out.

She began to eat like she had never eaten before. She saw a window and knocked on it frantically. When no one answered she kept knocking on the window. Someone finally opened the window with a sour look on their face.

"What do you want?" The question sounded aggressive.

"I was just wondering if I could have some orange juice or water please." Vinessa put in her request with a smile on her face.

"As long as you have calmed down." The orderly gained a small smile on his face.

"I have, I swear it." She raised her hand while she said it.

Before she knew it the slot opened back up and through it the orderly handed her a cup of water. She felt a little disappointed, but it gave her the hydration she needed. She smiled at the door as she returned the cup and tray. She turned around feeling a familiar energy. In the corner of the room was Dan, but this time he was curiously smaller than normal. It was like he was trying to hide from anyone that was not Vinessa.

"Dan, what are you doing here?" Vinessa whispered to the stick man on the wall.

"I am here because you are here."

"Man, I am so glad you never leave my side." Vinessa smiled at the *lifeless* figure.

"I would never leave you alone, Vinessa."

The more she looked at him the more Dan looked different. The figure now looked crudely drawn on the wall. It was like he was ripped from the place on her wall in her room and thrown on this one. She was starting to wonder if her friend was feeling okay or if someone hurt him. It was the energy that came off of him that made her keep her mouth shut. He felt different from when they had been in her room talking.

"What are we going to do, Dan. This room is kind of empty." Vinessa said with a nervous smile on her face.

"You need to kill him so we can leave this room."

"But if I kill him, they will call the police on me." Vinessa said her voice held a sense of concern about the situation.

"Then put me through the slot on the door."

"Fine, but I don't know what you are going to do." Vinessa said using her fingernails to pick at the wall around him.

"Good girl."

Vinessa picked at the wall until her fingernails started to bleed. She got a look of determination as the wall started to come apart. She bit her tongue to overcome the pain that she felt in her fingers. She grew a smile as blood slowly went down her throat and oozed from her fingertips. Dan told her what would happen in her dreams last night. It was strange to her that he had said it, but she trusts Dan with all her heart. She tore at it till she finally got it off. She handed the piece of padded wall to the orderly outside. As the window closed from the outside screams began to echo through the halls as someone's voice over the intercom yelling for everyone to lock the doors. Vinessa heard her door open as red lights flashed above.

What opened the door was not the Dan she used to know. It shook its head as it saw her rocking in the center of the room surrounded by stickmen drawn all over the walls in blood. She had a mad smile stretched across her face. She laughed as she saw all of the blood that covered the walls outside. Dan extended a handout to her, and she took it without a second thought. In Vinessa's mind he was her protector still; he was the one for her.

"Come you poor creature. Let us get you out of here."

"Yes, let us get out of here my prince." Vinessa spoke with a smile and skipped as they walked out of the hospital.

Travis stirred as a knock came across his driver side window. He rolled over and looked at the window to see a police officer. He sat up to roll the window down when he saw his eyes. His eyes flipped between a burning orange and brown each time he blinked. Travis shook his head when a real human passed through the police officer that was standing at his window already.

"Can you please roll the window down sir." The officer said from outside the car.

"Yes, sir I can." Travis said before rolling down his window.

"I was asked to check on you and make sure you are okay. I ran your plate and saw that you are a veteran. Do you have a place to go? I know this country has lost its care for the people that protect it." The officer had a genuine look of concern for Travis.

"Yes, I do have a home, but I pulled over for a nap. I guess I didn't realize how tired I was." Travis laughed this fact off.

"I am not going to write you a ticket, but I will say please be careful." The officer said before shaking Travis's hand and leaving.

Travis drove to his therapy office where Dr. Marron works. He had one thing to do before looking for his sister. He has to do it because he knows that Dr. Marron had something to do with it. As his car came to a stop in the parking lot his eyes glazed over with anger and revenge. He got out of his car and waited for Dr. Marron to leave his office. After an hour Travis stopped the doctor short of his car.

"Come with me, now." Travis said grabbing Dr. Marron by the arm.

"Where are we going you son of a bitch?" Dr. Marron asked.

"It doesn't fuck matter you fucking traitor." Travis said filled with anger as they pulled out of the parking lot.

"You have no fucking reason to take me anywhere." Dr. Marron said with his voice rising in volume.

"You say that, but I remember you putting a goddamn dart in my chest." Travis said putting his fist into the doctor's side.

The doctor doubled over in pain as Travis continued to drive to an unknown destination. Travis dropped a heavy-handed fist into the back of the doctor's head knocking him out. Travis drove for hours till he saw a canyon off the side of the road and decided that it would be just as good a spot as any. He drug the doctor out of the car and threw water on his face.

"What the fuck!" Dr. Marron yelled jerking awake.

"It is time for you to defend yourself mother fucker." Travis yelled throwing the doctor a knife.

The doctor picked the knife up with trembling hands. As he stood Travis took the stance he was trained to use in the military. The doctor charged at Travis who caught him under the arms and threw him onto the ground. The doctor rolled over in a pain that wrote itself on his face.

"Get the fuck up and face me goddamn it!" Travis yelled as tears of anger formed in his eyes which mixed with sweat as they worked down his face.

"Why do you care about her so goddamn much?" Dr. Marron screamed out as sweat dripped from his face.

Travis grabbed a handful of the doctor's hair and drug him to the side of the canyon. He held his head over the edge forcing the doctor to look at the bottom. He threw the doctor to the side and walked to his car. When Travis walked back holding a book titled *"rEVILaion"*.

"You see this book I have carried it with me ever since I got into the military. She gave it to me to remember her by. I will continue to carry it with me till I get her back." Travis yelled his hair sticking to his forehead.

The doctor tried to charge Travis again who threw him on his back once more. When the doctor turned to Travis, he found a gun barrel meeting him at eye level. He grabbed it with both hands and pulled it to meet his forehead. The doctor smiled while looking at Travis.

"I won't tell you a goddamn thing." Dr. Marron laughed.

"Fine then, suffer." Travis said shooting the doctor in his knees.

Chapter 31: Falling To Pieces

Travis drove to the church he and Father David had met at his first time back in North Carolina. When he got there, he could feel the emptiness that has been left behind from Father David dying. He walked within and collapsed into the pew closest to the exit. He placed his head on the one in front and closed his eyes. He hoped that this time the demon won't mess with him.

"Dear Lord, please help me through this as I try to find my sister. She is the only family I have left." Travis whispered to himself.

He sat in silence hoping that someone would actually answer him. He knew no one would, but he still held hope. When nothing happened, he got to his feet and went to the Father's old office. In honor of him the church left everything as it was. He looked around and someone was still bringing him spread sheets of how the church was doing. It brought a smile to Travis's face, but he couldn't help himself. He sat in the Father's chair and cried.

"I am sorry I couldn't save you." Travis said picking up a picture of the Father, Vinessa, and himself.

He didn't hear a word, but around him he could feel a comforting presence around him. It was like Father David was giving him a hug from the afterlife. His tears seemed to stop as this feeling made him smile. He lowered his head and laughed quietly.

"Thank you, father." Travis said with a smile.

He looked around the office one last time as he started to walk out. He heard a door open above him causing him to go back to the office and shut the door. He felt for the lock on the doorknob finding it just as someone grabbed it on the other side. His breath quickened as a voice spoke to him.

"Travis, I know you are in there. It is Sister Mary." The voice was soft and familiar to him.

"Name something you would remember from our time here when I was younger." Travis said just wanting to make sure it was her.

"When you had come on your seventh birthday you wished for your family to get better. You said that when you father got drunk one night and beat your mother." The voice was rich with sympathy for him.

He unlocked the door for her, and she stepped in. She was a small frail lady with grey hair and liver spots. She smiled at him when she saw him. The way she looked at him was like he hadn't aged a day to her. He smiled back to her, but it didn't send the same message. His smile was a hollow one.

"You have grown so much Travis, have you told your parents your secret yet?" She spoke with a I know everything tone.

"What secret?" Travis asked Sister Mary.

"The fact that you enjoy the love of boys and had your eye on that young Garett boy." Sister Mary said with a smile on her face.

"How did you know that?" Travis asked confused by her knowing this information.

"I knew when you were a child. God told me." Her smile seemed to only get bigger.

"Well, I am glad that you don't hold it against me." Travis said smiling.

"You must save her Travis." Sister Mary said in a raised volume.

"What?" Travis said confused.

"I said of course I didn't hold it against you." She said her smile normal again.

"I am glad that some people understand that not everyone is the same." Travis said turning around to get his cup of water.

When he turned around Sister Mary was gone, but the door had not opened. He looked around for her in every inch of the church but found nothing. He started to think his mind was playing tricks on him again before pulling out his phone. He typed in her full name which was Mary Williams. He found her name on a local news sight in the obituary tab.

"I guess I am talking to ghosts again." Travis laughed as he ran his fingers through his hair.

Travis walked out and turned around one last time and saw Father David standing with Sister Mary. They both waved at him as he left. He gave a small wave back as he shut the door behind him. As he got into his car, he looked at his sister's favorite book. He opened it and began reading it.

"This is rEVILation, she called it a book about taking your destiny and making it yours." He said to himself laughing.

He never understood why she read it so much. Even as he read it, the question stayed in his mind. He didn't hate the book, but he guesses that he just doesn't see the message that she does when she reads it. He closed the book and put it back under the passenger seat. He turned the car's ignition and drove off to a restaurant that was nearby. He entered the restaurant only to see the ghosts of his past again. He walked past the table he met Garett at when he confessed his love to him. He almost stopped because he thought he saw him sitting there.

"Damn." It was the only word Travis could think of.

He ordered his normal meal, but he found himself unable to enjoy it like normal. He paid and walked out feeling worse for eating there. He looked back through his messages to see one asking him to come by a lawyer's office to settle his mother's will. Travis went by and entered a depressing waiting room. He couldn't tell if it was the color of the paint or the fact it is a law office. He waited until a short fat man with a comb-over called out his name.

"In this office here please." The short man guided Travis into the first office from the door.

"What all do I need to sign sir?" Travis asked him as they sat down.

"It is all formalities that will acknowledge that you inherited all of her worldly belongings." The man said pulling out papers.

"Does my sister get anything?" Travis asked confused.

"Your sister is mentally unable to accept any of her estate." The short man slid the papers to Travis.

"How would you know? She has been missing for two weeks." Travis was confused at how he knew more about his sister then Travis did.

"Your sister was sent to a mental hospital after murdering an elderly couple." The short man said to him handing him a pen.

"That doesn't sound like her, but do you know which hospital it is?" Travis asked signing the papers and sliding them back to the man.

"I don't, but my best advice is getting everything settled at your mother's house. After you get some rest the place for this district that controls the hospitals is two towns over." The short man said sliding the keys to Travis.

Travis nodded before leaving for his mother's house. As he pulled up the sun was dipping below the horizon. He went inside and was met with the smell of mothballs and his mom's perfume. He started to clean starting with the couch. He decided that is where he wanted to sleep till the house was fully cleaned out. As he picked up her clothes and meds, he felt weak. The reality of everything hit him hard. He took a deep breath and leaned back. A feminine hand laid on both his shoulders and a voice came to him.

"My son why are you so sad?" His mother's voice asked him.

"I have lost everyone. I don't know where Vinessa is, Garett is gone, Father David has been killed, I even failed to see you." Travis couldn't fight the tears as he spoke.

He fell into tears and wails of pain as he fell forward his head fell into someone's chest. It smelled like his mother's perfume, but a younger version of her. She stroked his hair as he cried. Eventually she laid him down on the couch, but when he turned to look at her, she was gone. He decided sleeping was the best course of action.

"No matter what, you tried your best." He heard his mother's voice one last time before he fell asleep.

He awoke the next day to someone knocking on the door. He checked the clock and saw it was noon. He had never slept till noon before. He got up and answered the door.

"Hello?" Travis said followed by a yawn.

"Hello, I am Casey. I am answering your ad for a needed roommate. I know the ad said a few days, but I am also here to help you clean the house." Casey said with a smile on her face.

"I didn't post an ad." Travis said confused.

"I know. Your mom did, and she said to tell you that everything will be okay." Casey said ending it with a hug.

Chapter 32: Unknown Friends

Casey entered the house like she had been there before. She immediately got started cleaning up stuff around the house with a smile on her face. Travis shrugged and started helping clean the house with her. She exited the house and got boxes out of her trunk. It shocked him how prepared she was.

"I wanted to make sure that we could store everything that you didn't want to keep." Casey said her smile not fading one bit.

"I would like to save as much as I can." Travis said building up one of the boxes.

"We will do that, because she was a sweet lady that needs to be remembered." Casey said her smile falling to a look of melancholy.

"Are you okay?" Travis asked putting a hand on her shoulder.

"Yes, I am okay. It is just your mom used to teach in a class I had to sit in with." Casey had tears start to form, but only one fell when a smile formed.

"I remember her sending a letter about that before she quit sending me letters." Travis said holding an unfinished letter addressed to him.

He folded the letter and put it into a lockbox his mother had lying around. He was surprised to see many letters in the box that had been addressed to go to his unit. A note laid on top that said:

I am sorry my son. I know you will find this after my death. I meant to send these to you, but the chemo treatments have me beaten down. I even had to take a break from teaching. I hate that I have become this. I love teaching, and I already know you will think I hate you. I swear son if you do think that please know that I don't hate you.

I have come over the years to understand that I am here for letting you go to jail. It is my punishment. I have made my piece with death. I hope to see you at my last moments, but if you are not it is okay. I know you will take care of my home. This is your home now; I will be watching over you. I love you, Mom.

Travis put the note back with the letters feeling that it belonged with them. He felt his eyes becoming misty from looking at the letters. He was shaken back to reality by Casey putting a hand on his shoulder. He looked at her as she embraced him in her arms. It has been a long time since anyone has hugged him like this. It was causing him to feel a happiness that left him long ago. He let her hold him until she let go of him with a smile.

"I do feel I need to warn you that I am a very private person with stuff I keep in my room. Please knock when we get these rooms cleaned out. Till then, I have PJs and can sleep in my car." Her smile came back to her with this statement.

"No, you can sleep on the pull-out bed, I will take up the floor with a sleeping bag." Travis said as he went to his car.

While he was gone Casey began to prepare the pull-out bed along with finding a movie. Travis was surprised at how much seeing her sitting on the pull out reminded him of movie night when he was younger. It brought back memories of hiding under the covers from the aliens and zombies. He couldn't believe he forgot till now, but it had been so long ago. Casey was quick enough to turn and see the soft smile that had formed on his face. When he saw that she was looking he fell back into his pit of sorrow.

"So, would you like pizza?" Travis asked unrolling his sleeping bag on the floor near the kitchen.

"Yeah, sure we can get pizza." Casey said for the first time sounding awkward since she arrived.

"Okay let me order it. What kind do you eat?" Travis asked with on foot outside the front door.

"I will eat anything so order something you like." Casey said as dragons roared on the TV when she finally settled on a movie.

"Okay, pepperoni it is." He said stepping out the door dialing a nearby pizza shop.

Casey fell into her own thoughts. She worried whether Travis could tell how nervous she was or if he didn't like her being around already. The big thing was that she could never get rid of these thoughts. It was an issue that has haunted her since she was a young person–not that she is old. She noticed Travis coming back in, so she tried to look normal.

"The pizza will be here in a few. Till it gets here I am going to clean." Travis smiled and went to the kitchen.

"I will clean in here, so we aren't so suffocated." Casey chimed with a perky sound to her voice.

They began putting boxes in his mom's old room which was the largest in the house. It started to feel like they had more breathing room as each box was put away. Just as the seventh box of the evening was put away the doorbell rang. Casey looked at Travis with a hunger in her eyes and dropped the box to sprint to the door. He had never seen someone run for a pizza like that. We she brought it back in Travis couldn't stop the smile from forming on his face. Casey sat on the pull-out bed and patted beside her sitting the pizza beside her on the bed.

"Let us eat!" Casey yelled and clapped.

"Yes, I am coming." Travis said sitting down the box he had been holding.

They ate while laughing at the movie that had come on the TV. The night wore on bringing joy to Travis. It wasn't that kind of joy that you feel in your heart. She genuinely made him a happy person, but to him she was a great friend. Casey knew what she wanted and held hope this got her one step closer to her goal. She passed out halfway through their third movie pick. Travis tucked her in the bed before laying down himself.

Travis fell asleep within five minutes after laying down. His nightmares started to set in about ten minutes into his sleep. They took him back to war again and again. Each one took place within a different battle. From the outside looking in Casey just saw him jerking violently dripping with sweat and crying. She knew she was invading his space, but she couldn't help herself. She laid in the floor and held him close till it all stopped. When he finally calmed down, she started to get up to leave. As she moved his hand caught her, but he was still fast asleep. She decided to lay back down and sleep.

"What happened?" Travis said his vision still foggy looking around to find Casey's arm laying across him with a smile on her face.

"Good morning. I guess I should explain?" Casey asked sitting up to stretch.

"If you would like to." Travis said finally stretching himself.

"You had been having nightmares, and I felt like it would help you if I held you." Casey said shying away pulling her knees up to her chest.

"Thank you for doing that. It wasn't something you needed to do for me." Travis said standing as he checked the time.

"It was something I wanted to do. We need to get this place cleaned up some more." Casey jumped to her feet as energy flew through her.

They started packing more boxes as each one slowly worked its way into his mom's room. Casey was putting away boxes from within the room she would be taking when she found a baby book. She couldn't fight her impulse and started to look through the pictures. She giggled and laughed as she saw pictures of Travis sitting with his chubby cheeks in a shocked look as the camera flashed. Her personal favorite was one when his mom took a picture of Travis running in his white underpants.

"What are you looking at?" Travis asked before stopping short of Casey holding the picture filled book.

"Well, I guess you see that I found your mom's collection of embarrassing pictures of you. That I will never give back to you." Casey said in a playful tone of voice.

"I do see that in your hands right there, but can I take it off of your hands." Travis said as he tried to grabbed it taking it from her hands with force.

Casey blocked him from it as they both tripped back her landing on top of him as she pushed him. They both locked eyes causing the world to fall away only leaving the two of them. She quickly backed up quickly as she caught her body doing something on its own. She dropped the photo book beside Travis and said something that couldn't be understood as she ran out the door.

"What was that all about?" Travis asked himself as he grabbed the photo book.

He could hear footsteps walking up to him, and the bare feet was familiar to him. He looked up to see his mom standing there again. She didn't look very happy, but this time her spirit looked weaker than the first time she came to him. She wavered in and out of being seen by his eyes.

"You need to keep her close. I am not telling you to date her or love her. She spent months telling me how much she cared about you. She also promised me that she would take care of you. Please let her keep her promise." His mom said in a voice that seemed to fall out of reality.

"I am sorry for my thoughts!" Casey yelled as she walked through his mother's spirit and collapsed into his lap crying.

"Hey, it is okay." Travis said trying to comfort her his hands still gripping the book in his hands tight to himself.

"It isn't okay, I need to be honest with you before my thoughts destroy the dynamic in this house. You just need to promise me that you won't hold this against me or let it ruin the chances for us to form a friendship." Casey said clearing away her tears as she made contact with him.

"I promise nothing you say will destroy our ability to be friends." Travis said smiling not sure if he could believe his words.

"I have loved you since I saw you in school. I changed my clothing and my hair to try to catch your attention since my smarts didn't work. When you left for the military, I let myself fall back into the background. I told your mother I would protect you and be here for you. I made that promise after being her teacher aid and friend for two very happy years in my life." Casey said sitting back with her feet under her.

"See, I didn't get bothered by that. Thank you for telling me that. Let's go watch some more movies. We have plenty of time to clean." Travis said helping her back to his feet.

He doesn't know why but her confession made him feel strange inside. It made him feel the same strange feelings that he got when Garett sold himself to that monster that was hunting Travis just for one more day. It made him shiver when he sat on the couch after putting the bed away and she put her feet pointing towards him. She looked uncomfortable being curled in a ball in the corner of the couch. He couldn't help himself as he spoke up.

"I can move to another chair to let you lay down." Travis said looking at her with a smile on his face.

"No, it is okay I don't want to make you any more uncomfortable than I have already." Casey said looking back at the TV flipping through the channels.

"Then let me do this for you." Travis said pulling her feet into his lap forcing her to lay down fully on the couch.

She looked at him giving a playfully annoyed look then she was right back at flipping through the TV channels.

Travis became lost in his thoughts thinking about was what happened to Garett and Valieen. He was worried if they knew where he was right now and living in his mother's house with a woman's legs stretched across his lap. His stomach filled with anxiety.

*   *   *

"So, Dan where are we going to go first?" Vinessa asked the stick man that has become engraved on her arm.

"*We are going to have some fun around here.*" Dan's voice had an evil chuckle to it.

"Okie dokie!" Vinessa yelled skipping down the road with a lighter in her hand.

She skipped to a nearby store and went inside tucking the lighter into her pocket. It was a locally owned shop that had no cameras inside or outside. She walked straight to the back of the store where they keep racks upon racks of clothing. She pulled the lighter out of her pocket and started lighting the clothes on fire. As the flames caught the rest of the clothes she ran into the bathroom.

"I lit the clothes on fire like you wanted Dan!" Vinessa yelled looking into the mirror seeing Dan standing behind her in his true form.

"*Let us now leave.*" Dan gestured to the wall as a portal appeared which they both stepped through.

The entire building burned as Vinessa walked through a deep cut of woods only turning around to watch the building burn. People scrambled around trying to keep the fire from spreading to other buildings. This panic caused Vinessa to break down in a fit of laughter and joy. She pointed while looking at Dan who was now pasted on a tree that was beside her. She felt like she was fed by the pain and shock that each and every person felt as they ran around below her.

"Look at them trying so hard to hold their fragile lives together!" Vinesa laughed at the top of her lungs.

"Yes, it truly is one of the most beautiful sites I have ever seen."

As people started running up the hills Dan vanished from the tree and appeared on Vinessa's neck. Vinessa turned and ran from the scene trying her best to stay hidden. So far, she has the idea that people think she was murdered along with everyone else that lived in the hospital she was housed in. She had no plans on being caught anytime soon. She was too fast and disappeared within a forest that had an all-consuming feel to about it.

Chapter 33: The Girl With An Inferno In Her Eyes

Pillars of smoke cast ash across the sky visible for miles as Vinessa makes her way from the town she just set on fire. She held her hand out as ash began to rain from above her. She looked at it with curiosity. As she thought back this is the first-time seeing ash in this big of a flake. She felt a satisfaction with seeing the flake of ash. She continued down the road being careful to stay out of sight. Dan told her it was a game for them to play. He said it was like hide- and -seek, but if she got caught more people would die. She didn't like seeing Dan kill people.

"Dan I am starting to get better at this hiding thing." Vinessa said with a smile on her face.

"*Yes, you are my fair princess, but stay good or else I will have to kill.*"

"Oh no we can't be killing people anymore." Vinessa said her smile dropping a small amount.

"*That part will be decided by your ability to stay out of sight. Remember they want to take you away from me.*"

"I plan on being good at following your rules." Vinessa said as she dropped into a bush.

A phone she had taken began to vibrate in her pocket. When she pulled it out the local government had put out an alert which meant they had found the bodies and her cell empty with her nowhere to be found. It claimed she had killed everyone there. Only she knew the truth of everything that had happened. She broke the phone then tossed it into the river that cut the forest behind her. She followed the riverbank for three miles before cutting a ninety degree right turn away from the river. She knew doing this would distract search teams unless they have dogs with them.

"I think we will be fine." Vinessa said more so to herself.

"Yes, we will, because I will protect you from anyone who tries to hurt you."

"So, why do we have to kill all of these people again?" Vinessa asked taking a seat on a nearby rock.

"It is the only way I can bring my friends here to be with us."

Vinessa just gave a smile accompanied with a giggle. She had never been on her own in a long time. The fact that she was physically alone made her think. She knew that in every aspect except for physically not alone. Dan was there, but not there per se. To her it started to seem like they had been right, and Dan was no more than an imaginary friend. This idea was cleared out of her head as she watched the stick man appear on a rock right before her eyes. It looked like the figure was burned into the stone itself instead of being drawn or painted.

"You can't be thinking about stuff like that my dear Vinessa."

"Why not? How will you prove to me you are real?" Vinessa asks her voice sounding between confused and hopeful.

"Just watch, but first hold out your arm."

Vinessa did as Dan asked and held out her arm. As she watched on a cut slowly formed on her arms. She was surprised they didn't hurt, but wondering how they got there worried her. She watched as the stick man pulled himself off of the rock and climbed up her body to the cut on her arm. It laid flat on her arm over the cut. She could feel it draining her of blood. Soon it crawled back down to the rock it was on originally. It managed to stand on its own two feet jerking in random ways. As it jerked and writhed the true form appeared in front of her without a mirror.

"What are you doing Dan?" Vinessa asked.

She stepped back as screams of pain from what sounded like twenty different people came from the stick man. As Dan screamed, he began to grow and change shape. The screams got deeper and began wavering from one voice to twenty voices. She felt her skin crawl as if bugs had found their way underneath. She wanted to scratch, but she knew that nothing was actually crawling around under her skin. Even knowing that, the urge remained for her.

"This is my true form Vinessa. This is the form that will strike fear into those who try to stop us."

Vinessa felt like fear was supposed to wash over her, but instead she felt like she just found out her friends biggest secret. It made her smile to see how strong her friend actually was in reality compared to the form she was so used to seeing. When Dan made eye contact with her, she could feel her knees get weak from the amount of natural fear it caused. Her mind said one thing, while her body said another. It was an odd and unnatural feeling to have even if she just now felt it for the first time.

"You look so strong Dan!" Vinessa yelled while jumping and clapping.

Dan smiled with joy at her praise, but in the back of his mind he was confused as to why she didn't run in fear. He could see the fear, but he didn't taste it in the air around them. It was then that he realized that she was under his power now. It was the first step towards his goal. He wanted to bring this world to its knees, and free his brothers. Through Vinessa he could do that. She was the key to his goal of conquest.

"Come on, let us continue on our path." Dan said as he slowly vanished out of sight.

Vinessa squinted trying to see him in front of her, but when she couldn't all that could be heard was a sigh of defeat. She felt his invisible hand push her from behind–not hard enough to push her over–making her move forward. He guided her through the woods as if he had walked them his entire life managing to stay out of sight the entire time. When they finally emerged from the woods, she could see the top of the church she had once spent her childhood within.

*   *   *

"Casey, can you hand me the box?" Travis asked from the top of a step ladder.

"Yeah, sure here you go!" Casey stood on her tiptoes to make sure Travis didn't drop it.

They finally had gotten all of his mom's important items stored away in her room. As they scanned the room a smile managed to crawl across their faces. They both collapsed on the couch Casey throwing a pillow into Travis's lap before laying on it. He didn't move a muscle as she fell asleep shortly after making contact with the pillow. He almost fell asleep when a chill went up his spine. He couldn't tell what it was, but it felt like it was bad news.

Vinessa walked up to the front door of the home she had been abducted from. She pressed a hand to the door and could still feel the shadows that ran wild within the building. It had become a haven for monsters and ghouls that couldn't stay within the void that sat outside our realm. She slowly opened the door to be met with shadows taking stance atop the staircase glaring at her with eyes unseen by human sight. Dan pushed by her unseen and approached the center of the house's front room.

"All spirits in this home are now under my control!" He announced in a loud booming voice that echoed through the house.

The shadows shimmered and shot onto the walls before bowing to him. Dan exerted a pressure that could be felt around the entire house. It was a pressure that represented the power contained within the being known as Dan. He began to materialize in the center of the room once more showing his true form to Vinessa. His hand was raised commanding the shadows to stand once more. As his hand was lowered all of the shadows and all the pressure seemed to vanish from the air itself.

"I would like to ask that everyone here leaves me alone while I rest my body." Vinessa said as she went into her room and laid in her bed.

While she slept unknown to her cuts formed all over her body allowing several stickmen to swarm her and drink her blood. After drinking their fill, they made their way out of the house and around into other homes throughout the city. Unknown by children or their parent's evil has come into their homes, and it has no plans on leaving them in peace.

"Garton, when do we plan on making our next move?" Valieen asked nursing a cup of warm tea.

"We must build our numbers, but I fear we may not have that long." Garton said, sitting his cup down.

"You feel it, too don't you?" Valieen made eye contact to show how important the question was.

"I do feel it." Garett sat back keeping eye contact.

"Something is trying to force the ranks of the void free. An evil lives inside that void that can't be stopped even if the Devil sided with God." Valieen shook his head taking another sip of his tea.

They got up and looked out upon the village that they have built with bustling streets and filled with sounds of conversation. Garett picked up a mallet and slammed it into a nearby gong getting everyone's attention. He did it two more times causing everyone to kneel with their heads bowed facing the palace. Valieen pulled out a ceremonial dagger along with his arm. Everyone below copied him as they all slowly pulled the blades from wrist to elbow slicing open their arms.

As the blood covered the ground torches around them began to ignite with a purple flame. The more blood that fell the brighter the flames got until they burned as bright as the sun above. One by one the people fell over as the blood left their bodies. As they died fires came from the torches and engulfed the bodies one by one until no human features could be seen. After five minutes the flames vanished into the cuts on their arms. They rose to their feet, eyes made of purple flames. It was like their last bit of humanity was burned away from within them.

"You are now reborn as creatures of flames and magic!" Valieen yelled out over the crowd as the last one rose back to his feet.

In unison, they looked up and put up a salute to their two undying leaders. A new loyalty was felt in the air around the village. Each and every one of their newly born demon soldiers looked out from under their black cloaks with faceless eyes. Their soldiers undying and born out of darkness, brought to life with the fires of death. A chant made of everyone's voice present echoed out over the trees causing all life nearby to run out of fear.

Chapter 34: Danger In Marrion

Kids poured into the local hospital in Marrion with cuts that had appeared overnight, but when they got to the hospital seemed to have healed months earlier. The doctors became torn as families that have never had a history of abusing their children came in with their kids cut on their arms. This influx of children in the E.R. put the hospital in a tough spot of whether to believe the families or bringing the social services in to assist with the mystery—The children flooding the E.R, became a none stop thing all of them brandishing the mysterious cuts that heal for months overnight.

Travis had gotten a part-time job at the hospital as a security guard three days ago. He stood and watched as kids filed into the hospital confused as to why they had marks on their bodies. This caused Travis to feel the bad feeling he had felt just four days before. He knew this had to be what his mind was trying to warn him about. He knew it was the cult because this was not their—the cults—style. They had more of a sitting in the shadow's kind of style. They didn't want people to see them taking people away. Even the most direct attack Travis knew of was bombing a building with an acidic goo. This was something more, bold and not afraid to have massive casualties.

He stepped out and made a call to Casey. He felt she needed to be warned about what was going on. He wanted her to be safe and at home. He didn't know what is making him feel so protective over her. She had become very important to his life.

"Hey, Casey, make sure to paint over any stick figure drawings that are on the walls." Travis said trying to make himself sound urgent with his call.

"Yes, I will make sure to get that done right away." Casey answered being a lot more understanding than he thought she would be.

"Just remember this part. They are not just a child's drawing; something is majorly wrong with them. They will hurt you please be safe." Travis pleaded with Casey.

"Don't worry I will be safe." Travis's heart sank as Casey killed the call with no other words spoken between the pair.

Travis went back to the E.R. waiting room where kids had fallen asleep from how long the wait had become. All of them had become pale from blood loss but no blood fell to the floor. It was like their blood was just evaporating. It had no explanation, because pulsating cuts had opened all over each child's body that could be seen by everyone. Everyone scrambled with trauma kits to fix the cuts, but nothing helped them. He could feel his heart racing as he saw what was going on and his thoughts ran to what could be happening to Casey.

As the CDC arrived Travis raced out of the door and drove as fast as he could home. As he pulled up Casey was standing outside beside her car with tears rolling down her face. Travis jumped out and pulled her to him filled with worry. He rubbed her back trying to calm her down. When she calmed down her let go before asking his question.

"What happened?" Travis asked backing up to make eye contact.

"Your sister has gone mad Travis. She ran at me with a knife, but she didn't get me." Casey said putting herself back into his arms.

Travis looked over her shoulder to see a bloodied silhouette walk behind their house. It caused him to shudder a slight amount. Casey held him tighter as she felt him shudder from sight of the person. Travis helped Casey into his car's backseat so she could lay down before he went into their home. As he entered all of the lights had been turned off and shadows emanated from a dark figure that stood solid in the center of the kitchen.

"Who's there?" Travis said igniting the flashlight he brought from his car.

"*So, no ice cream?*" The figure looked like Vinessa but spoke with twenty voices as it shut the door to his freezer.

"You may look like her, but you are not my sister. You can't be." Travis said shining the light on the figure to confirm he was seeing what he thought he was seeing.

"*We are not your sister, we are Legion. We are power incarnate. We will take this town with our brothers and sisters of the void. We will use this body to become trusted and feed on those who get close to us.*" It was hard for Travis to hear this from his sister's mouth.

Travis could see something gleaming in her, its hand. It was on the side facing away from him which made it harder for him to get a good look at it. He knew that if he made one mistake on how he handled this his blood would be added to the blood he could already see on her. He stayed back as far as he could be when he was making his way to the front door. The bad feeling, he got before everything, and at the hospital had come back to him. He now knew it came from this thing posing as his sister. As he looked on the shadows that stood around her body fluctuated with the intimidating energy that came from her.

"We can smell the fear coming from you. It smells as strong as a freshly cut onion." The sentence was followed by twenty insane laughs that overlapped each other creating a drone that filled the air.

"I may have some fear of you, but I will not back down from you." Travis said feeling behind him for the doorknob.

Before Travis could react Vinessa's body charged at him full speed. The light from outside gleaned off of the knife's sharp edge as it came down at him. The first thing he thought of was raising his flashlight to block it. It blocked the knife, but the flashlight was destroyed in the process. He fell back into the wall out of the shock he recieved from her, it's sudden attack. His vision became blurred from the force of the attack causing him to struggle with all of the attacks after.

"Why are trying to fucking kill me out of all the people in this town?" Travis said, dodging an attack throwing himself into a nearby wall.

"The key must be destroyed before Valieen can achieve full structure." The twenty voices made a grinding sound this time as they spoke.

Before another attack could come Vinessa's body ran from the house and into the surrounding woods. Travis doubled over in pain holding his arm. The shock caused adrenaline to course through his body causing the pain to be slightly numbed. He tried to focus using his breathing as Casey came in to find him cradling his arm. She came over to him in a fright and checked his arm the best she could.

"We need to get you to the hospital." Casey said, trying to get her voice to respect how calm she was acting.

"The hospital is filled to the brim with children. It would take hours just to get into the lobby." Travis said with defeat in his voice.

Casey helped Travis to the couch and pulled out her phone speed dialing a doctor she has known who is retired. She quickly filled him in before taking a seat next to Travis trying to keep him comforted given the situation. She could see the pain that was in his eyes and how he felt defeated after the events of the day. To Travis for her to truly understand what he is going through she should have been in the room. She needed to see how the shadows and energy around Vinessa drained the light away. It didn't drain just physical light, but also light on the spiritual level.

"I am sorry I wasn't in here when all of that happened. I froze when I felt the energy that came off of her. I just had to run. It felt like the only thing I could do." Casey dropped her head when she finished talking.

"It's okay, I was almost unable to defend myself. I didn't want to hurt her, so I just rolled out of the way. I am guessing we are out of the woods for tonight." Travis said his eyelids starting to feel heavier with each word.

Casey moved to let him lay down to rest on the couch. As soon as his head came in contact with the couch, he was asleep. It made her smile to see him resting for once instead of worrying over someone else's safety. She couldn't wrap her head around the fact that even after getting hurt in the military and having a limp for the rest of his life why did he still wanted to protect everyone. He was truly an inspirational person. She just hopes he can keep up that fact after the conversation about publishing his mother's letters earlier that week. She didn't try to stop him, but she also didn't let him forget to leave out any that are too private for the world to see.

He insisted that he wanted to dedicate the publication to her and send all the money made to her favorite charity. He said that it would help tell the story of her final days. She thinks publishing it was more for his own sake than hers. She told him she would touch up the ink before sending them off to a publisher that was in the military with him on his first tour of duty.

"Casey." Travis said weakly in his sleep, his eyes fluttering around in their sockets.

She was about to say something before seeing he was asleep. Instead of saying anything she sat back and left him alone to work out his dreams. It pained her, but the psychology class she was taking online said that it was better to just be there for them than interfere. To keep herself from crying she put in her headphones and closed her eyes. She decided to continue her audio classes till he woke up.

"I hope your dreams are not too bad m-" She trailed off wanting to say what she was thinking, but her instincts protested.

In his dreams Travis fought alongside the men that had died in his last tour. They are sitting in the middle of an ambush guns firing full speed on both sides of a valley they had been tasked with taking. He remembered this day all too well. It was the day he had gotten the scar on his face and lost a very good friend. A scream came from across the valley as wooden bridges fell across the gap. He saw men running across with grenades in their hands, one finger laced through the pin loop.

"Get the fuck down!" Travis yelled looking to his brothers.

Everyone started to jump away from the wall as grenades flew over the wall. Explosion went off in various places on the wall that paired with screams from soldiers around him. Travis turned to see a man lying on against what is left of the wall, half of his leg missing. Travis pulled his arm over his shoulder helping him to his feet.

"We need to get you out of here." Travis strained to say as the soldier got to his feet.

Together they struggled to get away from the battle when a grenade rolled between his legs. Travis threw the soldier away as the explosion sent shrapnel tearing through his body. He felt every piece of metal burning and tearing every inch through his flesh as he fell back. His ears rang as his vision slowly began to clear from the brain rattling shock wave. Men ran towards him screaming and firing volley after volley over his head. He rolled over on to his side to see a pool of blood expanding from under his body. Looking beyond the blood he saw the enemy soldiers marching towards them.

"We will get you out of here!" Spooner's voice echoed as his ears started to clear up.

Spooner began to drag Travis from the battlefield using one arm to fire his side arm. He finally got to safety and dropped Travis to fight off more soldiers that managed to get past the defense line. When he looked down to talk to Travis his face turned between his normal face and one of decay. He shuddered right as all his senses cleared. Spooner put a knee on Travis's chest and leaned close enough to his ear where his breath grazed his skin.

"The key must fall before the skull king can rise." Spooner's voice filled with a hiss as he spoke.

"What do y-" Travis was cut off as Spooner's boot crushed his skull.

Travis shot up covered in sweat. He tried to speak to Casey to wake her, but every word scratched his throat. He checked the clock to see he had been asleep for four hours. He felt like he got no sleep in days. He got up to get water as quietly as he could trying not to wake Casey from her sleep. It warmed his heart to know that she stayed awake to make sure he was okay. He fell against the cabinet causing a loud crash. He looked over concerned about Casey waking up but was relieved to see she was still asleep. As the water was running two arms wrapped around him. He turned around only for Casey to wrap herself back around him.

"Travis, I was so worried about you. Please remember I am here for you." Casey said burying her face in his chest.

Travis hugged her back after turning off the water. He thought back to his mother's ghost telling him to keep her around. He was starting to understand why she wanted him to do that. She was putting her heart and soul into trying to help him. He began to hope that he was not being a massive burden on her. He took a sip of his water and cleared his throat.

"I know you will be here. I am very blessed to have you here with me. You have given me so much already, and I hope I am not a burden on your shoulders." Travis said, sitting in the floor with her still in his arms.

Chapter 35: Warnings

Travis found himself home alone as Casey went back to her job at the elementary school. He was working on touching up his mother's letters when a knock came on the front door. It was a heavy-handed knock that shook the wall around the door itself. He got up with urgency as the second set of knocks came nearly knocking a picture off of the wall. When he opened the door, no one was on the other side. He turned around chopping it up to a prank from some high school kids.

"Hello, you bastard." Valieen hissed throwing Travis against the door.

"We have some stuff we need to talk to you about Travis." The twisted voice of Garton came from over Valieen's shoulder.

"You're no longer Garett, are you?" Travis asked before taking a fist to his face, knocking him out.

"Come on Travis, wake up." Garton's twisted voice was far away and echoing.

"That almost hurt." Travis said laughing.

"You think you are funny, don't you?" Valieen hissed at Travis before spitting at him shortly after speaking.

"Ye-" Travis was cut off by Garton raising his hand to silence them both.

"We came to warn you. Your sister is dead. The Legion of dark spirits are too strong for her spirit to fight against. If they control her much longer then they will be able to take her body for themselves. They will be powerful if that happens. It will allow them to become one power instead of twenty individual powers. Watch out for her and trust nothing she says." Travis received another punch after Garton finished talking.

He awoke to see himself on the couch and a melted ice pack on his cheek. When he sat up, he could feel the pain in his jaw from being punched so hard. He got up and stumbled his way to the bathroom to check his face. When looking into the mirror he saw a shadowy hand slowly pull itself back behind his shower curtain. He slowed his breathing as he grabbed the curtain and jerked it open only to find no one. The door behind him slammed shut as he turned around.

"Who the fuck is in here?" Travis asked in almost a yelling volume.

He jerked to the door open bouncing it off the wall behind it and ran out looking for whoever pulled the door shut. He still found no one as he searched the house. He let out a sigh of disappointment when he didn't find anyone and decided to get dressed and head into work early. As he walked into work, he saw shadows plastered on the walls all around the hospital waiting room watching over the children that still poured into the building.

"Are you okay Travis you look pale?" His supervisor said putting a hand on his shoulder.

"Y-Yeah I am fine; I just can't believe this is happening to the children." Travis said as he turned to walk into the break room for his water.

"I can't believe it either, and it doesn't sit well with me that the doctors don't know what it is that's happening." His supervision sat across from him as he spoke.

They sat in silence as the sounds of kids talking in confused and frightened voices echoed in the halls. The entire situation confused everyone, not just the children. The part that makes it worse is the fact that this event has had no deaths in it, even with the children losing their blood. The CDC wanted to take some of the children for testing, but none of the parents could bring themselves to let their children go. It made sense to everyone around at the time. Why would you let your children go with people that don't even know how they would test what is going on?

"Can you please help me?" A woman walked in covered in blood carrying a pale bleeding child as she spoke.

He wouldn't stop bleeding after the first cuts appeared earlier that morning. That is the information she gave Travis as he rushed the child into the main part of the hospital. As he walked back from putting the child into a bed, he saw shadows bent over drinking the blood that covered the floor. It looked like rabid wild animals eating their freshly killed prey.

He left the hospital at the end of his shift to see Valieen and Garton standing on the roof of a building observing the hospital below. When he turned to look at what they had been looking at to see shadows crawling all over the outer wall of the building. It shook him to his very core. He finally felt like he had a firm grasp on the situation that they found themselves in. The town was under siege of hungry demons that were feeding off of the children. They turned to notice he was staring at him, and they all made eye contact with him. He lost count of how many he had seen trying looks between all of the demons.

"Fuck." Travis whispered to himself running for his car as they started to chase him.

Everyone around looked at him like he was crazy only to be cut where they stood by the demons that gave chase. They attacked everything in their path: adults, children, and pets. He heard everything that they cut screaming in pain through the growls and blood-curdling roars of the demons behind him. He jerked his car door open and shut it in time to see demons break against his vehicle like a wave breaking on shoals of rock. So many demons ran over his car that all light and sound from the outside was gone. It became nothing but darkness and thunder roars within his vehicle.

"I need to get the fuck out of here." Travis said as he struggled to start his car in the darkness.

When he got his car started the demons dispersed from around him. What he saw after they had fully cleared out was a parking lot covered in blood, and people screaming out in pain covered in cuts. He felt like his life had turned into a horror movie. He took several deep breaths before finally exiting his car to help the injured inside of the building.

"What happened?" Travis asked, helping a woman up from the ground.

"I don't know. I was standing here, and out of nowhere I got sharp, burning pains. I looked to find blood and cuts on my arm. It was too much pain to bear so my legs gave out." She dropped her head in shame as they passed the threshold of the hospital's doors.

Travis spent three hours helping people in and out of the hospital while the situation was cleaned up. He sat in his car staring at the steering wheel trying to work out why something like this would be happening. Did all of these people get hurt because of his actions? He may never get answers as to why this happened, he just knew it happened. He drove home when his phone started to ring.

"Hello?" He asked after hitting the answering button.

"Travis please hurry home; someone broke into the house. I just got home, and the door is open. I would go inside, but I have no idea if they are still in the house." Casey said her voice sounding panicked on the other end of the line.

"I will be there soon. Stay in your car with the doors locked." Travis said hanging up on her before she could say another word.

Travis got back to his house five minutes faster than he normally would. He was followed by a patrol car that he stopped and asked to come with him to his home. He through the front door, while the cop entered through the back door. When Travis got in the house, he found words painted on the wall in plain view of the front door. The words on the wall '***The key must be destroyed***' shook him to his very core. He had heard these words before when Vinessa broke into the house. He didn't know what it meant, but he knew he was in danger.

"I couldn't find anyone on the back side of your home sir." The cop said as he appeared from the kitchen.

"I didn't find anyone up here either. Thank you for coming to help me out." Travis said, shaking the cop's hand before they left.

Travis spent the rest of the day painting over the words while Casey cleaned up the stuff that had been destroyed.

He sat down looking at the wall while it dried to make sure the words didn't bleed through. He didn't see why he painted over it, because he knew they had still been there no matter the number of coats he puts on the wall. His mind wandered as to who had done this to his home. He figured he would find out soon.

Vinessa's body sat in the center of an empty dark room as shadows swirled around her. Her body sat soulless as it stared at a dot in the center of the wall across from her. Dan paced at the door impatiently as the shadows did their thing so they could take her body. Soon their swirling got faster and sounds of screams could be heard as they drew closer to her. Soon a black liquid made its way up her arm, and she leaned her head back with her mouth open. As it poured into her mouth, she gagged but didn't fight back. While the process was continuing, she had become covered in the liquid to the point you could make out her body. It looked as if the shadows had pulled her into the void just as she was becoming visible again.

"We are Legion, and we are one." They said as her eyes turned a deep purple showing Vinessa was no longer in her own body.

"Did it work?" Dan asked as Legion came from the room.

They gave him a nod before continuing to the bathroom. They sat checking to make sure the process was finished. As they could confirm no shadows had been left out a sinister smile crept across their face. A sense of victory could be felt coming from them as they exited the bathroom. For Legion, it has been a long time since they had a body.

That night Legion went out to test out their new body in ways they had long forgotten the feeling of.

"Help, help please I am lost." Legion used a voice that sounded just like Vinessa's old voice.

"Come pretty lady. I can get you home." A man from a nearby parked truck said in response to Legion's calls for help.

Legion ran over to him and climbed in the truck with the man. Legion found themselves riding down a back road in silence with a man whose eyes they could feel scanning their body. He soon pulled over, locking the doors so Legion couldn't leave. When eye contact was made with the man he started to speak once more.

"You got to give me some payment for the ride." The man said running a hand up Legion's leg towards their skirt.

"We can give you something for your kindness." Legion smiled as the statement left their mouth.

"What is it you going to give me?" The man said his hand disappearing under their skirt.

"This!" Legion yelled revealing all twenty of their voices as a blade slashed the man's throat throwing blood over the windshield.

Blood covered Legion's blood as they let out a sound of pleasure running their tongue slowly over the blade. They found the man's phone that was ringing. It was his wife calling to check on him. Legion answered it speaking in the man's voice telling his wife that *he* would be home soon. The very next day the news announced that six people had died that night–a father, his wife, and his six kids. They also released an image of a sentence that had been written in their blood which was *"Give us the key and the death will end."*

This set off a series of events that will change the town forever. Everyone started to wonder what they meant by *"key"*. It was everywhere from chat rooms to coffee shops. With Marrion being a small town, it spread like wildfire and everyone was talking about it. Travis avoided the news ever since he got out of the military and didn't know what happened until someone tried to talk to him about it while he was at work.

"Travis, did you hear about the Lovette family?" His supervisor asked as he clocked in.

"No, I have avoided the news ever since my time in the service ended. What happened?" Travis asked his face painted with curiosity.

"Last night they had been murdered. They said someone had killed and dumped the father three miles away. When they drove to their house and entered with the house keys. They said it looked as if a monster had attacked them with the way the bodies looked. Knife cuts, teeth marks, and claw marks." His supervisor shivered as he finished the description.

"That sounds like it must have shocked the police to find." Travis said as a distant look formed in his eyes.

"They said it was the worst thing they have seen in this town as far as the records could find." His supervisor walked away before he could say anything in response.

Travis was basically on autopilot during his workday. It sounded slightly familiar to something he had read in the church library. He spent most of his time searching back in his mind for the information. He finally found it which made it so much worse in his mind. It was a pattern for when shadows invade a vessel that can't embrace the shadow. To him this means they knew that none of the family could be a vessel for them and killed them out of the hell of it.

"I hope he gets the message." Legion spoke with a laughing undertone.

"You didn't have to do that." Dan said, trying to spread a sense of caution.

"We know, but something had to be done to get them to understand." Legion's voice gained a hiss as he spoke.

"Well, this will definitely get to him." Dan said as he turned the T.V. off.

Travis pulled out his phone and started doing research on the murders. If he was right, then he knew he would find one sentence somewhere in the articles. He got frustrated when he noticed not that many newspapers had covered the murder yet. He was on the internet for hours before he found it. As he read the article it confirmed his worst fears.

"I just fucking knew this was going to get worst." Travis said, dropping his phone and laying back in his chair.

Chapter 36: Shadow Wars

It had been a month since people started showing up to the hospital with cuts that appear overnight. Every tenth visit that was made to the hospital resulted to me and some others having to make a visit to the morgue with a body. The church took the chance to move more of their resources into the city and has been blessing three houses a day. It also seemed that everyone was showing up to church every Sunday now. The demons got what they had wanted. The entire town was pungent with the smell of fear.

No street corner was safe from the view of demons and to the point where a priest could be found at the corner of every city block. Travis took a vacation from work due to the influx of accidents that had over-filled the hospital. With each and every person he saw coming into the hospital it was like he was being sent further and further back into his past. He never wanted to return to his past ever again. He didn't even want to go back if he had a way to make the events of the past better.

"I don't know if I can go back to the hospital until these demons are taken care of." Travis said, his head laying in his hands.

"Well, that is okay they waved at anyone having to pay anything bill wise while the Catholic Church is combating these demons." Casey said twirling noodles around her fork.

"Yes, that is good I just don't want you to think I am useless after these events. I also feel like it may be my fault that things are this bad. Since I came back to Marrion things have gone downhill. I love this town and I don't want to see it destroyed." Travis gave a weak smile to his statement.

"The fact you love it just shows that it was not your fault that any of this has happened." Casey placed one of her hands over his hoping it will help him to stop worrying.

His mind raced at a thousand miles per hour ever since the increase of demon attacks. He couldn't even lose himself in a show without it being stopped by the news networks or being framed by one of those breaking news bars. Each and every one of them was just to update everyone on the new body count that the demons had claimed. No one ever dared to leave their house and the ones that did ran a chance that they will never coming home again. Many of them that didn't come home usually ended up on Travis's yard with their guts ripped out and strung in a nearby tree.

Every so often you would hear about a large crowd of people fainting from a massive amount of blood loss all at once. You just have to hope that the church can make it to the area fast enough to stop even just half of the demons from leaving. Another thing people became confused about was how a large population of demons—the church said it was around one thousand—showed up. He didn't even know who to ask that type of question.

A month and a half ago Dan and Legion had gone to a rural farm on the outskirts of Marrion. While they had been there, they killed the farmer and his entire family. They used their blood to draw symbols all around the property. After they had finished all of the trees and buildings had been marked to create a circle around the home that spanned for three miles in every direction.

"Are we ready to do this Legion?" Dan asked as they looked out over the property from the roof of the house.

"Yes, we are, but you do remember what this will cause?" Legion asked their eyes alternating between twenty outlandish eye colors as every demon took a look at their handy work.

"Yes, it will mark the beginning of the second holy war." Dan said a smirk creeping across his face.

They lured every farm animal to the house in the center of the home locking all of the doors to keep them from escaping. After giving a nod to each other they set the house on fire exiting through a portal that closed right behind them the screams of the souls that got used to make each one echoed with each wave of screams becoming more and more quiet till they had been no more. They looked on as the blaze consumed the house that stood before them. The air became filled with smells of burning fur and the sounds of the animals crying out in pain as they burned alive.

Soon they began chanting their voices becoming one sound. As they chanted the fire turned a deep shade of violet and the animal cries became a united roar of something outside of this earth. As the chants continued a white flame broke the other flames in half and slowly began to expand. One by one shadows slowly began to come from the flames vanishing once more as they came in contact with the moonlight. Dan never stopped chanting, but he had a look on his face that spelled out pride.

"Our army has arrived, Legion." Dan said as the last shadow came from the flames.

"Let's use this as a chance to kill the key instead of going after Valieen." Legion said poking Dan in the chest.

"You are right my friends. I already have a plan to do it with." Dan's face twisted into the most evil expression even Legion has never seen before.

They spent three days going over the plan that he wanted to put into play. It was one of spreading terror through the entire town of Marrion. He wanted to crush their key from the inside out. Starting with his sense of purpose. Shortly after they finished their ritual and started to execute their plan people in Marrion started to die. Travis became the prime suspect because bodies kept showing up on his lawn. In their home Dan and Legion had three T.V.s turned onto the local news. They smiled every time the body count total rose by any amount.

"This can be counted as a victory Legion." Dan said with a hardy laugh.

"Yes, but this will be slightly troublesome." Legion said, showing Dan an article saying the Catholic Church had become invested in Marrion.

"Yes, that could be-" Dan said as Legion spoke up.

"There is no could about it! This is a goddamn issue Dan! If they are involved, you know that Valieen will come to claim his key!" Legion said as they stormed out of the door slamming it behind them.

Dan poured over his plan which to his surprise didn't include combating the church. He didn't know how he could have possibly missed such a big piece to his puzzle. It would attract a ton of attention knowing that the biggest church on the planet would be coming down on their heads now. He still wanted to hold steady with his plan but make one small change to it just for the church. He made it a rule and a point to kill any church officials.

"I guess it is all out war with the church then." Dan said to himself sitting at his desk.

Valieen and Garton caught the same breaking news from their contact in Marrion. They looked at each other with looks that combined concern and opportunity. It was their chance to take Travis from his home, but they also need to protect him from the demons from the void. They both have decided that Marrion will be the foreground of the next holy war.

"It seems that it has begun Valieen." Garton commented as he sat back in his throne.

"I think it has." Valieen said, taking a deep breath of frustration.

They both stood and walked outside looking out over their town of newly born demons. They held hope that they may be all that they need to win this new war. The crowd below roared to life as they stepped out on their balcony. Garton gestured to the town gates which began to glow a bright red and hummed as it went through changes before their eyes.

"When you go through you will be in the town of Marrion. While you are there look for the key and kill anyone that stands in your way." Garton announced as they began marching through the gate.

Garton and Valieen followed behind their demons through the gate as the village was set ablaze in a dazzling orange and gold light that melted the snow fifty feet in every direction. Everything feel silent as the last gate opened. No one had the intention of coming back if the war turned against them. This was Valieen's last chance to secure his empire on earth. He had no plans of going down without a fight, and Travis was the deciding factor of all of it. He was the win or lose for both sides.

"Goodbye my dear legacy." Valieen said one last time as the village faded from his sight.

Casey placed a blindfold over Travis's eyes and tied him to a chair before he could react. No matter how much he begged she wouldn't let him off of the chair. He could hear her moving glass objects around in the Kitchen along with the sounds of other people entering his home. He began to yell for someone to let him loose when the room fell silent.

"Okay, I will let you go." Casey laughed as she loosened the ties around his arms.

"What is this?" Travis said as he saw people standing around him holding cups full of alcohol.

"We are here to celebrate you." Casey said, handing him a cup full of brandy.

"I guess this is okay." Travis shrugged and drank his drink.

They had a night full of booming music and laughter. Travis had felt joy with every second that passed. Casey stayed close to him while bugging him for a dance. Travis gave her a smile and finally gave in just as a slow song came over the speakers. He had never danced with a girl before, but he had also never enjoyed a girl's company the same way he enjoyed her being around. After a few drinks he felt like his thoughts had become fuzzy, but he knew what he had always been wondering.

"I am sorry." He didn't know why he was apologizing before he leaned over and kissed Casey.

Casey's face became flushed with a red color as she buried her face in his chest. He could feel his own face becoming red and hot. He knew he had to process what had just happened, but for now he only knew he wanted to enjoy himself. They partied for a few more hours before people started finding places to sleep. He went to his old room and passed out on his newly bought king-sized bed. He had no nightmares on that night which was welcomed the next morning. The sunlight began shining through his eyelids forcing him to awake.

"What time is it?" He asked himself rolling over to find Casey laying over his chest in the nude her breasts pressed against him.

He shook his head to see if he was still slightly dreaming, but nothing changed. He looked under the cover to see that he was still wearing his normal sweats and boxers. When she started to stir and hold him closer, he didn't protest as she pulled him closer. He still didn't know what this feeling was that he felt for her, but he was starting to accept the fact he might not be what he thought he was. She made him smile and made him feel butterflies.

"I think I love you." He said to himself looking at the woman sleeping over him holding him like no one has before—To him it felt caring, loving, full. He was used to people feeling empty, filled with pitty, selfish.

"I know I love you." Casey said sleepily with a smile on her face.

"Did we do what I think we did last night?" Travis asked.

"No, but you did tell me to sleep as comfortably as I wanted which was sweet of you." Casey gave him a squeeze before falling back asleep.

"I am defiantly bisexual." Travis said as a smile crept across his face while he looked at the only girl, he loved more than family.

Chapter 37: Marron in Marrion

Dr. Marron crawled his way up the final length of the hill as his body starts to give in to its exhaustion. Even as he lays against a tree to rest a smile creeps across his face. He was ready to finish his job at any cost, but first he needed a shower. His eyes finally started to slowly close as he drifted off to sleep. He awoke to a man in a black suit using their cane to poke his foot.

"Wake up fella, you can't sleep here." The man in the black suit said as Dr. Marron's gaze drifted to their face.

"The fuck do you want?" Marron asked the man.

"I assume you are here for the key?" The man in the suit asked crouching down to look Marron in the eyes.

"Key? What do you mean and who are you in the first place?" Marron asked, struggling to his feet.

"Who I am doesn't matter, but I can do this." The man in the suit said, tapping his cane to Dr. Marron's knees.

A light came from the end of the cane before going into Dr. Marron's knees. He felt a warmth as his ability to use his knees without being in pain came to him. As he tested his newly healed legs a ravenous grin came over his face. He licked his lips causing unease to appear on the man's face. Before the man in the black suit could react, Marron had shoved a knife into his gut and jerked it to his left side causing his organs to fall out of his gut. He fell to his knees making eye contact with Marron.

"W-w-why?" The man said blood coming from his mouth as he coughed.

"It doesn't matter." Marron said shoving the knife into his eye socket.

He took the knife out of his eye and grabbed the cane from the ground. He faked a limp as he walked into town with the cane in his hand. To further make his disguise more believable he forced his breathing to be labored. Scars still covered his body along with dirt that was caked on his body and clothes. As he finally came upon the house that was to his knowledge the home of Travis and his sister Vinessa rain began to fall. He scoffed thinking it was only proper for the storm to give his already dark mission even more depth.

"Hello, is anyone home?" Marron asked as he knocked on the front door with a heavy hand.

"Who are you?" Legion asks as Marron charges and shoves them into the wall knocking them out.

"Legion who was it?" Dan asked coming around the corner to find rain entering through an open door.

*   *   *

Travis's phone went off the display showing "*Vinessa.*" He answered it to only hear breathing and thunder in the background. Just as he was about to say something the line dropped. Two seconds after the call dropped a picture text came through. It was a picture of his *sister, the* back of her head matted with blood. He closed the phone getting up for his coat.

"I am leaving for an hour or so." Travis announced hearing the water still going in the bathroom.

Another text came through with a message of where to meet to get her back. He was skeptical about if he actually wanted to save Legion since the person—who he didn't know was Dr. Marron—didn't know about his sister's soul no longer being in control of her body. He just wanted to try to bring back Vinessa's body back without it getting any more damage done to it. He jumped in his car driving as fast as he could taking one more look at his phone while he went down the highway.

Meet me at Bridget Lookout. -Marron.

"This mother fucker is going to be in pieces for this bullshit." Travis said through gritted teeth.

As Marrion pulled the car to a stop he pulled a gun from his jacket checking it to make sure it was loaded. He got out and pulled Viessa's unconscious body from the trunk and tied it to a wooden pole next to the cliff. He braced himself as a pair of lights appeared around the bend of the road, but it wasn't paired with the sound of an engine running. Still, he fired when they made it around the bend. Two men fell yelling out in pain and holding their chests.

"What the fuck." One of the men groaned.

"You walked up here at the wrong time." Marron said walking over and putting a bullet into each man's heads.

He struggled to pull the dead men to the cliff and push them over allowing them to limply bounce off the rock on the way down. He struggled to catch his breath as Travis's car came around the corner blaring loud rock music. Marron fell to the ground and let out five quick shots causing Travis to hit the wall of rock that sat parallel to the sharp cliff. He laughed getting to his feet as all that could be heard was the hiss of the car's radiator spewing hot water.

"I finally got your ass." Marron said walking towards the car unleashing more bullets into the passenger side.

"Fuck you!" Travis yelled as he fired three shots out of the window barely missing Marron's head and chest.

Travis kicked the door open, shoving Marron into his parked car making him scream in agony. The rain made their hair stick against their faces and foreheads. Marrion backed up breathing heavy. Travis did the same thing looking for a reason to buy more time to think of what to do.

"Do you understand what the fuck is wrong here! You are the key to a beautiful world! What did you do to me when I tried to help you! You fucking shot me in my goddamn legs! You are a stupid son of a bitch that thinks the world can be fixed by humanity! We destroyed this planet and have no fucking idea how to fix it! You are meant to carry a k-" Marron stop as he took a deep inhale.

Marron looked down as rain dripped from his shirt red as a palette of fresh paint. He laughed looking at Travis over for a gun. Behind him stood Legion with an arm inside of his chest. Black liquid moved from Legion's shoulder and into Marron who screamed out in pain as it moved through his body burning his veins. His screams turned into choking gurgles as the liquid spilled out of his mouth. It stained the shirt as it created streaks of black all the way to the bottom. He fell down seizing with blood coming from his pores streaking down his body like running mascara.

"He was very annoying." Legion said as they started to repeatedly stomp on Marron's head.

"I guess I could say you're welcome since I distracted him." Travis let out a groan of pain as he held his stomach.

"While you did stop him, I am also obligated to kill you since you are the key." Legion said, letting out a sigh of conflict.

"I am sorry. I really don't know what that even means." Travis said, throwing his hands out to his sides.

"It means that if Valieen takes your body then he can become the skull king. This means he will be the strongest creature in existence. By existence means earth, hell, heaven, and any planets beyond." Legion said looking at Travis from below a furrowed brow.

"I don't plan on letting him take me, and I for damn sure don't plan on dying anytime soon." Travis said, raising his weapon.

Before any actions could happen or words could be exchanged a blue light appeared. Dan stepped through looking at the situation and waved Legion through the portal. He scowled at Travis as he went through himself. After the portal closed Travis struggled to his car for his phone. He sifted through broken glass and rock. With his bleeding hands he dialed 911 and collapsed onto the ground next to his car.

"I hope your body isn't here when they pick me up." Travis said with his voice fading into laughter.

His vision was blurry, but he could make out Valieen picking up Marron's body. He gave Travis a salute as he carried the body through a portal never to reemerge. The ambulance could be heard throughout the entire valley as its siren bounced off the rocks that made up the walls. He was picked up and put onto a gurney, but he couldn't bring himself to open his eyes. He was afraid to see the looks on the faces of the paramedics.

"He is badly injured!" He could hear a paramedic yell.

"Get him into surgery now, I will be there in a moment!" What he could assume was a doctor yelled back.

He could hear every voice echo weakly in his mind like he was still in the valley. They sounded panicked as he could feel their needles and scalpels enter his body. He wanted to tell them that he could be okay without the surgery, but he knew he would die without it. He still thought that he would die with or without the surgery being done. Two armies had begun fighting over him so no matter what he will probably die in the end, or at least that's what his thoughts had been telling him.

"Looks like I am alive." Travis groaned as he opened his eyes to the cold air of a hospital room.

"Oh my God you're alive!" Casey yelled tears in her eyes throwing her arms around Travis.

"Hey Casey, I am still sort of in pain." Travis groaned.

"Sorry." Casey said, sniffling clearing the tears from her eyes.

"Listen Casey, I have to ask you a question." Travis said, taking Casey by the hand carefully.

"Yes?" Casey asked, picking at the end of her skirt from her nerves.

"I have been thinking over some stuff, and I just have one question. Would you like to be in my arms after all of this is over? Like as my, um as my significant other." Travis said nervously.

"If I am thinking you are asking what you are then I have been waiting for you to ask that." Casey said lightly squeezing Travis's hand, tears dripping off the tip of her nose.

"Good, that makes me extremely happy." Travis said his voice hoarse from being thirsty.

Travis turned on the T.V. to see a house up in flames. He took a close look and could see it was the house that was left to him from Father David. He couldn't find the words to say, all he could muster was silence. He looked close and could faintly see a figure being dragged out of the back of the house by another. The sight brought on a sense of dread around him. He was quite sure it was heavy enough for Casey to feel it as well.

"Isn't that the house you and your sister had?" Casey asked her eyes bouncing between him and the T.V.

"Um, yes, it is." Travis said, still unable to believe what he was seeing.

"I am sorry that you are seeing it this way?" Casey said her head dropping down leaving her gaze on the floor.

"It is okay, I am pretty sure the church still held the deed to the house." Travis said as he let out a pained laugh.

Travis kept thinking about the figures in the background of the video. The one gave off a hint of familiarity to his mind. The other one intimidated him. It struck a fear down to his very bones. He shuddered at the thought of what that other one could be. He looked at Casey for comfort. When he looked at her the sun gave her skin a soothing almond color. He smiled without thinking about it at the sight of how soothing her complexion was.

"I am going to stay here till you are able to go home Travis." Casey said walking from the room to talk to the nurses about it.

Travis spent two weeks in the hospital bouncing between bed rest and rehab. Every step pained him, but he knew it was required to help him walk again later. He still pushed himself through it for the fact that Casey was by his side with every bit of the process. On the day they had been able to go back to their home the door had a note pinned to the door. His heart sank in his chest at the very sight of it. It was like his body already knew what it was going to say.

I have taken Vinessa's body to the place in which your father taught. I know you want her body back at the least so you can bury her when this is over. I personally don't want to drag this fight out any longer. I know you are a very stubborn person Travis. This is why I am willing to let you make the choice. Either way someone is going to die. It can be Legion aka Vinessa, or it can be you. You won't really die completely. You will just be moved to the backseat in your mind. Valieen will control your actions from there. You two are meant to rule the world as one. You are meant to become part of the skull king. The sooner you accept that fact the sooner you will be able to save everyone in this fucking town. Good luck with that on your mind.

Chapter 38: Ice Cream Forever

Travis let the note fall to his feet after staring at it for half an hour. He slammed his fists on his knees as he shook his head out of disbelief. He could feel anger and frustration rising in his body like a wildfire. He felt like he was going to explode at any second as a portal opened in his living room and out stepped Dan–whose body was covered in burns on one side. Travis glared at him as Dan sat across from him in his mother's favorite chair.

"Get out of the goddamn chair." Travis said, trying to keep his cool.

"I am not here to wage a war with you." Dan's voice held a sense of pain with every word he spoke.

"Then leave!" Travis yelled shooting up out of his chair.

"I didn't know where else to go, but you can kill me if you want. Me being killed and even Legion being killed won't stop the events I have put into motion. Not anymore at least." Dan let out a pained chuckle at the end of his sentence.

"You act like you have won, but I swear if her body doesn't come back home, I will torture you." Travis leaned in close and whispered into Dan's ear.

"We did win, in a way. You have no idea who here is on my side and who is still human." Dan let out a pain laugh that ends in a cough that was accompanied by blood.

"It looks like that fire did some damage to you." Travis said standing up straight making eye contact with Dan.

"Y-yes it did." Dan gave a smirk with these words as he closed his eyes and sighed.

"You know what, you can stay there and bleed inside and feel every second as your blood floods your organs while squeezing them as well. Casey can decide your fate." Travis put a bottle of water in front of Dan as he walked out of the door.

Dan laughed as he coughed up more blood. He looked at the blood bringing on a sense of mortality that he hadn't felt since he died in 350A.D. He began to think back to the time he had died. His village was being invaded as he and his sister ran through a field of flowers in fear of their lives. The sound of his parents yelling for them to keep running and never stop. That is exactly what Dan–his name back then was Alicari–did even though his sister suffered from the flu. He would end up ending her life at his sister's request. She would pass at the age of seven from a knife to the heart.

"I am coming home my dear sister." Dan passed away with a tear covered smile.

It was like he could feel his soul finally being put back together. His tears began to run dry as a bright light started to open in the wall revealing a hallway. It was dressed in marble and gold accents. He could hear a familiar voice calling for him.

"Come home brother. Come to me like you have promised all this time."

He walked towards the voice and looked back to see his mutilated body sitting in the chair. He looked down at his body and saw he was human once more. A smirk spread across his face followed by more tears. He looked down to the end of the hallway where a silhouette stood. He walked closer shielding his eyes from the light. There stood his sister looking as young as she did when she died.

"I am home sister." Alicari said his tears continuing to fall.

"*Took you long enough!*" His sister said pulling him into the light as his passes his final look at the world he is leaving behind.

Rain began to fall as Travis found himself walking among the graves behind the church he knew too well. It used to be a place he found comfort in. He saw his mother was not buried next to the bastard she married after his father left which made him kind of happy, but he still felt terrible for not being there in her final hour. He looked down at her headstone rain falling from his chin.

"Wow!" The word called out after the sound of a camera snapping a picture sounded out.

"Who are you?" Travis asked his voice stern.

"I am just a passerby taking pictures. Here look at yours!" The little man was excited to show off his new photograph.

"Wow look at that." Travis said pointing at the group of spirits glowing a deep dark blue laced with purple streaks that surrounded him.

"I know right!" The little man dancing around excited trying to be careful with his camera.

"I might have to look for you after I am done here." Travis spoke through a smile.

"I work here." The little man gave Travis a card reading *Johnson photos East Main.*

"Thank you." Travis walked away ending the conversation.

As he walked away a wave of dark blue and purple burst from his back as the phantoms of his family appears. He looked left and right smiling to see Vinessa, Susan, Johnathon, and Father David. This means that he can confirm they have all left their bodies and what he is dealing with is no longer human. He could feel their power flowing through him. He tried to focus his breathing as his body broke and reformed the energy healing him as he began to glow himself.

"I am a goddamn superhuman." Travis said shaking his head at how corny he was.

He entered the church which seemed to have aged decades since the last he had been in it. Cobwebs hung from the ceiling above decayed pews. The rocks looked like they had been crumbling around him. He could see cracks forming on the walls and chips of cement falls from the places where the cracks met. He looked toward the front of the room and there he saw them. Legion was tied up by ropes and iron chains. Behind them stood Valieen who had a massive smile on his face.

"Welcome." Valieen held out his arms, Garton grabbed Travis from behind.

"You are going to see the beginning of the end." Garton hissed into his ear followed up by a cackle.

"What the fuck is going on!" Travis yelled as a bandana gagged him.

Graton tied his arms and his legs pushing him into a pew. They both began to chant as the roof above them began to pull apart. Soon the roof began to collapse, but instead of falling to the floor the rubble disappeared before they hit anything below. Rain fell through a portal that had ripped open in the sky above Garton and Valieen. Screams echoed from the portal as it spit out fire and burnt body parts.

"And here we send the shades back to the darkness in which they had been born." Valieen chanted to the sky as he and Garton put glowing black hands on each of Legion's shoulders.

Legion's veins began to turn black as they seized and black liquid made of hands slowly reached out of their mouth. Screams of twenty-one different people came from the body as their head shot so far back it sounds like the bones cracked in their neck. The screams got louder as more hands emerged from their mouth causing black liquid to drip from the corners of their mouth. He looked at their eyes, and he could see Vinessa coming forward, producing tears of pain.

Legion fell over jerking on the floor with so much force that splinters embedded themselves in their body. The bindings on their arms broke allowing Legion to grab at their throat to no effect with how little strength they had left. They began scratching to try to get air in any way causing blood to ooze mixing with the black liquid. Soon choking noises came from Legion as their eyes began to grow dim. Their arms began to reach for Travis who ran to Legion and laid their head in his lap. The black liquid began to run thin as a familiar voice came from their mouth.

"So, T-t-travis. C-can we g-get that ice cream now?" Vinessa asked in a fading voice as a smile emerged.

"Yes, yes we can get all the ice cream you want sis." Travis said as his voice began to choke up and tears flowed from his eye.

"Thank y-" Vinessa let out one last gasp as her eyes and smiles faded away.

He sat as rain fell heavy from above paired with thunder. He sat tears running from his face running his thumb against his sisters now lifeless cheeks. His mind was racing as his last family member left him. Loud footsteps echoed as Valieen walked to his side. Without looking up Travis threw a weak punch against Valieen's leg who kicked him away from Vinessa's body.

"Get away from her you stupid bitch." Travis yelled so loud his voice cracked.

"This is what you get for not knowing who was in charge here!" Valieen yelled as he pulled Vinessa in half.

Travis could hear every fiber and ligament ripped in half. Blood showered over everyone in the church. Travis could hear his heart in his ears and every pulse of blood could be felt through his body. His teeth began to grind as he charged at Valieen. When his body made contact Valieen fell back dropping Vinessa's body—or at least both of the halves—causing Travis to be startled.

"Fuck you!" Travis yelled as he threw punch after punch into the sides of Valieen's head.

Valieen let out groans of pain with each hit as blood began to run from his nose. Garton shoved Travis off as he opened a portal behind them that caused the church to catch on fire. Valieen and Graton laughed as they exited through the portal. Travis watched flames catch the pews through fuzzy vision. He frantically looked around for Vinessa's body. When he found her, he crawled over each movement causing him pain. He took a deep breath sitting up to pull her head into his lap. He let out a sigh as he cleared the blood matted hair from her face.

"I am sorry that I failed you." Travis said looking around watching as the flame danced a violent dance around them.

He closed his eyes as he accepted the fate that has been laid out around him. To raise the mood, he flipped through his phone music and turned on the orchestra song he had been hooked on for a week now. He smiled as the track added to the drama. He nodded as his mind ran through all the things that could have happened to him and seemed to settle on the fact that this was what he deserved.

"This was exactly what I thought would happen to me. I knew I was destined for the flames of hell for the path I had carved for myself. I just didn't know that trying to save you would get me here, but I am glad I got to speak to you for my last moments on earth." He said as something collapsed behind him.

"You know I think that demon broke your leg." His sister's spirit said as it sat cross-legged in front of him.

"Oh, yeah and I think a couple of ribs." Travis said coughing from the smoke that was building up around them.

"Well, if that is the cause be careful with that cough." His sister said.

"Yeah, it kind of hurts." Travis smiled weakly.

"I can't wait for this to be over. I am wanting some ice cream." His sister rubbed her stomach.

The fire began to roar louder as wood began to crack and one window could be heard busting somewhere around them. Travis's sister pulled her corpse off of him and helped him down to the office that used to hold a man that smiled every day he was in it. Travis pulled the rolling office chair under him as she sat him in the chair. He smiled as he relaxed back into the chair.

"How does it feel to be in this chair?" Father David said from behind Travis.

"It feels so comfortable." Travis said turning the chair around to see Vinessa sitting on the desk and Father David standing with a big smile on his face.

"I am glad that you are here, I wanted to tell you something." Father David crouched down to eye level.

"What is that father?" Travis groaned sitting up in the chair.

"You are not going to burn in hellfire, even if this inferno takes you." Father David gave Travis a quick hug and backed up to where he stood before.

"Thanks for the confidence Father." Travis held his chest as he spoke.

"Son, I am so proud of what you have done with your life." He turned to see it was his mother that spoke the words, but she wasn't young like back at his home. She was a healthy-looking older lady.

"Mom." The word took all of the strength he had not to cough saying it.

"Son save your strength and just listen. You have grown in ways I never thought you would have ever to have been. As a young boy you were always so shy, but now as a man you carry yourself showing the world who you really are. Even I couldn't do that, even as I was dying. I know you still beat yourself up over not being home when I met my end, but I was actually happy you had not been there. I was screaming at the top of my lungs from how much pain I was in." His mom stopped as tears formed on her face.

"Mom I know about the letters you wrote." Travis said to change the subject.

"I wrote those and meant to send them to you, but the chemo had made me so weak. It was the one thing I regret not being able to finish in my life." His mom looked away as the tears fell from her chin.

"I read them, and I hope that is what matters for you mom." Travis's voice got weaker as his breathing began to get harder for him.

"Son, I am sorry I left you and your sister to that monster." The deep voice of his father came from behind him.

"Dad?" Travis turned around tears covering his chest mixing with his sweat.

"Yes son, I am here for you for once in my time on this earth." His father wrapped his muscular arms around him.

"Dad I swear it is okay. I tried to protect her, but I failed and now she is laying on the floor above us ripped in half." Travis said as the sadness and smoke caused him to choke on his words as they came out.

More wood about them began to scream out from the heat caused by the flames. The smoke filled the area around him so thick that you couldn't see much around the room. Travis reached forward and grabbed the picture of Him, Father David, and Vinessa. He hugged it to his chest as something fell above him. He sat back in the chair as his breathing slowed.

"Travis this place is going to fall soon." Spooner said sitting on the desk locking eyes with Travis.

"Yeah, it is, isn't it?" Travis said with a smirk on his face.

"Are you not going to call someone?" Spooner asked as he started to pace around the desk.

"Will you stop that please? It brings up bad memories." Travis said, taking a look at the picture he was holding.

"Are you going to call someone?!" Spooner yelled the question this time pulling his rank.

"I can't call anyone, because my phone is crushed above us!" Travis yelled back at Spooner.

Travis took a look at where Spooner was supposed to have stood, but nothing was there. He felt like he was going crazy as he thought he could see faces in the flames that had built up around him. His hearing began to fade as all he could hear was someone singing slow and moody opera. It made his eyes well up with tears once again. He looked up to see the faces of all of his family fading in and out of the flames talking with no words.

"I am so sorry; I couldn't save anyone. I fucked it all up so badly!" Travis yelled as he slammed the picture onto the ground.

He could hear as the roof gave in and fell onto the floor above him. He tried to laugh, but his chest protested. He sat back in the chair as his body felt it reaching its limits. He watched as the heat caused reality to ripple around him. He held hope someone would find him. He didn't care if it was dead or alive. He remembered that he wouldn't be able to tell if any of them that did the finding would be human or demon.

"This is probably for the best. If I were to stay alive, I might have put Casey into so much danger." Travis came to notice he couldn't cry any more cause his tears evaporated right away.

The sounds of the singing woman—the one that was in the opera—continued making his emotions run wild. His life started to flash before his eyes. It was a life that would consist of hiding his true self and go even to the other side of the world to try to leave himself behind. He could hear someone yelling over the flames, as his vision went black.

Dedications

I would like to dedicate this book to all my friends that have kept telling me to carry on writing and to not let my dreams die. Some I would like to thank specifically.

My friend J.D. Toombs he not only read this as I wrote it but took time out of writing his own book to do it.

Susie Layell who was like another mom to me and has always driven me to achieve my dreams.

I would like to make a special thanks to Lara Rouse for helping me edit for the first editions release.

My co-workers at my day job who put up with the tapping of the keyboard the entire shift.

My final dedication is to my fiancé, roommate, and my dogs who have to share a house with me along with hear all of my stupid writing ideas.

Additional thanks to @donidraws on Twitter for the cover art

Author Notes

This book was started with a visit to a therapist. He thought it would be good to put my emotions onto paper. This was my way to do that. I hope that you enjoy the story, and maybe find something within it to help you.

If you did not like it enough to read it a second time, please pass the story on. I hope that this story finds its way to help someone in a dark place. I know we all find ourselves in a dark place. I also know that sometimes we cannot get out on our own.

I am so thankful that you read this story. Thank you so much for helping my dream to get one step to coming to reality.

www.ingramcontent.com/pod-product-compliance
Lightning Source LLC
Chambersburg PA
CBHW071550030726
47593CB00001BA/100